THE VISCOUNT'S FORBIDDEN FLIRTATION

SARAH RODI

HISTORICAL

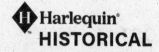

Harlequin®
HISTORICAL

ISBN-13: 978-1-335-54004-1

The Viscount's Forbidden Flirtation

Copyright © 2025 by Sarah Rodi

Recycling programs for this product may not exist in your area.

For questions and comments about the quality of this book, please contact us at CustomerService@Harlequin.com.

TM and ® are trademarks of Harlequin Enterprises ULC.

Harlequin Enterprises ULC
22 Adelaide St. West, 41st Floor
Toronto, Ontario M5H 4E3, Canada
www.Harlequin.com

Printed in U.S.A.

A Season to Wed

*The brand-new Regency quartet from
Virginia Heath, Sarah Rodi, Ella Matthews
and Lucy Morris!*

As the 1816 London season gets underway,
it promises to be the most talked about yet,
as we have four new eligible suitors fresh
from the battlefields of Waterloo...

Soldiers Adam, Ezra, Ash and Hawk might
find themselves out of step with the expectations
of the *ton*, but they're duty bound to make
advantageous matches.

Yet, if they're to be victorious in the marriage
mart, they'll need to venture beyond the sanctuary
of their card games at White's and enter the
tempest of society's ballrooms!

Book 1:
Only an Heiress Will Do by Virginia Heath

Book 2:
The Viscount's Forbidden Flirtation by Sarah Rodi

Available now

Book 3:
Their Second Chance Season by Ella Matthews

Book 4:
The Lord's Maddening Miss by Lucy Morris

Coming soon!

Author Note

What an honor it has been to write a collaboration series with authors Virginia Heath, Ella Matthews and Lucy Morris. It was fun to create our heroes, Ezra, Ash, Hawk and Adam. The four men met at Oxford University and have been friends ever since. They joined the cavalry to fight Napoleon after their graduation, assuming the war would be over within months. Years later, they have returned from Waterloo, scarred inside and out. Ezra Hart thinks war is behind him and knows he must find a match for himself this season, but when he encounters French émigrée Seraphine, he realizes his battles in the ballroom are only just beginning. She is the embodiment of the enemy he has been fighting—and he is disturbed to find her attractive, and his anger with himself, and with her, leads him to snub her. Seraphine is all too aware of the soldiers' presence at Lady Bulphan's ball, especially the formidable Ezra Hart, and she decides never to forgive his humiliating treatment of her.

I loved every second of immersing myself in the opulent Regency ballrooms, and I hope you enjoy Ezra and Seraphine's story as much as I enjoyed writing it.

Sarah Rodi has always been a hopeless romantic. She grew up watching old romantic movies recommended by her granddad or devouring love stories from the local library. Sarah lives in the village of Cookham in Berkshire, where she enjoys walking along the River Thames with her husband, her two daughters and their dog. She has been a magazine journalist for over twenty years, but it has been her lifelong dream to write romance for Harlequin. Sarah believes everyone deserves to find their happy-ever-after. You can contact her via @sarahrodiedits or sarahrodiedits@gmail.com. Or visit her website at sarahrodi.com.

Books by Sarah Rodi

Harlequin Historical

Claimed by the Viking Chief
Second Chance with His Viking Wife
"Chosen as the Warrior's Wife"
in *Convenient Vows with a Viking*
The Viking and the Runaway Empress
Her Secret Vows with the Viking
The Viking's Princess Bride

Rise of the Ivarssons

The Viking's Stolen Princess
Escaping with Her Saxon Enemy

Visit the Author Profile page
at Harlequin.com.

For the Gurneys.
Thank you for your friendship,
and all the family fun and laughter.

Prologue

Oxford University—May 1809

The four men swayed down the rain-washed cobbled streets, singing out of tune and laughing heartily, their arms wrapped around each other's shoulders as they made their way to their favourite inn. And there was nowhere else Ezra Hart would wish to be on his last night at Oxford.

He had found happiness here and if there was one thing this place had taught him, it was just how essential his friendships were. Friends, he'd discovered, were far more important than family.

They managed to secure a cosy corner at the Crown in Cornmarket and began to make light work of another bottle of cognac. The inn was alive with the buzz of conversation and men downing drinks, smoking, some even brawling and taking it out on to the street.

Ezra tipped up his glass. 'To the future!' he said, before knocking back some of the amber liquid, feeling the burn in his throat on its way down.

'To us,' Ash, Hawk and Adam replied.

They had been through a lot these past four years

together and Ezra was sad it was all coming to an end, that they would now be going their separate ways. He'd had a taste of freedom here, of adventure—he had been able to make his own choices. And as of tonight, he'd made another one. A life-changing one.

'To freedom,' Ezra said.

He wondered if he would ever see them again, as tomorrow he was signing up to fight the French in the war against Napoleon. Not that he'd told his friends yet. He was waiting for the right moment, because he knew they would call him a fool and try to talk him out of it.

But this was something he had to do.

During his time at university, he'd taken a keen interest in politics and the fate of their nation. He'd been watching Napoleon's ambitious advance across Europe with growing unease. The man was a threat to British order and he had to be stopped. Ezra was prepared to stand up and fight him, to risk his life for his friends and his country. And he didn't think it would hurt to exorcise some of his own demons on the battlefield.

He felt he needed to do something brave. Something notable. He wasn't ready to go back to London—not yet. He had to accomplish something on his own terms, to prove his worth. And what could be better than seeing more of the world, earning a reputation of being a damn good soldier and winning glory in battle?

He would not return to Artington Hall—home—without it.

Home.

Could he even call it that?

It had never felt like it. Not since the day he'd gone to live there eleven years ago. Only these three men sitting around the table knew the truth of his heritage; it wasn't something he was keen to share with anyone else. In fact, it was a truth he went out of his way to keep hidden.

He'd never forget that one bright autumn afternoon, not long after his tenth birthday, when the colours were starting to change to rust on the trees, the leaves beginning to fall. Ezra had been playing with his siblings in the garden, catching frogs, chasing butterflies around the pond, when he'd been called inside to bathe and dress in his finest clothes. His mother and father had ushered him into the drawing room, trying to tame his damp, wet curls, and presented him to his father's patron, the Viscount Hart and his wife. He hadn't known much about them—only that they provided his father with a modest living at the rectory on the Harts' estate in Derbyshire.

As his parents and their important guests had sat and talked, Ezra had been preoccupied, staring longingly out of the window at his brother and sisters still frolicking outside, wondering why he'd been the one made to miss out, willing the adults to finish their tea in the stuffy room so he could get back to the others. Finally, they'd all stood and, looking up, he'd seen their gazes were focused on him and they had begun congratulating him, clapping him on the back. Unbeknown to him, it seemed something had been decided. Something huge. And that something had been his fate.

William Hart and his wife were grieving the loss of their only son, a boy Ezra's own age, and wanting to fill that void, it seemed the role of the Viscount's heir had somehow been granted to him. There were no other living male relatives that the Harts knew of. And due to the lack of a legitimate claimant, the Viscount's title would fall into abeyance. While there was nothing Lord Hart could do about that, he *could* leave his property and lands that were not entailed to someone of his choosing. Someone he and his wife had brought up as their own, moulded into their way of life.

Ezra.

And it seemed they had offered to compensate his family handsomely.

Ezra didn't know what he'd done to deserve it—this blessing, this burden. No one had even asked him if it was what he wanted. And it hadn't been. He felt as if he'd been put up for sale and bought by the highest bidder.

As his trunk had been packed, he'd begged his father to let him stay; he had pleaded with his mother, tears rolling down his cheeks. They'd had to prise his fingers from her dress.

'Do not cause a scene, just go,' his father had said, trying to hold back his own emotions as Ezra was escorted to the coach, the door slamming shut with him inside. 'One day you will understand,' his father had whispered, as the carriage began to pull away, heading for London. 'This will change your life—and ours.'

And it had. Ezra's life as he'd known it had ended.

He'd become heir to the Viscount's fortune overnight and later his name had been changed from Whittaker to Hart so he could one day inherit the Artington estate. But he hadn't seen or heard from his family again and the wound ran deep.

At first, he and the Harts had tried to get along, but all too soon it became apparent just how misguided their attempts to fill the hole in their hearts had been. Too trapped in their grief, it became obvious that they couldn't love Ezra like their own son and, what was worse, he seemed to be a perpetual reminder to them of what they'd lost.

He had been sent off to Eton boarding school, returning only at the weekends. And the Viscount had been hard on him—strict, determined to at least mould him into a man suitable to inherit.

Ezra had hated him, blaming him for taking him away from his family, destroying his happiness and for making him feel unlovable—a disappointment for never living up to their expectations.

He had always felt like an imposter at the imposing Artington Hall, because although his fortunes might have changed, he could never inherit the title of Viscount—a constant taunt of his modest heritage. An affirmation that he would never quite be good enough for that. And as if the Viscount felt the same, it had been kept a secret, always.

Besides, it seemed the Viscount was more concerned with a suitable heir taking over the estate than the title. But then, the Harts wouldn't be around to bear the consequences when the truth finally came out, would they? The scandal that might occur when they eventually passed and Ezra inherited—and people found out he could not be made Viscount as he and the Harts were never related. The Viscount wouldn't have to deal with the judgement of society, but Ezra would and it weighed heavy on his mind.

In the end it was a relief when he'd finally left for Oxford and escaped his guardian's watchful gaze. He'd finally been able to live a little.

He'd worked hard, needing to be the best at everything, needing to make it on his own terms to be reassured of his value. He wanted to fill his own coffers without having to rely on the allowance the Harts had given him. And he wondered now what they'd think about him using some of it to purchase a commission into the Thirteenth Light Dragoons rather than returning home to take up his duties on the Artington estate. But by the time his guardian found out, Ezra would be halfway to the Continent and there would be nothing the Viscount could do about it.

He was just considering the best way to tell his friends about his decision, when one of his classmates slapped a copy of *The Times* on their table.

'Bloody Napoleon is on the advance again! Completely unstoppable. He'll be coming for us next.'

'Well, we can't defeat France without more men prepared to stand up and fight against him.' Ezra got to his feet and started pacing, restless. 'I loathe Napoleon with every fibre of my being. I'm not going to sit by and wait for him to attack us. That's why I'm going to do something about it.' He took a breath and raked a hand through his unruly hair. 'I'm joining up tomorrow to do my bit to stop him, purchasing myself a commission in the cavalry. You should all know tonight is my last hurrah as a civilian.'

Silence descended on the table as they all stared up at him, aghast.

'Don't be an idiot,' Hawk finally scoffed. 'You wouldn't last five minutes in the army without us watching your back.'

'He's right,' slurred Ash. 'You'll end up dead without us.'

Ezra placed his hands on the table and leaned in. 'Then put your money where your mouth is and join with me.' Ezra slowly stared at each of them in turn and when he was met by stony silence, shook his head. 'Somehow I didn't think any of you would risk your cosy futures for King and country.'

It was a challenge. He knew it and they knew it. And he wasn't even sure if it was one he wanted them to accept. He didn't want to be responsible for making sure they came back unharmed. Was he being selfish? Yet he'd come to realise he didn't belong anywhere apart from with his friends. And he was reluctant to let them go. This was his way of holding on to something of his own—his friendships and his pride.

'I'm wondering how you'll cope as a soldier when your respect for authority is all but non-existent?' Ash said.

'They'd better promote me up the ranks and put me in charge, then.' Ezra winked.

There was a long silence before Adam spoke. 'Well, seeing as there is nothing cosy about my miserable future and I loathe the prospect of being a vicar with every fibre of my being, how much is a commission?' Adam was just as reluctant as Ezra to return home—he wanted to be a lawyer, yet his father was insistent he go into the priesthood.

'Seven hundred and fifty pounds—but you'll make that back in no time in salary and pension.'

He could tell his friend was tempted.

After a beat, Adam placed his glass down on the table with an air of finality. 'Then I'm in. For King and country.'

'Me, too,' said Ash out of the blue.

Ezra frowned at his best friend. 'Because you have a sudden, visceral loathing of Napoleon, too, that you've kept hidden from me all this time?'

'Because I don't want to be left out if you and Adam are going and because I've never been to the Continent and I am due an adventure,' slurred Ash as he reached for more cognac. 'Besides, how on earth would I live with myself if you two idiots got yourself killed simply because I wasn't there to save you?'

Hawk glared at the three of them and then huffed. 'Thanks a lot.'

'For what?' asked Adam.

'For ruining my graduation, all my plans and my life in one fell swoop.'

'How is us joining up to fight the French ruining your life?'

'Because we all know that none of you will last five minutes in the cavalry without me constantly watching your backs.'

'So you're really coming with me?' Ezra said, surprised, worried at what he'd got them all into, but also excited that perhaps their adventure together wasn't over—not yet. They were delaying the future for a little while longer.

'Of course. We're always with you, Ezra.'

'Then I feel, gentlemen, that a new toast is now appropriate.' Ezra raised his tumbler. 'To the cavalry and victory!'

'To the cavalry and victory!' they said in unison, clinking their glasses and tipping back the rest of their drinks.

And in a few months' time, he'd be back—and able to prove to Viscount Hart that he was a soldier and a man to be respected, worthy of all he was set to inherit.

Chapter One

London, England— seven years later, 1816

This wasn't the first time Ezra had an appointment at dawn. But for a renowned Waterloo Lieutenant Colonel, he could think of no better way to settle a dispute than with a duel—after all, he was used to defending his honour and his country on the field.

Back to back, he and Baron Mounier began to walk to the count—ten paces apart over the hard, frosty ground of Hyde Park. Shoulders down, chest forward, Ezra blew out a breath as he took long, steady strides.

'One, two, three…'

Time seemed to slow down and he became increasingly aware of his surroundings—the snapping of a twig underfoot and the thick morning mist swirling around him. He knew it would make it harder to hit his target, but he had experience on his side.

'Four, five, six…'

He heard his opponent cock his pistol, the distinctive sound of metal scraping against metal reverberating around the enclosure, and his fingers tightened on his own trigger. It felt good—powerful—to have a weapon in his hand again. But was Baron Mounier losing his nerve?

'Seven, eight, nine...'

He turned, but the Baron fired early, the loud crack shattering the still silence and sending a flock of birds in the trees soaring into flight before circling overhead.

Ezra stood stock-still and, in that moment, he wondered if he really cared whether he lived or died. It was a sentiment that had made him reckless, although effective, on the frontline. Hell, it was why he had gone to war in the first place, prepared to die for his friends and his country. And over the past seven years, the battlefield had become his domain, his normality, and he realised now that he kept finding himself in these situations, starting a fight, putting himself in harm's way, perhaps chasing the high he'd experienced during the war.

The bullet flew past his left ear, narrowly missing him.

'Ten.'

He grinned. 'It would appear you missed, Lord Mounier,' he said, propelling his steady voice across the distance between them. 'I, however, shall not.'

He saw his opponent's lips tremble, the Baron's weapon fall to his side in defeat and, finally, even though the man was French, Ezra took pity on him. He knew deep down it was his own anger that was to blame for this situation and, suddenly, wanting to put the Baron out of his misery, he lifted his arm aloft and aimed his pistol upwards, firing his shot at the sky. The boom carried over the landscape, sending squirrels scarpering and bringing the matter to a close.

Baron Mounier glanced up, his eyes wide with relieved shock.

'I will not add injury to insult, Lord Mounier. I admit I lost my temper the other evening at White's,' Ezra said, walking back to the Baron swiftly, looking him directly in the eye. Ezra gave a small, dignified bow. 'I am sorry you took offence at my words quoted in that political pamphlet. You were right to demand satisfaction in defence of your character.'

'Well, why the devil didn't you say so at the time? Why bring us out here and make us go through all this?' the Baron asked.

Ezra shrugged. 'I admit I find it hard to decline a challenge—and hard to forgive and forget our countries were recently at war, that my friends and I fought and bled against your kind.'

He had been brought up by the Viscount to mistrust the French and for these past twelve years, France had been Britain's most constant enemy. Napoleon's war had taken over years of his life. He had returned a changed man—scarred, inside and out. But despite there still being tension between the British and French, he knew those who had fled France, seeking asylum here, were not at fault and he must try to remember it. He needed to let go of some of his memories, his anger.

The man shook his head, his face ashen, clearly still shaken by the duel. 'We came to your country in peace when I was a boy. We have always been on your side against the Revolutionaries. We pose no threat to you.'

Ezra nodded. 'I hope your honour has been satisfied and we can now settle our quarrel?'

But a loud clamouring of a horse's hooves approaching drew his attention, making Ezra's pulse quicken once more, for they would no doubt be in trouble with the law if they were to be found here. Yet to his astonishment, out of the thick London fog appeared the figure of a lone woman on horseback. She was wearing a grey riding coat with striking blue braiding, but it was her hair that caught his attention. She wore it down and loose, as if she had left this morning in such a rush, she hadn't had time to fix it, the strawberry-blonde strands tumbling down over her shoulders, and his heart slammed against his ribs at her raw beauty.

'Whoa.' She brought the horse to a halt just feet away from Ezra and Lord Mounier, with the control of an experienced rider, and gracefully swung herself down from the animal. 'Aunt Malvine told me you had gone, you fool! You had me worried half to death.' And she threw her arms around the Baron.

Ezra's brow rose in surprise. He hadn't known the man was married. He had done well for himself. Exceptionally well.

And then she turned, focusing her bright angry gaze on him. Eyes as blue as the Atlantic he'd sailed on his voyage to the Continent held him in their grasp, a jolt of awareness rushing through him.

'You were a soldier?'

'Yes.'

'Then shame on you,' she spat. 'For you should know better than most that the days for fighting are long over. I insist you stop this nonsense at once. This man is all I have in the world and I will not let him throw his future away on the likes of someone like you.'

He was taken aback by her sharp words. He had never

seen a woman show such open contempt for him before. No one but the Viscount had ever chastised him so.

Despite often wondering if he deserved to be respected, knowing his true roots, Ezra was used to being well regarded in society. The Harts had moved here when he was ten and they had relied on people making assumptions—people believing him to be their own flesh and blood. They saw no point in correcting them, and the lie had been easy to maintain.

It wasn't until he'd grown up that he'd realised their ruse had done him a disservice, because now it felt like a loaded cannon, just waiting to go off. Now he had to keep up the pretence or face the humiliation of confessing the truth of his background.

Baron Mounier stepped forward, placing a hand on the woman's arm, perhaps not wanting to give cause for another challenge. 'Calm yourself, Seraphine. This is Mr Ezra Hart, heir to the Artington estate.'

'I know who he is.' She spoke in a very slight, melodious French accent as she continued to hold his gaze. 'It was you who spoke out about us in that pamphlet distributed around the *ton* last week, was it not? I believe you called us "the plague"?'

'Seraphine!' Lord Mounier admonished her. 'Not now. Mr Hart was a Lieutenant Colonel in Wellington's army and I was just about to accept his apology. The matter has been resolved. All is well. And you should not be here.'

'Neither should you,' she said.

'Think of your reputation.'

'Think of yours.'

Baron Mounier blew out a breath. 'Forgive me, Mr

Hart. Allow me to introduce Miss Seraphine Mounier, my sister.'

'Sister?' Ezra queried, a peculiar feeling of relief and renewed interest coursing through him. 'It is a pleasure to meet you, Miss Mounier. As you can see, I did not harm him,' he said, offering her his best smile.

'I am pleased about that, for your sake, else the consequences would have been great indeed.'

He raised an eyebrow. 'Is that so? Your family is important to you?'

'It is everything to me.'

It had been to him, too, once. Not any more. His family was dead to him—they had been since the day they'd given him up. As for the Viscount, things had been different since Ezra had returned from the war—after all, he'd been to hell and back out there, in a position where he'd made decisions that determined life or death for others, so no situation could ever be as dire as that, even his stifled life at Artington.

Ezra had returned to find the Viscount grieving for his wife. She had died from a fever the previous summer. Ezra and the Viscountess had never been especially close, but he still felt sad he hadn't been able to say his goodbyes. And now it was just the two of them, practically strangers, rattling around the grand estate.

In his overwhelming grief for his wife, the Viscount seemed to have lost himself, lacking interest in life. He had been mildly pleased to hear Ezra had progressed through the officer ranks on merit, and had surprised Ezra by entrusting him to take over the running of the Artington estate. It had been a huge moment for Ezra, though he wondered why he sought validation from someone who didn't even seem to like him.

'Come now, Brother, we must leave this place, before the authorities arrive and find us here,' Seraphine said, before turning back to Ezra. 'If I were you, I would flee, too, while you still have the chance.'

'Thank you for the advice,' he said. 'But no one got hurt. There has been no wrongdoing.'

'Only in my eyes then.' And her icy, reprimanding look told him she meant it.

He wasn't used to a woman being so cool towards him, so immune to his charm. He guessed, in this instance, he deserved it. So why did he feel his blood heating? He had the feeling if the Baron knew the thoughts he was having about his sister, he'd take up his pistol once more and this time he wouldn't miss!

Whatever was the matter with him? He even found himself offering her his hand, to assist her ascent back on to her horse. There was a long moment while they stared at one another, her leather-gloved fingers avoiding his.

'I hope you will allow me to make it up to you both?'

'And how do you propose to do that?' she asked.

'Lord Mounier, you must join me for a shoot at Artington Hall some time.'

'I would like that very much,' the Baron said.

The lady pulled a face and he knew instantly she disapproved—of him, or the activity?

'You do not endorse hunting, Miss Mounier?'

'It is not how I would choose to spend a morning, but as for you, it seems you cannot get enough of having a weapon in your hand, wishing to cause another creature harm.'

He grinned. He had never met a more spirited woman.

'I assume you will be attending Lady Bulphan's ball this evening?'

'My brother is insisting that we do so, despite my pro-testations.'

His brows rose again. 'You do not care for balls?' If not, she certainly wasn't like the other ladies in the *ton*, whose only care seemed to be the next glittering soirée at which they might ensnare a potential spouse.

'Not when we are so obviously unwelcome. I would rather avoid the people and places who discriminate against us.'

Baron Mounier clicked his tongue, interjecting, 'Hush, Seraphine. Of course we would not miss Lady Bulphan's ball.'

'Then perhaps you would allow me the honour of a dance?' Ezra asked her.

The lady swung herself up on her horse unaided and settled herself astride the animal, shocking him once more, before staring down at him, lancing him again with a look. She gripped the reins tightly in her hands. 'My apologies, but I believe my dance card is full for this evening. And I am certain you would not want to dance with the likes of me—a disease.'

Pressing her ankles into the horse's sides, she spurred her animal into action, taking the lead as she and her brother galloped across the rolling parkland, leaving Ezra confounded—and, for the first time in a long while, feeling strangely glad to be alive.

Seraphine threw her cloak on to the hook and stormed up the stairs of their Mayfair town house to the first floor, then up the second flight of steps to her room, her brother hot on her heels. She threw open the curtains, ignoring her unmade bed that she'd jumped out of in such a hurry, and turned around to see Henri leaning against the door frame. Breathless but invigorated from the morning ride, she steeled herself for his reproof.

'Sister, you know our situation here is unstable. Why do you insist upon being so wilful and making things worse?'

'How could me turning up to try to save your life possibly have made things worse? That arrogant, appalling man was about to kill you.'

'But he did not. And you think that you arriving half-undressed, hair dishevelled, riding astride and offering him a few stern words, is going to help? How exactly? Do you know who that man is?'

'Hateful, that is who he is. Henri, how can you forgive the things he said about us?' She had read that pamphlet with disgust. Mr Ezra Hart had said the French immigrants were a daily reminder of the enemy the British soldiers had fought. The article was so damning, it was enough to turn the whole *ton* against them.

When she had heard of his subsequent quarrel with her brother at White's, and then of their meeting at dawn, her frustration had flared at the unjustness of it all.

She and Henri had been just children when their parents were executed by an angry crowd in the terrors of the Revolution. Devastated and afraid, they had been taken in by their aunt and uncle, fled the brutality in France and made their way to London. No strangers to court in Versailles, upon their arrival here their aunt had quickly become an acquaintance of Queen Charlotte, allowing them to mix in aristocratic circles. Yet Seraphine had always felt like an outcast growing up in London society. She knew the other ladies in the *ton* whispered about her behind her back, even now.

When the war was over, she had hoped the prejudice would be, too. But with the soldiers' return from Waterloo came a fresh wave of anger towards her people, highlighting their difference and wanting them gone. And while she knew it was a sentiment only felt by a small minority, exacerbated by the crop failures and food shortages this past winter, their security had been threatened.

This morning, she had felt her own anger burn—that enough was enough. She had thrown on her cloak, knowing she must go and put a stop to the duel. She could not let the narrow-mindedness of a few—the likes of Mr Ezra Hart—ruin her brother's life.

'He is one of the most influential men in the *ton*!' Henri said.

'Exactly! The things he said…'

'Never mind the things he said. He admitted he was drunk and did not mean half of it.'

'And the other half?' she asked, cocking an eyebrow.

Henri sighed. 'Seraphine,' he warned, 'while I am trying to calm the situation and improve our reputation, you seem intent on destroying it.'

'I just do not see why I should have to be pleasant to everyone, when they are not pleasant to us!' She sighed, sitting down on the edge of the bed. 'How is it right that he thinks he can say such things, then challenge you to a duel just because you are standing up for yourself for being born in France? A country you have not set foot in for two decades because our parents opposed its regime. It makes me livid.'

Henri crossed his arms over his chest. 'Rightly or wrongly, these people are still angry about the war. As are we. But it is hard for them to distinguish us from our compatriots—those they fought against in Napoleon's army.'

'We have faced prejudice and discrimination for years. We are victimised by the very people who are meant to offer us protection. We are classed as outsiders and always will be.'

She knew they would fit in better in England if they forgot about their heritage, but she could not. Forgetting about it would be traitorous to her parents—it was her link to them, keeping them in her memory.

He sighed. 'Please, Sister. Try to remember these people, this country, offered us a safe haven in our time of need. Would you rather have returned to France to face the guillotine?'

She swallowed.

Henri sighed and came into the room. 'I do not understand you,' he said, shaking his head. 'Do you not think it is time you at least tried to fit in here?'

'I have tried!' she said. 'But you think I should change who I am just to please society? Because of a need to be accepted by others? We may have left our homeland, but it does not mean I wish to forget my heritage. You think I should try to be more like others in an effort to blend in?'

'I do not think you could blend in if you tried!'

She wasn't sure if that was a compliment or not.

He blew out a breath. 'Can you not put aside your stubborn pride and try to be happy?' he said.

'I am happy.'

'No, you are not. Seraphine, I have been much too lenient with you—feeling bad about everything we suffered, the things we saw, about Mother and Father dying, having to leave our home. I have wanted to make it up to you. Perhaps I have spoilt you. I have tried to protect you here and bring you up properly. And I am proud of you—the woman you have become. You are beautiful, intelligent, kind… But you are much too wilful. Something needs to change. Which is why I have made my decision…'

She looked up at him.

'I have decided the time has come for you to marry.'

'What? Henri, no!' she said, launching herself back to her feet in outrage.

'Yes. I cannot have you sitting around here, reading, or playing pianoforte all day, walking out into the city alone doing God knows what—and I certainly cannot have you meddling in my affairs, trying to fight my battles.'

'I am sorry–'

'Let me finish! You making a good match will help our situation. Help us all. It will expand our horizons, strengthen our position. And you cannot expect me, and our uncle, to support you for ever.'

His words were like a punch to the stomach. Hurt, she tried to defend herself. 'I make my own wage—through teaching French, my dance lessons.'

'It is not enough!'

She slumped back down on the bed, running her hands over the soft fabric that matched the elaborate bed hangings and wallpaper. She knew given their background she was lucky, compared to some, to live in such a high level of comfort, but still…

'I have no desire to be a man's wife,' she said miserably.

'What about a mother?'

'Why do I have to conform to another role everyone wants to pigeonhole me into? I always had far greater ambitions than marriage and raising children,' she said, shaking her head.

'Oh, really? Like what?' Henri asked, coming to sit down beside her.

She shrugged. 'I want to help people. Make a difference. You know that.' Henri was aware of her charitable work with émigrés less fortunate than themselves. Besides, she had always thought if she were to marry, it would be for love. She would not settle for anything less. And how could she love or be loved here, when no one understood her? And when she struggled to trust anyone?

She didn't remember much about her mother and father, but she did remember the way they used to look at each other, dance with each other—as if her father couldn't bear to let her mother go. As if they knew what the other was thinking without even speaking. She had re-enacted it many times with her dolls growing up. But she knew it was rare to find someone like that. And if you did, surely you were just opening yourself up to hurt if something should befall the person you cared about? No, it wasn't worth the pain.

Henri took her chin in his hand and turned her head to look at him. 'You can make a difference by being a wife, Seraphine. By having a family. Just imagine what that would do for people like us if you were to wed an

English gentleman. Someone who could help us to be accepted here.' He rose off the bed. 'And you can start by looking your best at Lady Bulphan's ball tonight.'

She groaned and collapsed back on to the bed. 'I have nothing to wear.'

'You went to the modiste just last week!'

'I mean I have nothing anyone will approve of to wear.' She smiled.

'Oh, dear God. You had better show me.'

She propped herself up on to her elbows. 'You really care to see them?'

'Yes, when I have a vested interest in what it could do for us,' he said.

And she couldn't help but laugh.

She padded over to her wardrobe and threw open the doors.

'You will look lovely in this one,' Henri said, getting up and pulling out a white tulle gown.

She held it up against her body, looked in the mirror and pulled a face. 'It is very demure.'

'That is a good thing,' he said reproachfully. 'Most of the *ton* will be wearing white—you will fit in a dream.'

Which was exactly why her eye was drawn to the Imperial blue-silk gown. It had a high, under-the-bust waistline in the French style and elaborate detailing on the skirt. It was less boned, more naturally fitting, so it clung to her body and showed off her curves.

She sighed, realising her brother had a point. Perhaps she could try a little harder to conform.

'I hate balls,' she said.

'I do not know why.'

'Yes, you do. People overlook me. Snub me. They do not like me. I would rather stay at home.'

'And how will you find a husband here? We are going. No more buts.' He stalked towards the door. 'I am going out for a while. Have a good day. Try to be good,' and then he paused and turned back to look at her. 'Despite my displeasure at your behaviour this morning, thank you for coming after me, caring about me.'

'I am glad you are all right,' she said, before scrutinising the white gown against her skin in the mirror.

'And, Seraphine? Go for the French blue one. You will look stunning in that and you know you want to give the *ton* something to talk about.' He winked.

Chapter Two

Ezra took a steadying breath as he began to push through the crushing crowd in the ballroom of the Mayfair mansion, alongside the other guests arriving in a swirl of sumptuous silk, feathers and pearls. The glass doors were thrown open at the side of the room and the guests spilled out on to the terrace in the fading light, their animated voices raised to be heard above the clinking glasses and tuneful strumming of the band.

Ezra scanned the hall. There were now perhaps eighty people in the room, yet apart from Ash at his side, no one he especially had the inclination to speak to.

Where were they? Adam, Hawk...

Ezra caught a glimpse of his reflection in the ornate mirror on the wall and he drew a hand across his bleak face. He looked tired. The result of too many late evenings spent at White's and too many restless nights' sleep, his dreams darkened by images of battle. Unfortunately, he'd discovered it would take a lot more than downing a bottle of whisky before bed to forget the things he had witnessed over there.

He tried to shake away his thoughts. It was funny how he had been able to give a rallying battle speech to his men, inspiring them to take up arms time and time again, yet he could barely motivate himself to conjure up the courage to join in the revelry and dance. He had grown up having the rules of society drummed into him, so he knew how to behave and how to make polite conversation when he had to. Only he would feel better participating in the superficial interactions of the evening alongside his friends.

He knew tonight was different, important. But his starched linen cravat, tied tightly with precision, and the collar of his crisp cotton shirt were choking him in the cloying, glittering ballroom, the air thick with the scent of women's perfume and strict etiquette governing his every move. It almost made him wish to be back on the frontline at Waterloo, fighting, free of restraint.

Almost.

He was all too aware his presence this evening made a statement—it declared he was looking for a wife.

He adjusted his cravat, loosening it a little, feeling suffocated by the expectations placed upon his shoulders. He may have promised the Viscount he would fulfil his duty this Season and find a respectable bride, the old man insistent that he marry to sire an heir and secure the family legacy, but it didn't mean he liked the idea.

The man seemed to have become even colder, even more distant, if that was possible, in the years Ezra had been away. And it was why Ezra tried to spend as little of his time at Artington as possible. He got the paperwork done, spoke to the staff, then retreated to his bachelor lodgings. But it was his staying away, his nights out on the *ton*, which had been the cause of the latest argument between them and the Viscount had given him an ultimatum.

The man had reasserted that the only reason he and his wife had taken Ezra on was so they would have the chance to continue the family legacy—and the time had come for Ezra to marry and produce an heir. He said if Ezra didn't rein in his behaviour, if he refused to wed, then he would strike him from his will and prevent him from inheriting at all. He would reveal the truth about who Ezra really was.

It had come as a huge shock. Would his guardian really do such a thing, after all this time? He couldn't be sure. But he wouldn't take the risk.

Ezra knew how fortunate he was to be here tonight, when many of his comrades had fallen in battle, and to be mixing with the most fashionable elite in such safe and opulent surroundings. He was aware of the impressed hush that had settled on the room as he'd walked in. He imagined the women and their mothers found him handsome and his wealth and connections meant he was considered one of the most eligible bachelors in the *ton* this Season. Yet still only Adam, Ash and Hawk were familiar with the truth of the situation—his real self and where he had come from.

Ezra could only imagine the shame he would feel if the Viscount revealed the truth now—after all he had suffered in trying to prove himself worthy. It was the worst thing that could happen; it would be humiliating to have people know that he hadn't been wanted by his birth family, and it would bring great embarrassment if the *ton* was to discover he didn't deserve the riches bestowed upon him by the Harts.

Status, he had been taught, or at least the impression of having it, was everything—the very essence of your importance and power, not family or love.

So he would find a wife before the Season was over. If it meant the Viscount would honour his promise and make him his heir—and keep his secret—then he would do it.

Fortunately, he had no interest in a romantic match—he had learned a long time ago that caring only led to grief, so choosing a bride who would please the Viscount shouldn't be too hard.

Thoughts of how foolish he'd been, going ahead with that duel this morning, putting his reputation—and his life—at risk, entered his mind. As did the woman he'd met. He searched the room once more to see if he could see Baron Mounier and his sister, the vivacious Miss Mounier. The image of her standing up to him this morning dressed in just her nightgown and cloak, her eyes shimmering with a fierce determination, had strangely stuck with him all day long.

Glancing around, it wasn't hard to find her in the crowd—she stood out due to her grace and poise. A tall, statuesque beauty amid all the flowers and flamboyance, talking to an older woman on the far side of the room. Her blonde hair with titian streaks was fixed properly tonight, parted in the middle and pulled up into a simple, elegant bun. It was adorned with pearls rather than the outlandish ostrich feathers of the debutantes, and her attractive face was framed with soft tendrils of curls.

While most of the women on the marriage mart wore white-silk dresses, elaborately encrusted with jewels and puff sleeves in a bid to make them dazzle the brightest,

Miss Seraphine stood out for her beauty alone—her slender curves accentuated in a vivid but elegant blue-silk gown with a low neckline that hinted at the pert swells beneath. Her sleeves were small—sophisticated—and she wore long white gloves that offered just a glimpse of smooth, tantalising bare skin above the elbow. He wondered at her age—slightly younger than himself at eight and twenty perhaps, but older than most of the debutantes. Still, she looked stunning in the flickering golden light of the ballroom.

As if she could sense his eyes on her, her condemning gaze lifted, meeting his across the room, and a shot of recognition, appreciation, as powerful as that flare from his pistol this morning, spread through him again. He inclined his head, but just as quickly as their eyes met, she turned away, giving him the cut, which only increased his interest in her.

He cursed himself once more for drunkenly giving his overly harsh opinions, offering a quote or two about the émigrés in that pamphlet, saying that their presence was a reminder of the war. And that after such a terrible winter, which had caused crops to fail and a shortage of food, the situation was worsened by having extra mouths to feed. He was certain he would not have been so vocal had he been sober. It had been his anger and the whisky talking. And perhaps his guilt, for their presence was also a reminder of the things he had done—the lives he had taken, people of her kind. He deserved her disdain, yet still she fascinated him.

He clicked his jaw, cross with himself. He did not want to be attracted to her. He knew he should not be. For she was headstrong. She was French. She would be deemed unsuitable by his guardian—and perhaps by a few in society. And it was vital he made a match worthy of the Viscount's respected, noble line. In his former life, he might have been able to pursue her, but not now he was a Hart. Besides, he didn't even know why he was thinking along these lines, as she'd hated him at first sight.

No, he would have to turn his attention elsewhere, yet his reluctance to do so disturbed him, and he realised it would be better for his sake if he did not dance with her. She was a danger to him, in the way an attractive woman was to a man who had to make a choice with his head, not his body. She was a danger to his reputation. No, he realised now—a dance was out of the question and the best course of action in this circumstance would be for him to maintain his distance.

Finally, he saw his comrades. The only people here who would know what he was thinking, how he was feeling—ready to offer up a wink and a wicked grin, a glimmer of mutual understanding in their eyes, and make light of more than one of them having to find a wife this Season. Now they could go into this fresh battle for a bride together.

Seraphine was all too aware of the soldiers' presence at the ball, especially the arrogant Mr Ezra Hart whom she'd had the displeasure of meeting this very morning.

She had not been able to stop thinking about her brother's duel at dawn and that man and what might have happened. The things he had said about them…

'There are plenty of eligible men here tonight, Seraphine,' her aunt said, breaking her out of her reverie.

The older woman looked magnificent this evening, in a wig to rival that of the Queen.

'Aunt Malvine,' she warned, taking a sip of her punch, 'despite what my brother might have told you, I have no desire to find a husband.'

'It seems such a waste, my dear. Just look at you. You are beautiful.'

'Thank you, Aunt. You flatter me. But I am quite content with my lot, believe me. It is Henri who I would like to see settled and have children. I only wish to be a doting aunt, just like you.'

'But you deserve to be happy, too, as your parents were. I did tell Henri I could ask for an audience with the Queen to see if she could do anything.'

'No, Aunt, really, I assure you, there is no need.'

Being French, they were both aware she had been unable to make her debut in society like the many beautiful young debutantes here tonight. Her lips twisted at the meaning of the French word—*female beginner*. In what, she wondered? Courting? Love? She supposed that did describe her, but she was far too old to be thinking about that kind of nonsense now.

Besides, marriage meant compromise. Compromising her culture and values, her personal goals, when she wanted to maintain control of her independence.

Her aunt glanced over her shoulder, unwilling to give up her cause. 'That is Lord Wentworth over there, dancing with Miss Andrews. He is a widower. Most charming and he has five thousand pounds a year.'

Seraphine's eyes reluctantly followed her aunt's across the room. The man was a great deal older than her, and looked a little out of breath from the vigour of dancing.

'Or there's Lord Barrington, surrounded by a flock of eager young ladies. Rather handsome, do you not think?'

'Perhaps.'

But her eye had already been drawn over to the corner, where Mr Ezra Hart stood with an acquaintance. He was brazenly staring right at her and their gazes collided across the ballroom, causing her breath to hitch.

Not one of the men her aunt had pointed out was his equal. He was taller than the rest, with dark, wavy, almost untameable hair and even darker eyes. He was impeccably dressed and held himself upright, an aloof air of superiority surrounding him. He looked different to the reckless, pistol-wielding man she had seen on the duelling ground this morning.

'And I see you have noticed the Viscount's son, Mr Ezra Hart.'

Seraphine blanched, embarrassed that she'd momentarily forgotten herself and been caught staring.

'Have you been introduced without my knowing, Niece?'

'Henri knows him,' she said, abruptly turning away. '*Unfortunately.* His character is questionable.' She thought back to his wicked grin this morning as he had blatantly tried to flirt with her—after duelling with her brother!

Seraphine hoped her aunt and uncle had not read the despicable words that had been written in that pamphlet. She always tried to shield them from such things.

'Really? I have heard he is quite the catch of the Season.'

'Is he?' She shrugged, feigning nonchalance. 'What do you know of him?'

Her aunt gave a knowing smile and Seraphine could have kicked herself for showing even the slightest bit of interest. 'Well now, let me see. He is said to be a war hero—a favourite of the Duke of Wellington. He was rumoured to be wild on the battlefield—and just as wild now he is back in the *ton*,' Aunt Malvine said with a wink. 'Some would consider him a rake.'

'See! I told you,' Seraphine said, triumphant. She knew she had been right about him. His open assault on them still made her seethe with anger when she thought about it. She pitied the poor woman who ended up married to him.

'But if that is even to be believed, he is a very rich rake.' Her aunt lowered her voice and leaned in. 'I have heard he has twenty thousand a year. His father, the Viscount, has been fragile lately, since the recent death of his wife, meaning rumours are rife the young man is on the cusp of inheriting the Harts' grand estate at Artington on the outskirts of London. I think his past could be overlooked for such a fortune, no? They are a very respected family—generous benefactors to the *ton*, donating to the church and the veterans. You could do a lot worse than becoming a viscountess.'

Seraphine tutted. 'You are not listening, Aunt. My time has long passed to make my debut in society. I do not wish to marry and especially not to that man!' Seraphine chastised her. 'I am grateful I have not had to spend months practising my curtsies. I was merely intrigued to know more about the man my brother has spoken of. That is the extent of my interest.'

'If you say so, dear…'

Unable to help herself, Seraphine glanced back to see Mr Hart's eyes light up as he welcomed two other men into his group, their deep laughter drifting across the room. Thick as thieves they looked, as they talked among themselves, almost oblivious to the rest of the attendees at the ball, and she wondered at their closeness. Had they fought alongside each other in the war, perhaps? She and Henri were close because of all they had been through together.

She forced herself to turn away. She refused to give the Viscount's son any more of her attention.

'More punch, Aunt?'

Ezra still wasn't used to seeing the men out of their uniform, looking clean and refined—and dancing as opposed to fighting. He wondered at which was a more dangerous pursuit. He loathed the ridiculous courting ritual with a passion, yet he knew it was imperative—a chance to converse with a woman and gauge her suitability as a wife.

He had reluctantly danced the first quadrille with Miss Fletcher, and a cotillion with Miss Galpin, much to the smug satisfaction of their mothers. He knew what he embodied to them. Yet he found their daughters lacking. No doubt they could read and write and sew and sing, but he wasn't even sure the Viscount would approve of them—they seemed so fawning and similar, saying whatever they thought he wanted to hear when he would much rather discover their own opinions. Even the Viscount's late wife had been a formidable woman with a strong personality, despite her delicate constitution.

* * *

He had been careful not to dance with the same partner twice. By the end of the third set, which had been no better, he bowed to Miss Hoskins and escorted her to a seat, before seeing his chance to escape. Swiftly excusing himself, he hoped no one would notice his absence for the next turn. Only just as he was making his way outside, he was commandeered by a couple and, much to his consternation, the woman had tears in her eyes.

'Lieutenant Colonel Hart?'

'Yes.'

'We are Lord and Lady Baines. Our son—he fought with you in the Thirteenth. He wrote home about you often. He said that you cared for the welfare of your men. It is an honour to meet you.'

Ezra cleared his throat. 'Major Walter Baines?'

'Yes.'

He swallowed. 'I knew Walter well. It is good to meet you,' he said, shaking the man's hand.

They looked at him in wide-eyed hope, waiting with bated breath, and he knew what they wanted. They needed to know their son had been brave—a Waterloo warrior. That he'd had a good death.

He didn't have the heart to tell them there had been nothing glorious about any of it, not as he'd thought there would be when he'd signed up after Oxford.

He would never be able to forget that final bloody and brutal fight that had lasted all day. The carpet of lifeless bodies and the smell of burning flesh on pyres. The mass graves. Thousands of dead horses. The screams of the wounded that raged on even after the battle had ended and night had fallen.

He felt the familiar sickness swirl. No, he could not tell them that.

An image of Walter's face flashed before his eyes.

They'd received their orders to charge and broken their enemy, before charging again and again. 'Drive them back, Thirteenth!' the rallying cry came. And so they had. But not without sustaining heavy fire.

At one point, he'd seen Walter dispatch an opponent, then the next, before taking a lance to his chest. And Ezra had charged at the men responsible, knocking them down in fury and retaliation. He'd often wondered in the months since—what kind of person did that made him? His stomach churned. If you took a life, did you deserve to have one yourself?

They had won, but how could it feel like a win, when they had lost so many?

He knew Walter's parents needed him to give some meaning to their loss. But he still struggled to comprehend it all himself.

He was sick of the fake slapping of backs and offers of congratulations among the men, as they all tried to pretend, to forget the horrors of what they'd witnessed. Of course he was patriotic, pleased they had toppled Napoleon's power, but when he thought back to how he'd gone off to war, desiring those very words of praise and accolades, thinking it would be easy and they'd return within months, he felt like such a fool. And he would do anything to have his fellow soldiers back.

'He was brave until the end,' he told them. 'One of the best fighters we had. He did you both proud.'

The lady brought a handkerchief up to her eyes. 'Thank you. We miss him dearly.'

Lord Baines put his arm around his wife's shoulder and, after nodding his thanks to Ezra, he led her away.

Ezra felt around in his coat pockets for his hip flask, but they were empty. Damn, he wished he had some of Hawk's strong Scottish whisky right now.

He pushed through the crowds, the haze of body heat, out of the doors and on to the terrace, needing some air, putting as much distance as he could between him and his dark memories, and the throng of women all vying for his attention.

He drew in a few deep, ragged breaths. The thick scent of lavender was heavy on the evening air and the stars glittered in the night sky. Flower borders were bursting with colour, yet not even they couldn't brighten his melancholy thoughts.

There were groups of people milling around, conversing, so he took the steps down into the gardens and rounded the corner, seeking quiet, but instead he rushed headlong into someone coming the other way, his shoulder colliding fiercely with theirs.

'Watch where you're going!' he spat.

'I could say the same to you...'

And he realised he knew that voice. 'Miss Mounier! Always getting in the way, aren't you?' he snapped.

'Oh. It is you,' she said, glaring at him, rubbing her arm. 'And you have no regard for anyone's safety.'

He reared back. 'As lively as I remember.' He gave a slight bow, recovering himself and his manners. 'Forgive me, I was not looking where I was heading.'

'Perhaps you should take more care.'

'I said I was sorry.'

'Sometimes that is not enough.'

His eyes narrowed on her.

He had come out here, trying to outrun the onslaught of his memories, but coming face to face with this beautiful émigrée seemed to shine an even greater light on his behaviour during the war. It plagued his conscience, filling him with remorse. He placed a hand to his clammy brow, the images of battle warring with the sight of Miss Mounier before him. It made him want to run, yet, perversely, he also couldn't bring himself to step away.

He glanced around them, discomfort assailing him as he realised they were out of view from the other guests at the ball.

'I trust you have recovered from this morning's excursions?' he said.

'Indeed. Although I think I now know why that track in Hyde Park is called Rotten Row.'

His lips curved upwards. 'From a French phrase, I believe?'

'Yes. *La Route du Roi*.'

He looked around again at the empty gardens with unease. He could do without a scandal right now. The Viscount had already read him the riot act about his drinking and late-night card games and his ladies of the night, threatening to take away his allowance—and much more—if he didn't toe the line. But in a way it was good they couldn't be seen. He didn't really want to have to explain himself to anyone—why he was conversing with the type of person he had so recently and very publicly criticised.

'You are alone again, Miss Mounier. Is it a habit of yours, I wonder?' Now the censure was on his own tongue.

'It is how I like it. The air is cloying in there, so I decided to take a turn around the gardens.'

'In the dark?'

'Should I be afraid of who I might bump into?'

'Without a doubt.' He smiled. 'Interestingly, you told me your dance card was full, but I am yet to see you take to the dance floor.'

'I am surprised you noticed, you have been inundated with partners yourself.'

'Do you not wish to meet any suitors?'

She stiffened and he instantly realised he'd been too bold, too forward.

'Should women only dance when they want to meet a man, not for their own enjoyment?' she asked.

'I have not seen you partake in the revelry even for your own pleasure.'

'My pleasure is no concern of yours.'

'Seraphine,' a woman's voice called.

'Saved—by my aunt. And on that note, I shall bid you a good evening,' she said, walking past him. For some reason, he found her easy dismissal of him—for the second time today—maddening.

She rounded the corner, heading back towards the ballroom.

'Seraphine, there you are! Aunt and I have been looking for you,' Ezra heard her brother say.

'And here I am.'

Ezra took a breath and came round the corner after her, a walk in the gardens no longer holding such appeal to him.

'Hart! I have been meaning to find you all evening. Please allow me to introduce my aunt, Madame Auclair.'

'It is a pleasure to meet you, *madame*,' Ezra said, turning to the older woman with the huge hairstyle, offering her his best smile.

He sensed Miss Mounier slant him a look, perhaps thinking him disingenuous.

'How are you enjoying the ball, Mr Hart? I expect you are glad to be home and getting back to some semblance of normality, are you not?'

'Indeed,' he said, yet his muscles tensed. He hoped she wasn't about to launch into an enquiry of his endeavours abroad. He did not want to get into that again tonight—especially not with this French woman and her family.

'I have heard many great things about Artington Hall.'

He breathed out a sigh of relief—so it was his home she was interested in, not discussing the conflict. He supposed talking about Artington was the lesser of two evils. 'And all of it true,' he lied smoothly, having had years of practice.

'The architecture and grounds were inspired by your grandfather's Grand Tour and his frequent trips to France, I believe?'

Grandfather...

'Correct, *madame*. You have done your research. We have some beautiful French stained glass—designed and made in Paris.'

'Oh, how delightful.'

'And where is it that you live, Madame Auclair?' he said, humouring her.

'Mayfair. We are very fortunate—it is central to all

the modistes and parks for an afternoon promenade and White's for my husband and Henri, of course.'

'Where is your husband tonight?'

'I admit, he is no fan of these occasions. He is much more at home in the outdoors, walking.'

'A man after my own heart. You know, the route from Mayfair to Artington is a pleasant four-mile walk, past the villages of Fernside and Frampton. Once you head out of town, the terrain involves mostly flat grass and gravel paths. Artington is open to visitors, *madame*, and you and your husband would be most welcome to come and take a tour should you ever be in the area.'

He wondered what had possessed him to extend such an invitation. The Viscount certainly would not approve.

The woman clasped her hands together. 'We would be delighted to.'

'I am sure you were hoping not to see me again so soon, Lord Mounier,' Ezra said as they made their way back inside the ballroom.

'On the contrary, Hart, you promised my sister a dance. I intend to hold you to it.'

Ezra halted. 'Alas, I am afraid I must decline…'

Seraphine felt a punch to her stomach. She wasn't sure if it was her imagination, or if the band had paused playing at that very moment, but it seemed as if everyone had heard Mr Hart's cruel words of dismissal and turned around to stare. It was as if the slight compounded her difference and she had never been so humiliated.

She told herself she hadn't wanted to dance with him anyway, but to be snubbed in such a way, in front of this grand assembly, was mortifying to say the least. It seemed to add weight to the words he'd said about them in that interview and she hated him more than ever.

Did he think himself superior to her because she was French? Did he think their connections less than his own? Maybe that was true, but she would never make anyone feel the way he had just done.

'You forget, Henri, I told Mr Hart my dance card is already full,' she said, trying to defuse the situation, and fast, before her brother took offence on her behalf and caused an even greater scene.

'Indeed, you did, Miss Mounier.' Mr Hart gave a stiff bow, giving her one last look before he left them.

Her contempt for him roared within.

'Well, I never!' said her aunt, under her breath.

'I told you. He is most disagreeable,' Seraphine muttered.

'I was going to say I found him rather charming, until–'

'No matter,' Seraphine said, cutting her off. 'It is not as if I ever intend to see him again,' she added, raising her chin in the air. 'In fact, I am determined Mr Hart will not have any more impact on my night.'

So why, then, could she not get him out of her thoughts all evening? She watched as he danced with Miss Jennings and Lady Frances Fairfax, a peculiar burning sensation searing through her stomach. She wondered what made those women more appealing than her—yet why did she even care?

She couldn't believe he had questioned her non-participation in the dances. It had made her feel…what? Like the spinster that she was? But why should she be concerned about his opinion? She had already heard the worst of it.

Yet his rebuke of her behaviour made her want to rebel, to create more of a reaction from him. It was absurd. And it led her to accept when her brother's friends asked her to dance. She asked them questions and responded to their own with faux enthusiasm. And she made sure they danced well, and wide, laughing loudly, right under Ezra Hart's proud, snooty nose.

But once it was over, she felt foolish, as she watched the Viscount's son mix with the guests in the room, greeting old friends warmly and being introduced to new acquaintances, and she bitterly wished she had never met him. She certainly would never be able to forgive or forget his undignified treatment of her.

Chapter Three

Seraphine stepped down from the carriage outside the King's Theatre. She was so glad to be going to the opera, instead of another ball. Music was a passion of hers, so this was at least something she could enjoy. She could sit in the dark and listen to the performers without having to make polite conversation.

'Why have you never brought me here before?' she asked, taking Henri's arm as he escorted her inside and, for a moment, the spectacle took her breath away. She was struck by the lavish, magnificent interiors and such an outlandish parade of beautiful gowns and decorative headwear.

'Because one does not really go to the opera to see a performance, but to put on one, and I figured you have to do enough of that already,' he said, squeezing her arm. 'You see, going to the opera is as much about the audience and the fashion, who is who in society, as it is about the singers and the music. Now remember, the purpose of tonight is for you to meet people.'

'Can I not just enjoy the music?' she whispered. She really had no interest in conversing with strangers, especially those she had to hide aspects of herself from to try to fit in in the hope that they might like her. What was the point?

'I am afraid not.'

She grimaced, but she wasn't sure anything could diminish her excitement right now, especially when she heard the strings of the orchestra warming up in the distance.

She smoothed her gloved hand over her dress as a waiter carrying flutes of champagne came towards her and she accepted a glass, graciously. When she took a sip, the bubbles helped to warm her stomach, easing a little of her tension.

'Miss Mounier,' a greeting came from her side.

They turned to see Lady Frances and her friend, Miss Jennings, who Seraphine recognised from Lady Bulphan's ball the other evening.

'Go. Make friends. And be pleasant,' Henri hissed in her ear.

'I am always pleasant,' she said and then her brother was gone, swallowed up by the crowd.

She took another sip of her drink, hoping it would bring her courage and fast.

'How delightful to see you here,' Lady Frances said with what sounded like a distinct lack of sincerity in her tone. 'I did not know you were *the sort of person* who liked the opera.'

And what kind of person was that? Seraphine wondered.

'Neither did I. It is my first time.'

Lady Frances feigned a gasp. 'First time? Did you hear that, Miss Jennings?' she said with a trill of laughter, turning to her friend with wide, mock-shocked eyes.

'Yes, but I love music, so I expect I shall enjoy it very much.'

'I have no doubt you will.' Miss Jennings smiled kindly.

Mr Hart and a male acquaintance chose that very moment to stroll past and Seraphine's heart sank. The evening was rapidly taking a turn for the worse. She glanced around. Where had Henri gone?

The ladies turned and preened, offering the men their best smiles, almost blocking Seraphine from view.

'Lady Frances, Miss Jennings,' Mr Hart said, bowing his head. 'How do you do this evening?'

The women giggled, fanning their faces, and Seraphine tried to stop herself from rolling her eyes.

Then he gave Seraphine a curt nod. 'Miss Mounier.'

'We have just discovered Miss Mounier has never visited the opera before,' Lady Frances said, slanting a glance at her. 'Can you imagine? And at her *older* age? I think this must be at least my seventh or eighth time.'

Seraphine bit back a tart remark and glanced Mr Hart's way, but he avoided her gaze, finding a spot just above her shoulder, making her want to turn to see what he was looking at. Was he really trying to snub her for a second time and pretend they'd never met in front of his important friends?

'Can I get you ladies a glass of something?' he said, looking between Lady Frances and Miss Jennings.

He was!

She wished she could do the same and ignore him, but with his tall frame and broad shoulders, she was finding that harder than she'd like. She didn't want to admit he looked handsome in a dark-blue wool coat and breeches, with a carefully tied pale-grey neckcloth. No wonder the ladies were practically swooning.

'What a beautiful gown you are wearing this evening, Miss Mounier,' Miss Jennings added, trying to include her.

It was a sapphire-silk gown, with gold brocade, which the modiste had created for this very occasion, saying it was Seraphine's colour.

'In the French style, I believe?' Lady Frances interjected and Miss Jennings gave her friend a withering look.

Seraphine smiled tightly. 'Yes, a personal preference.'

'How nice. Some might call it unpatriotic, of course.'

'I thought we were beyond all that. The *ton* is partial to French literature, art and cuisine, is it not? It follows suit that we should also like French fashion,' Seraphine said. 'I think the contribution French people have made to British culture over the past century should be celebrated, not slighted.' She had promised her brother she would behave, but she was finding it increasingly difficult to do so with every passing comment. She had never felt so judged.

'What do you think, Mr Hart?' Lady Frances said, trying to bring him into the debate. 'We know you have had something to say on all things French recently. What do you think of Miss Mounier's gown? Could it be right I saw my servant in something similar only recently?'

Seraphine bit down on her tongue, hard, until she tasted blood. The woman was insufferable.

Mr Hart seemed to hesitate, as if deciding whether or not to be drawn into the conversation. Finally, he looked up at Seraphine, their eyes meeting briefly, before he turned back to the others.

'My valet manages my own wardrobe and I am certainly not equipped to comment on female fashions, Lady Frances.'

'But we do so enjoy hearing your views on *all* subjects,' she said, flattering him.

And Seraphine couldn't help herself any longer.

'And yet I am not sure I asked for anyone's opinions on the matter, especially not the narrow-minded, inconsequential views of *some*. I do hope you do not have to eat your words when I see you and the rest of the *ton* wearing a dress just like this before the Season is out, Lady Frances.' And she tipped her glass up and finished her champagne in one large gulp, before placing the glass down on a nearby table and walking away. 'Enjoy the opera,' she called over her shoulder, ignoring the woman's dramatic gasp, hoping her trembling legs would carry her away and into the theatre to find her seat as quickly as possible.

She was relieved when Henri finally came to join her and the opera began, the arias reverberating around the hall, yet the opera was already ruined—Seraphine couldn't enjoy it as much as she wanted to. Her heart was still beating fast and she was too busy reliving the scene out in the lobby—Lady Frances's malicious comments and Mr Hart's second snub in as many days. And she was furious with herself that she'd let them get to her.

The truth was, Lady Frances didn't bother her so much, but Mr Hart? He had hurt her with the things he'd said in that pamphlet, more than she cared to admit. She knew he hadn't been speaking about her personally, as he'd given the interview before they had met, but every word had hit her hard, playing on her greatest fears of being an outsider. And he'd made it worse with his treatment of her at Lady Bulphan's ball.

She glanced up to where he was sitting in a box. When she realised he was staring right back at her, instead of at the stage, her heart lurched. Their gazes connected, causing her face to heat, her pulse to pound, and she immediately glanced away. She had so desperately wanted to enjoy the performance, but somehow she couldn't concentrate on anything but him, the things he had said, the way he'd behaved. It was infuriating.

Towards the end of the act she whispered to Henri she was stepping outside for a moment and removed herself from her seat and made her way along the aisle and out into the lobby. Usually, music would rejuvenate her, kick her out of any mood, but not even the comedic moments of the opera had been able to lift her spirits tonight.

Outside, in the lobby, she took a few deep steadying breaths. She sat down and picked up the playbill on the table, her eyes flicking over the page and studying the list of instruments that made up the orchestra, needing the distraction.

'Not enjoying the opera, Miss Mounier?'

She baulked. She hadn't been aware of anyone's presence—let alone Mr Hart's. How long had he been sitting at the table next to hers, watching her? Her skin erupted in goose pimples.

She glanced at him, considered ignoring him, then thought better of it. There was no way she would give him the satisfaction of knowing he unnerved her. She didn't want him to think he had any effect on her whatsoever. She put down the playbill and feigned a sigh.

'I usually love Mozart.' She shrugged. 'I am just not in the mood for it this evening.'

'*Don Giovanni* is certainly an acquired taste.'

She pinned him with a look. 'Are not all arrogant noblemen who infuriate everyone with their misdeeds?'

His lips twisted.

She had learned to cover up her hurt and anger with nonchalance and wit and was rather pleased with her comeback. 'I do hope I am not missing the part where he gets what he deserves and descends into hell,' she added.

He quirked one perfect dark eyebrow. 'I thought you had not seen it before?'

'I have not, but I am an avid reader, even when I do not like the subject matter.'

He inclined his head. 'You are referring to what I said in the article in that pamphlet. Still upset?'

'You're wrong,' she said, shrugging one of her shoulders. 'As I said earlier, I could not care less about your opinion.' She looked around the lobby and realised, apart from the serving staff, they were alone. 'It is interesting that your memory of who I am has improved so quickly now we do not have an audience.'

She was no fool. He was ashamed to know her. That was why he hadn't acknowledged her properly earlier when he'd approached the other women. Was that because she was French, or because he felt he had to stand by the things he'd said about her *because* she was French? She thought it interesting he'd invited Henri to hunt at Artington Hall. He'd said her aunt could visit.

But now she realised he probably didn't intend to honour any of those invitations. Yet if he didn't like her and was embarrassed to be seen with her, why was he even bothering to talk to her now?

'I presume it is because of where I come from—and that is why you did not want to be seen dancing with me the other night, as well?' she said, unable to help herself and refusing to let him off the hook. 'Worried the *ton* will talk, Mr Hart?'

He leaned forward. 'May I remind you it was you who said you did not have a spare slot to dance with me?'

She turned to look up at the staff again, until she sensed him lean back against his seat, smoothing his palms over his thighs. 'And given my father's orders—his strict criteria for me to find a suitable wife this Season— I thought it unwise.' He shrugged a broad shoulder. 'It is complicated…difficult to explain.'

'For someone who went to Oxford, I find that hard to believe.'

'How did you know I went to Oxford?'

She scowled. 'I assumed. Privileged people always go to Oxford, do they not? No doubt it is where you learnt your lessons in elitism and prejudice. Your lofty position in life has made you unable to see past the end of your own patrician nose. But if you would rather not acknowledge me in public, that is fine. In fact, I shall make it easy for you—let us simply agree never to speak to one another again.'

Ezra watched as Miss Mounier abruptly got up and stalked away from him, heading through the door of the theatre and out on to the street, and instantly he knew that, by implying she was unsuitable, he had said the wrong thing.

But her open assault on his position in life had taken him aback. If only she knew the truth—how he'd been brought into this world in a family that was far from privileged. How his family had struggled to put food on the table in those years before he'd been given up by his parents. Yes, maybe he had experienced riches greater than most people had ever known in the years since, but he'd always felt uncomfortable in such surroundings, like a fish out of water, as if he didn't belong.

And he lived in fear of people finding out the truth— of the underprivileged life he'd been born into, of discovering who he really was. That he was a fraud. That he would never be able to inherit the Viscount's title because he wasn't his 'proper' son.

He knew, one day, the truth would out. Perhaps when the Viscount died—or even sooner, if he didn't obey the man's orders and find a bride. And there would be people who would relish seeing him disgraced. Money only counted for so much.

He supposed if he got engaged, he would have to tell the woman the truth about him. He just couldn't picture doing that. He'd had many mistresses over the years, more than was probably appropriate since he'd returned from the war, temporarily helping him to forget the things he had seen and done. But he never shared his feelings with them, never got close to them. He was reluctant to open up to anyone. For so long, he had kept people at a distance, believing if his own parents could let him down so badly, anyone could, so he had never wanted to get close to anyone, to care.

He got up out of his seat, heading for the door, going after her. 'Miss Mounier, wait!'

Ezra had made himself her adversary when he'd given a quote for that pamphlet and she had been hostile ever since they'd met. He'd found it irritating that she'd ignored him, as she and her aunt had taken a turn around the room at Lady Bulphan's ball. And he had felt a niggle of dissatisfaction when she'd danced with other men.

He should have been pleased she was keeping her distance, staying away from him, yet her indifference was maddening, bizarrely making him take more of an interest, not less. All of which had made him behave more aloof towards her than was perhaps wholly appropriate when he'd approached the women earlier. Damn, he wasn't handling any of this very well.

He caught up to her on the street. 'Where are you going? It is dark. Late. Please, come back inside.' He felt bad. He knew he deserved her scorn.

'Stop following me. I am no concern of yours and we have nothing more to say to each other.'

She was giving him a get-out, telling him after tonight, he'd never have to see her or speak to her again— so he had to wonder, why wasn't he taking it? Why was he following her out here, trying to talk to her alone, once more?

She reminded him of a beautiful exotic bird in her bright sapphire gown, like the ones people kept as pets or in menageries that held a certain fascination. They had vibrant blue plumage and the ability to speak like others... And he wondered, did she feel trapped in a cage here, trying to impersonate others to fit in? Like him?

Yes, she was like a bird who perhaps wanted to be

set free. Save for the claws, he thought. No, they were reserved for Lady Frances. He had been impressed with the way Miss Mounier had handled the other woman, leaving her speechless. He'd had to bite back a smile of admiration. But Lady Frances's behaviour had shone a light on his own—that he, too, had insulted Miss Mounier through his own words in that damn pamphlet and his frosty behaviour this evening, and he knew he must apologise.

He gripped her elbow. 'Miss Mounier!'

She snatched her arm back, shocked. 'Get your hands off me!'

He raked his fingers through his hair, glancing at the row of carriages lined up outside the opera house, the footmen talking among themselves, and he wondered if they had seen. 'I did not mean to cause offence.'

But at least his actions had finally brought her to a stop as she looked furtively up and down the street herself. She was rubbing her arm as if he'd hurt her.

'I feel as if we have got off to a bad start,' he said.

'Oh, please, how could we ever have got off to a good start, with you calling us a disease, then trying to put a bullet in my brother?'

He inclined his head. 'I can see why I might have earned your instant hatred.'

'I do not deny it,' she said, tilting her chin up in defiance. 'It is true I took an immediate dislike to you. I think it was the moment I read the line "Times are hard enough for our own people without additional French mouths to feed."'

He sucked in a breath, embarrassed at his own words.

'I am impressed that you expand your mind through reading political literature—and operas.'

'It is not my intention to impress you. I merely like to be informed on the public's opinion, that is all. And now I know yours. Are you always so vocal?' she said, pulling her cloak tighter around her.

About everything bar his family history.

Ezra allowed himself the liberty of taking a step towards her. 'I confess I'd had a lot of whisky. I should not have been so outspoken. The truth is,' he said, 'seeing so many of your people here, knowing they need help, just reminds me of the war. The struggles we faced, the battles we fought in. It is not something I am keen to relive, to be reminded of every single day. But that is no excuse.' He shook his head. 'I am truly sorry. It seems your brother has forgiven me—can you not?'

She sighed, looking all around them again, eventually lifting her gaze to meet his. 'I am willing to forgive, but it does not mean I will forget.'

A sentiment after his own heart, especially where the Viscount and his family was concerned.

Then she relented. 'Yet I did promise my brother to keep my ill feeling towards you in check, so I will try to do my best.'

He smiled. 'I am very glad to hear it.'

He wondered if she had been told to behave, just as he had for so many years. Or had his inappropriate touch of her skin shocked her into compliance?

Damn, he had no right to touch her. None. It was amazing she hadn't caused more of a fuss about it.

She looked uncomfortable for a moment, wringing her hands. 'We had better head back inside, although

I should imagine the opera is nearly over now and we can soon go home.'

'You really do not care for these events, do you?' he said, as they began to walk back towards the theatre.

He shared her feelings, preferring his own company, or that of his friends at White's. He thought it stemmed from the stifled family dinners he'd experienced growing up at Artington, when he had only been allowed to speak when spoken to and only on topics that interested the Viscount. When he was constantly corrected on his posture or use of his cutlery. He had always tried so hard to please—but he wasn't sure he had ever pleased anyone, especially himself.

'Actually, I was looking forward to tonight, mainly because of the music. It is a passion of mine.'

His heart lifted, pleased she was sharing something about herself with him. What else delighted and enthused her? he wondered. 'You play, I presume?'

'Yes, the pianoforte. I would like to be better at it than I am.'

'I am sure you are better than you make out.'

'No,' she said, shaking her head. 'I am not one of those people who exaggerate their accomplishments to appear more impressive.'

He rubbed his hand over his chest. Did he do that? He was certainly stretching the truth about his identity.

'And my brother is brutally honest with me, which I am grateful for.'

'Yes, I know what that is like. The Viscount is the same.'

She slowed and turned towards him. 'I was sorry to hear about your mother, Mr Hart,' she said.

Her change of tone, and subject matter, took him off guard.

Mother...would it ever sound normal to hear the Viscountess called that?

'My aunt said she died recently.'

'Yes, it came as a shock to us all. Your parents?' he queried, as they started to walk once more.

'They died. In France. When Henri and I were very small.'

Something they had in common then. They'd both had to grow up without their parents being around.

'I am sorry for your loss, too.'

She lifted one elegant shoulder. 'I was young. I wish so desperately that I remember more about them,' she said.

He thought she was lucky. He wished he didn't remember his parents. It would make it all so much easier to bear. He often wondered if they ever thought of him. How they could have forgotten him so easily. He had tried but failed to wipe them—and the hurt—from his memory.

He had thought about writing to them over the years—at least to his brother and sisters, as they weren't to blame. But every time he'd gone to put ink to parchment, he couldn't bring himself to form the letters on the page. He didn't know where to start, or what to say. It was like picking off a scab of a wound and he wasn't sure he wanted them to know he still cared. Plus he had known the Harts wouldn't approve.

As the doorman held open the door for them to re-enter the theatre, he heard a crescendo of music and knew the act was coming to an end. Soon the audience would be out of their seats and heading back through the lobby towards them.

He inclined his head. 'I shall not take up any more of your time, Miss Mounier. If you go now, you might just catch the final part of the performance and see Don Giovanni meet his fitting end,' he said, offering her a smile. 'Enjoy the rest of your evening.'

'Thank you,' she said, heading off in the opposite direction.

'And by the way,' he called, halting her progress. She turned back round. 'Despite what Lady Frances said, your gown is exquisite, Miss Mounier, especially because it brings out the colour of your eyes.'

Chapter Four

Seraphine was woken by the alarming noise of a window smashing. She threw off her blankets and rushed to investigate, meeting her concerned aunt on the landing.

'What is it, Seraphine?'

'I am unsure. Is Henri back yet? Perhaps he has had too much brandy,' Seraphine said.

'Perhaps. Or is it your uncle? He went downstairs a while ago. He could not sleep.'

'Then stay here, Aunt, while I check all is well.'

The woman nodded, fretful. 'Be careful.'

As Seraphine reached the gallery, she gasped. Flames were engulfing the room—it looked as if someone had thrown something through the window, smashing the glass and setting the place on fire. She was shocked to see her uncle was already trying to fight the blaze, dousing it in whatever liquid he could find.

She worked quickly, calling for help from the servants, before trying to assist her uncle in putting out the flames. But the blaze was already too great. The heat forced them back. And just as they retreated, the fire caught hold of her uncle's robe and he roared in pain.

Thinking fast, Seraphine yanked the curtains from

the windows and threw them on top of him, rolling him over, patting him down. But not before the skin on her right hand—and on his chest—had been scorched.

Knowing they needed to get out of there, to seek assistance, she helped her grimacing uncle up, holding him under his arms, and made a hasty retreat.

Walking as quickly as possible down the landing, they found her aunt. Seraphine knew they'd have to evacuate the property and wait for the authorities to help. But would they arrive before the damage was too great?

Out on the street, Seraphine wrapped her arms around her waist as she stood in her nightgown, looking up at their beloved home in dismay. Thick, curling smoke was rising up into the sky and flames were licking along the roof.

'Did we leave the fire on? Or a candle burning?' her aunt asked, lowering her uncle on to the ground. Despite his pain, he sent Seraphine a warning look that told her not to say a word. He clearly didn't want to worry his wife.

'Perhaps,' Seraphine said. But as she watched the flames swallow up the gallery, she shuddered, knowing this had been no accident.

Memories of the Terrors in France came back with force. She had been just five, but she still recalled an angry mob outside Notre Dame, storming the cathedral, looting its treasures. Statues had been decapitated, followed by people, and flames had begun to consume the sacred building, just as they were demolishing her home now. But despite the chaos and violence, it was the people's wrath she remembered and feared most. It had her shivering at the recollection.

She couldn't believe someone had set fire to their house on purpose. Someone angry. Someone who meant them harm.

But who? Who could have done such a thing?

All she knew was they could not let her aunt know—it would upset her far too much. She had to keep the truth from her while they investigated what had happened.

The street was a spectacle as Seraphine, the volunteers and the authorities attempted to get the fire under control. A physician on site gave her uncle some laudanum to ease his pain and her aunt tried to cool his skin with dampened blankets.

It had been such a strange week. A most bizarre start to the Season in which her brother had said she must marry.

A carriage came trundling down the road, distracting her from her thoughts, and relief threatened to overwhelm her when Henri leapt out.

'Good Christ, what on earth has happened?' he said, looking up at the scene, aghast.

'Henri, thank goodness,' Seraphine said, rushing over to him. 'We have been fighting the flames for a while, but I fear it is no use.'

'How did this happen?'

'Brother,' she said, lowering her voice, 'it was no accident. Someone threw something through the window. Oil, tar…'

'What are you saying—that someone wilfully set the house on fire? While you were all inside?' She could see his face pale in the moonlight. 'Are you hurt? My God, you could have been killed.'

She gave an involuntary shudder, the realisation sink-ing in. 'Just a few burns,' she said, holding out her hand. 'Nothing that will not heal. Uncle—he is a lot worse than I.'

And then a figure appeared from behind her brother and her breath caught. She wondered how she hadn't seen him before.

Mr Ezra Hart. Here! Why?

For some reason, she did not want him to witness such a scene, to see them so vulnerable—and her standing there in her nightgown!

'Who could have done this?' he said, approaching them and looking up at the burning building.

'What is he doing here?' she said to Henri, immediately going on the offensive.

'Sister!'

'What? Do not tell me you two are friends now?' She was irritated at both of them. Henri, for the stench of brandy on his breath and his poor taste in company, and Mr Hart for his mere presence.

She thought back to the events at the opera the other evening and her storming out on to the street, Mr Hart coming after her. She still couldn't believe he'd grabbed her arm, triggering an alarming ripple of awareness through her body.

'Hart was kind enough to give me a ride home,' Henri said. 'I admit I have had a little too much to drink. Yet if this has not cleared my head, I do not know what will.'

It was certainly a sobering sight, seeing their home overcome with flames.

'I thought you had agreed to keep your ill feeling towards me in check, Miss Mounier?' Mr Hart said.

'Perhaps I am finding it harder than I thought.'

He grinned. 'How can we help?' he said, stepping forward, and, to Seraphine's surprise, the high-and-mighty Viscount's son removed his tailcoat, handing it to her. 'Here,' he said, his eyes raking over her, making her feel exposed. 'You need this more than me.'

She accepted it almost grudgingly, her fingers brushing against his, her heart strangely skittering. Reluctantly, she put it on and she could feel the warmth of his body heat on the material, the smell of his spicy scent on the collar.

Then he removed his neckcloth and rolled up his sleeves. Her stomach flipped. So he wasn't prepared to dance with her, but he was willing to get his hands dirty and help them? After the comments he'd made about them? It made no sense. And the sight of his muscular arms, his tanned, exposed skin at the base of his throat, was disturbing.

He approached the authorities and the volunteers, asking what the plan was to get the fire under control, and she could barely comprehend it when he picked up a pail and began to climb a ladder, throwing bucket after bucket of water on to the raging flames.

Why did it have to be he who had come to their aid? Of all people.

'Miss Mounier, take your aunt and uncle and sit in my carriage to stay warm,' he called down to her. 'Your uncle must be in shock. You all must be.'

She shook her head. 'I want to stay and help.'

Henri crouched down next to their uncle, assessing his wounds. He put his arm around his shoulders and assisted him up, before heading towards the safety of the carriage.

Seraphine was aware Mr Hart was staring down at her from halfway up a ladder. 'Do you ever do as you are told, Miss Mounier?' His stern face was rigid with disapproval.

'Rarely.'

He shook his head. 'Did you get any sign of who did this?' he asked, as he came back down the rungs and began to refill his pail at the pump. 'I do not like the thought of you lingering here. The perpetrators might come back.'

'There are enough people around now to scare them off.'

A natural leader, he began to give some of the men orders, telling them where they should concentrate their efforts, and they listened, clearly respecting his judgement. He moved with confidence and she imagined he must have been just like this on the battlefield—a man the men could believe in and follow. No wonder he had climbed so rapidly through the officer ranks. Six years he had been at war, and he had reached Lieutenant Colonel in that time—based on merit, not by purchase, her brother had said. Had he enjoyed the fight and the glory?

She imagined he liked being at the heart of danger. Yet he had admitted to her so honestly the other night that he didn't like to be reminded of the war, making her wonder at the things he had seen and done. He was trouble and she must remember it. But she had to admit, she was glad to have him here. His presence offered reassurance and just his powerful strength and determination alone helped to dampen some of the blaze.

Finally, with a little help from the heavens as the clouds burst with welcome rain, they began to make progress, putting out the last of the flames. But deep down, she knew it was too late to save the first floor of the building—it was in ruins.

As the men began to put down their pumps and buckets and head for their beds, she thanked them for their help and, eventually, the street was all but empty. She was exhausted, soaked through and dithering. Staring up at the blackened walls of their home, she felt at a loss. They had done all they could tonight, but what would happen now? She knew it would take a great many months and an awful lot of money to put it right for it to be liveable again.

Mr Hart took out his pocket watch. 'It is late,' he said, turning to Henri. 'I suggest I take you all back to Artington with me. There is a cottage on the estate you can stay in tonight.'

'No!' Seraphine said, her head whipping round, suddenly panicked at the thought of spending any longer than she had to with this man. And she certainly did not want his charity. 'We can stay at an inn. There is one just down the road.'

He shook his head. 'My lodgings will be much more comfortable, especially for your uncle, and I can have my staff attend to his wounds—and yours,' he said, his dark, concerned eyes dipping to her hand. She hadn't been aware he'd noticed her own injuries.

'That is very good of you, Hart,' Henri said.

Seraphine went to protest, but her brother halted her. 'It would save us going from inn to inn, trying to find a room for the night at this time, Seraphine. So thank you, Hart, we shall accept.'

'I do not want to be an imposition. What about your

father? And surely you do not want to harbour the likes of us?'

His eyes narrowed on her. 'Let me worry about that, Miss Mounier.'

Reluctantly, she allowed Henri to help her into the coach. No sooner had the footman shut the door and they'd set off then Henri passed out, no doubt due to all the liquor he had consumed, and her aunt drifted off to sleep on her dozing uncle's shoulder. At least the laudanum was working for now. The silence stretched inside the cramped carriage and Seraphine wondered if she should feign sleep, too. That way, she wouldn't have to talk to the imposing man sitting opposite her, staring at her, in the dark.

She looked out of the window at the grand houses rushing past, the horses' galloping hooves echoing around the moonlit, lonely streets. She had hoped the view would distract her from him and the weight of his piercing gaze on her. No such luck. With every bump in the road, their knees brushed, causing a peculiar heat to flare in her stomach, and she pulled her body back. Her hands twisted in her lap. The one was smarting and she turned it over to look at the blisters forming.

'Is it very sore?'

She glanced up. 'Not as much as my pride.'

'I am trying to determine if you are brave, Miss Mounier, or very foolish.'

She sighed, suddenly weary, the events of this evening darkening her thoughts. 'I understand that like so many others you do not approve of me and you are entitled to your opinion, but for tonight, perhaps you could keep your criticisms to yourself?'

'You mistake me, Miss Mounier. I was intending to compliment you, not criticise you. I cannot imagine any other woman I know helping to put out a fire. It was very brave.'

She reared back, surprised, feeling a little foolish that she had snapped at him. Then she sighed, relenting. 'I wanted to save it.' She shrugged. 'Our house.' And to her horror, she felt tears well up in her eyes and furiously blinked them away. She did not want to appear weak in front of this man.

'That is understandable. It has been your home since you were very young?'

'Yes.' She nodded. 'It is not our possessions as much as the memories.' She knew from experience it was unwise to get attached to anything—belongings and people— after having to leave her life and everything behind in a hurry once before. Forming connections meant getting hurt. 'Although I very much wish I had retrieved my father's pocket watch before we left the building. It was very dear to me.'

He nodded, thoughtful. 'Perhaps it can still be salvaged. Do you have any idea who would have done this?' he asked again.

She shook her head. 'It could have been anyone. There are a few groups who take offence to us being here. It is one thing émigrés living in London, another if they have wealth. I guess if we were not safe in our own country, why should we be safe here?'

'Why did your family choose to come to England?'

'Things were getting progressively worse in France. Tensions were high. When my parents were killed and their property confiscated, my uncle, who had heard

England was a safe harbour for French émigrés, decided to bring us here.'

It had been a long and arduous journey, not knowing what they would find when they arrived here or how they would be received. An unsettling time for them all.

'And has it been a refuge, for the most part?'

'Yes, mostly. And I realise we are more fortunate than some. But it is hard to change the people's deep-rooted opinion of us. Those who are suspicious of us, believing us to be spies, or thinking we are here to take their work or their homes from them. I imagine your words in that pamphlet didn't help—stirring up a hornet's nest,' she said accusingly. 'Perhaps *that* is why our house was targeted. That, thanks to you, we were very nearly killed.'

His brow furrowed and he went silent.

And goodness knew why, but Seraphine instantly felt guilty for putting this on him. After all, without his help this evening, they might never have got the fire under control and she knew she ought to at least extend her gratitude to him for that.

'But I thank you for your assistance tonight. And then, to put us all up, as well. It is…good of you,' she admitted.

'I bet that was hard for you to say,' he said, his lips twisting, then he was instantly serious again. 'But it sounds as if it was the least I could do, given the circumstances. If I am to blame for tonight's events, I am deeply sorry. That was never my intention.'

The gentle rocking of the carriage and the small, enclosed space added an intimacy to their conversation, especially as she drew his tailcoat closer around her and seemed to breathe in more of his peppery, intoxicating cologne with every breath she took.

His apology surprised her—that he was willing to concede. She had thought him arrogant. Conceited. Someone who thought he was always right. It took a strong man to admit when he was at fault and, somehow, she found herself softening towards him—just a little. But she knew better than to ever trust someone like him.

Ezra knew the moment the footman had turned on to the long driveway up to Artington—the movement of the carriage changed as the horses trotted over the rougher terrain. He wondered if he had lost his mind, bringing this French family home with him. The Viscount would most definitely not approve. Yet what else was he meant to do—leave them stranded in the street? His conscience had not allowed it.

No, when he'd seen how they'd been mistreated, he knew he must help them.

Her.

There was an empty cottage on the estate where they could stay for the night, or even for as long as they needed—until their uncle had recovered and the damage to their home had been repaired.

He was shocked by the destruction caused. Thank goodness Miss Mounier and her family hadn't suffered any greater injuries. The burns to her uncle's chest were severe and he knew they would need fresh, dampened bandages applied as soon as they arrived. Miss Mounier's hand would need attention, too.

Was she right—had he stirred up a fresh wave of anger against them? Was this all his fault? He felt sick with the thought of it. Damn him, he was such a fool. When was he going to stop being so impulsive, his rash words getting him and others into trouble? Had he learned nothing?

He had been to blame for his friends signing up to fight the French six years ago. He'd goaded them into it because he'd wanted them to stick together. Like a desperate, drowning man, he had clung on to his friendships, selfishly pulling them down with him.

'Then put your money where your mouth is and join with me.'

Those words haunted him. To think what could have happened just because he'd wanted to keep his friends with him. What if he'd got one of them killed? Instead, they all had to deal with the horrors they'd witnessed, trying to obliterate the memories with their banter and Hawk's strong whisky.

And had he done the same again now? Had he almost got these people killed? Simply because he'd been too loose-tongued? It was a wake-up call indeed. He needed to grow up.

'Are we here?' Miss Mounier asked, sitting forward and peering out of the window. And just at that moment, Artington Hall rose up before them in all its glory, a vast golden-brick mansion that never failed to make Ezra feel both awe and dread at the same time.

'Yes.'

'It is magnificent,' she gasped.

Looking at it through her eyes, he knew that it was. But it didn't mean it was a happy home, as hers had clearly been. If Artington was on fire, he wondered if he would be as desperate to save it, this vast heirloom he felt unworthy of.

He was sure he was meant to feel grateful—for wasn't it every man's dream to climb the ranks of society? But his rapid ascension felt hollow, as it had come at a great cost.

He'd never asked for a fortune, an estate. And he couldn't help but resent the Harts for taking him away from his family and home. Every day he'd missed his brother and sisters and wondered how his parents could have offered him up to another couple, how much coin they had been given in compensation. Had it earned them a better life? Had they wanted that for him? Nevertheless, it was the fact they had never stayed in touch that hurt the most, even now.

Would he always feel like their boy at heart, not the Viscount's? A Whittaker, not a Hart? Different to those around him?

He returned his gaze to the beautiful woman sitting opposite him. Was that how Miss Mounier felt? For she, too, had been displaced, removed from everything she knew and cared for, just like him, only she'd had it worse. Her parents had been killed. She'd had to flee to another country. He wondered how the loss of her family at such an early age had impacted her. She'd had to put up with the blatant contempt of some in society and she did it well. He could tell she kept people at a distance. Did she struggle to trust people, as he did? Yet at least she had known her parents had loved her to the end, that they'd never abandoned her.

He wondered what it was about her that was making him think about his past and tried to pull himself away from his thoughts.

'We shall head straight for the cottage, if that suits?'

'Yes, thank you.'

The carriage stopped just in front of the small, private dwelling and the ceasing of movement woke everyone inside. The footman opened the door and Ezra stepped out, before turning and extending his hand to assist Miss Mounier down. He thought she might avoid his help, but tonight, she accepted it, although a little reluctantly. She placed her uninjured hand in his and, the moment his fingers tightened around hers, his skin burned.

Damn.

Ezra instructed the coachmen to fetch the servants, then busied himself with finding the small key under the plant pot and pushed open the door. Squatting down on his haunches, he hastily lit the fire and some candles, before assisting Henri with bringing his uncle inside. They laid the older man down on the bed, making sure he was as comfortable as possible.

When two servants arrived, they brought with them sheets out of which they made some bandages and set to work, wetting some strips of material to place over Monsieur Auclair's skin, as he groaned in pain.

'You are probably all in need of refreshment. Mounier, there is some whisky and wine in the cabinet over there,' Ezra said.

Henri nodded and began to pour them all a drink.

Then Ezra turned his attention to Miss Mounier. 'Shall we see to your own wounds?'

'That will not be necessary. All that is required is a good night's sleep, I think. You have done more than enough.'

But stealing one of the servants' bandages, Ezra came

towards her and took her scorched hand in his, not tak-ing no for an answer, making sure he was gentle.

'Do you mind?' she said, trying to snatch her hand back.

But he didn't relinquish her fingers, giving her a stern look. Instead, he turned her hand round in his, inspect-ing the damaged skin to her palm, and he noticed she went rigid, perhaps staying still so he could get this over with as soon as possible.

He began to carefully wind the damp material around her hand, hopefully soothing the burn, keeping the wound clean and cool, and for a moment, he wondered if she'd stopped breathing. Her floral scent drifted under his nose—a mixture of lilies and vanilla—and he had to stop himself from leaning in closer.

'You have done this before,' she observed stiffly.

'There were plenty of injuries to keep us busy over on the Continent,' he said, grimacing, as he tucked the end of the bandage in. He finally, reluctantly, let her go. 'Any better?'

'Yes, thank you,' she whispered, holding her ban-daged hand to her chest.

'Good.'

'We will be gone by morning.'

'Nonsense. You must stay until your uncle is recov-ered. We can arrange for any belongings that survived the fire to be brought here—starting with some clothes.' And then he inclined his head, lowering his voice. 'This is the second time I've seen you in your nightgown, Miss Mounier.'

She tugged his coat tighter around her, then realisation dawned. 'Oh, here, you must take this back,' she said, flustered, going to take the garment off.

'Keep it, Miss Mounier. You might be glad of it—it may get cold in the night.'

Henri came towards them and offered them both a glass of whisky.

'Not for me, thank you, Mounier. I shall leave you all now to rest.'

'Very well, Hart. Thank you, once again.'

'If your uncle is comfortable, you must both take a tour of Artington in the morning,' Ezra said, as Miss Mounier escorted him politely to the door. 'Perhaps it will take your mind off the events of this evening.'

Ezra stepped outside. The rain had stopped and the moonlight lit up the path. Thinking about Miss Mounier's words in the carriage, still wondering whether he was to blame, he turned to face her. 'I do hope I was not the cause of this evening's events, Miss Mounier. But please know, whether I was to blame or not, I do intend to make it up to you.'

Chapter Five

Seraphine looked all around her with wonder out on to the rolling parkland, where deer were aimlessly grazing, birds melodious chirping from the trees, and the beauty of the place stealing into her heart. Imagine waking up to such a view every morning, it would surely start every day right. She drew in a large breath of fresh country air. The Artington estate was so vast, so peaceful, so different from being in London. She imagined Mr Hart must gain a great sense of freedom from living here.

She had woken early and, after checking on her aunt, uncle and Henri, who were still fast asleep, she'd pulled on her boots and Mr Hart's coat and crept out into the cottage garden, just as the early morning mists began to rise.

She had tossed and turned all night, images of Ezra Hart taking her hand in his, the warmth spreading across her skin as his fingers curled around hers. And more disturbing wispy images, flickering through her dreams, of him picking her up and carrying her out of a burning building, saving her from harm. It was absurd. What did it mean?

This man had been the cause of her misery, not the

saviour of it. Yet she couldn't stop her mind wandering back to the way she'd tried to prise her fingers from his, but he'd held them fast, not relinquishing her hand until he'd fastened the bandage with skill. She had stopped breathing, heat blazing in her fingers where he was touching her and low in her stomach, causing her body to tremble.

But she did not want to think about that. Him.

Instead, she tried to focus on Artington House, towering in the distance. It truly was resplendent. It was built in the Palladian style, with a central block flanked by two smaller buildings, all in beautiful golden Bath stone. And as the sun rose, it took on a glorious glow. It looked as if much work had been done to the face of the house over the years by the various owners. It was imposing, yet handsome, and boasted character and charm, much like the man who had brought them here last night.

She knew he had done a good deed in helping them, but being a guest in his home made her feel worse, not better, for she didn't want to be indebted to him. She had determined to hate him. She shook her head, making her way back inside.

She must not forget he was fickle. Yes, he had been nice to her, taken care of her and her family last night, but that didn't mean he would behave the same way in public. No, she must always keep her guard up against him. She knew the only people she could trust in this world were all within the walls of this cottage.

There was a clock tower set apart from the rest of the house, in the same stone as the hall, and when the clock face told her it was ten, the housekeeper of Artington

Hall knocked on the cottage door. She introduced herself as Mrs Dawson and said she had brought with her a physician to inspect Monsieur Auclair's wounds, along with pastries and teas. She was delighted to have guests in the cottage, revealing it was somewhat of a rarity.

'Where is Mr Hart this morning?' Henri asked.

'The young master went to London early, Lord Mounier.'

'Back to London?' Seraphine questioned, surprise and something that felt oddly like disappointment crashing through her. But he *had* told her he meant to make amends—was it so wrong that she had expected him to stay?

'Yes, on urgent business. He instructed me to look after you all this morning, until his return, and to give you a tour of the estate, if you would like one. He is a modest man—he would not wish to show you around himself. He is certainly not one to boast.'

'Why is it that you do not have many visitors to Artington, Mrs Dawson?' Seraphine asked, as she took a sip of the hot, comforting tea. 'I would have thought you would be inundated.'

'The house is always open, yet Viscount Hart and Master Ezra are such private men. They rarely encourage visitors,' she said. 'I was told to bring you some of the Viscountess's old clothes for you and your aunt to wear, while you wait for some of your own to be fetched or remade,' she added, as another two maids brought in a trunk and set it down. 'I was so sorry to hear of the unfortunate events of last night.'

'That is very kind of you, thank you. However, we shall not be staying long,' Seraphine said.

Henri sent her a warning look.

'Yet we are most grateful for the garments for today,' she added quickly.

It was good of the kindly housekeeper to let them borrow such exquisite clothes, despite them being rather dated and heavy—the thick lace clawed up her neck, restricting her movements somewhat. But for now, they'd have to do.

Henri offered to stay and watch over their uncle, pleased to have a quiet morning, perhaps still nursing his own self-inflicted headache, while Mrs Dawson set about showing Seraphine and her aunt round the house. And Seraphine had to admit, she was just a little bit curious to see the inside of Mr Hart's home, to find out if it told her anything about the man that she didn't know.

'The house stood empty and neglected until Viscount Hart and his wife returned from the north several years ago, finally deciding to make a home here for themselves and their boy, re-establishing themselves in the *ton*,' Mrs Dawson said.

'I assumed they had always lived here,' Seraphine said, surprised. 'Where did they reside before this?'

'Their other estate in Derbyshire. I believe the Viscountess had some health issues and was partial to taking the waters in Buxton. I cannot claim to know much about their life before, as they had all new staff when they moved here, wanting to keep their former lives separate, and a skeleton staff in place in the north should they ever return. Like I said, they are very private.'

Aunt Malvine leaned in. 'Rumour has it there was a great scandal between Lord Hart's father and mother and the Viscount had never wanted to return to live here. But when his son was of the age to go to Eton, it became a necessity,' she whispered.

'Aunt! How ever do you know such things?' Seraphine asked her in surprise.

'You may enjoy reading your political literature, Seraphine, broadening your mind, but I cannot deny I like to stay abreast of the gossip pamphlets of the *ton*,' she winked.

Seraphine laughed lightly, shaking her head.

'The Viscount set about restoring the house to its former glory,' Mrs Dawson continued, drawing back their attention. 'It was his desire that it should reflect his inheritance, wealth and taste. And he has done the most wonderful job, has he not?'

'Indeed, it is most spectacular.'

Seraphine wondered how Lord Hart could have stayed away from such a place for so long—and what had happened to him to keep him from it? So it was a house full of secrets, was it? Was his son a man of mystery, too?

They strolled through the richly decorated hall and up a spectacular staircase, on to the first-floor gallery, Mrs Dawson pointing out things of interest. And Seraphine was mesmerised, trailing her fingers over the polished handrails, the fine furnishings, looking up at the intricate plasterwork on the ceilings and the beautiful crystal chandeliers. She had never seen a finer home.

'You probably heard the sad news of the Viscountess passing away last year. The Viscount took it very badly indeed. He is not the same man now—he misses his wife dearly. It has been hard on the young master, too...'

Had they been close? Seraphine wondered. Despite her aunt being a wonderful substitute, she thought of her own mother often. Was Mr Hart still grieving for his own?

'But he has graciously taken over the running of the estate, and he does it so well, despite not being here as often as we should all like,' Mrs Dawson continued. 'He is so kind to us all.'

Seraphine tried to reconcile this glowing report of him with the man who had so openly criticised her family and snubbed her. Yet he *had* been gracious enough to apologise.

'We are hoping he will marry this Season, which means we shall soon have a new mistress—perhaps then the young master will settle here. At the moment, he rarely stays at the country seat for long, preferring to stay at his bachelor lodgings and the company of those in London.'

Was he spending his time with the men Seraphine had seen him with at Lady Bulphan's ball, perhaps? Or was it women who stole his attention away from being at his father's side at home? After all, her aunt had called him a rake. A strange burning sensation erupted in her stomach at the thought.

They walked through an exquisite ballroom and on into an adjoining library, decorated with rich wood panelling and grand paintings hanging on the walls.

'The portraits date back to the earliest of the Harts, right up to the present day,' Mrs Dawson said.

Seraphine stared up at the paintings. She had always been a lover of art and they were so beautifully portrayed. She followed the faces around the room from the sixteen-hundreds until she came to the present day, to the one of the Viscount—a proud-looking man—and next to him a painting of a woman. She was elegant, beautiful, but looked fragile, like a porcelain doll.

'These were painted a good while ago now,' Mrs Dawson said.

And then Seraphine came to the most recent one—of Mr Ezra Hart.

The painting showed him in his soldier uniform—a bell-topped shako and a dark-blue jacket, adorned with many war medals, and it fascinated her. Her eyes raked over every detail. He looked impressive, annoyingly handsome.

'There is not much likeness between the two men, is there?' her aunt said, leaning in to speak to her.

And her aunt was right—there was not much similarity between him and his father, or him and his mother, for that matter. His features were darker and much more defined.

'The young master fought in many battles in the war,' Mrs Dawson said. 'His regiment—the Thirteenth—is renowned for their courage and skill. They defeated three times their numbers at the Battle of Campo Maior,' she said proudly. 'He also had several commands at Badajoz, Nive and Toulouse, and, of course, Waterloo. They charged repeatedly during the day—and he earned a commendation from the Regent. We were very concerned about him during the years he was away and are so glad to have him home, safe. We know many who have not been so fortunate.'

Seraphine once again wondered what sights Ezra Hart had seen out there and how he had coped. Had he suffered any injuries? Had it made him tougher, stronger? She hadn't heard many of the soldiers talk of their expe-

riences, except for surface-level details. And suddenly
she wanted to know what the reality of war had been
like—rather than the glorified versions that were spoken
of in society. Had it been as terrifying as the atrocities
she'd seen in France? What impact had it had on him?

After the things she had witnessed, she had become
more cautious and had struggled to trust people as much,
wanting to protect herself from harm. Was it the same
for him? She knew the death toll had been great and the
barbarity of battle would certainly help to explain some
of Mr Hart's anger towards the French—even those who
were innocent and on his side. Not that it excused his
treatment of her.

'Shall we move on to the drawing room?'

As Mrs Dawson escorted her aunt to look at the beautiful French stained glass in the next room, Seraphine
followed, feeling the eyes of Mr Ezra Hart's family on
her as she walked. And rebelliously, she turned and stuck
out her tongue at the portrait of the man who had brought
her here, before leaving the room.

Listening to the two women talking, she wandered
through some adjoining doors into a study. It was a beautiful room, much like the library, with dark mahogany
panelling and a huge desk in the middle. Out of the window she could see the clock tower and she listened to the
housekeeper tell her aunt it was a water tower, serving
water to the house. 'There is a staircase on the one side
that you used to be able to climb, but the Viscount doesn't
allow it any more.'

Seraphine studied all the books on the shelves and
picked up one or two and inspected the spines, thinking

she must go after the others. Their voices were becoming fainter and fainter.

'Margaret?'

She gasped and swung around to see a frail, older-looking man leaning on a stick in the doorway, staring at her. His faded eyes were wide, as if he'd seen a ghost.

She recognised him instantly from his portrait. The Viscount, Lord Hart.

'You are not Margaret,' he said, startled, clearly feeling foolish. 'My apologies. For a moment, you looked just like my late wife in that dress. So familiar…'

Seraphine suddenly felt dreadful for wearing it. 'Lord Hart, it is an honour to meet you.' She curtsied.

'And you are?'

'I am Miss Mounier, My Lord. Your housekeeper is kindly giving my aunt and me a tour of the house. You have a beautiful home.'

His pale blue eyes narrowed on her.

'Mounier. You are French?'

She swallowed. 'Yes, My Lord.'

'Then you are not welcome here,' he spat, stomping his stick on the floor. 'My housekeeper should know better than to let any old person in here.'

She inhaled sharply and the familiar feelings of being an outsider, an outcast, suddenly came back with force, stealing her breath away. She knew they should not have come.

'I am sorry. We were invited. I did not mean to impose.'

'By whom? Who invited you?' he said, clearly agitated.

'Your son, my lord.'

His frown deepened. 'Ezra?'

Did he have another?

'Ezra asked you here?'

'Yes.'

'I might have known,' he scoffed, his lips thinning. And the disapproval and censure in his stern eyes made her wither inside. He was formidable. 'Is it not enough that he stays out all night, doing God knows what? Now he has the audacity to insult me by bringing his French flirtations back here.'

She gasped at his rudeness.

'Get out of here! Go on. Get out right now!' he said, coming towards her, shaking his stick at her.

And she was so shocked, she dropped the book on the floor, turned and ran. She raced along the landing, down the steps, taking them two at a time, and out of the door on to the terrace, tears blinding her eyes. She didn't see him standing there before it was too late and crashed straight into the solid chest of Mr Ezra Hart.

His arms came up to steady her and he stared down into her face.

'Whoa, steady! We have to stop meeting like this!' But when he saw her face, his amused look instantly turned to one of concern. 'Miss Mounier! Whatever is the matter?'

She shook her head. 'We must leave. Immediately. We should never have come,' she said, unable to meet his gaze.

'Are you not well? Come, sit down.'

He took her arm and led her to a chair, gently touching her elbow. She was conscious of his fingers grazing her skin through the material of her long gloves, reminding her that she should most definitely be leaving, not letting him coax her into sitting. And yet her legs felt like water—weak and trembling—and she was glad of the seat for support.

'I am fine. It is just… We have outstayed our welcome.'

His brow furrowed. 'Nonsense, Miss Mounier, I invited you.'

'And your father uninvited us!' she shot back, wiping her eyes, trying to regain her composure. She cursed herself. She had sworn she would never let him see her shed any tears. Especially not tears he or his friends or family had caused.

He reared back. 'You met the Viscount?'

'Yes. And it seems your sentiments towards us are hereditary, Mr Hart.'

The corner of his mouth caught and his forehead furrowed. '*That* is very unlikely,' he muttered. He took a step towards her. 'I apologise. He is not himself and he is not used to having visitors.'

'Certainly not French ones.'

He looked grave, removing his hat and placing it on the table 'What did he say?'

'Never mind what he said,' she replied, still mortified at the older man's words. That he'd dared to call her one of his son's flirtations.

'Well, I am sorry for it. Whatever it was. He is prone to anger. I know better than most how he can be.' He paced away, dragging his hand over his jaw, before turning back.

And she wondered—did Mr Hart not get on with his father? She could only imagine what his upbringing had been like, growing up under that overbearing man's strict rule. And she felt a moment of gratitude that she had been brought up under the loving care of her aunt and uncle.

'It is his house. He is quite entitled. But that does not mean we must stay and endure it,' she said.

'I felt the same on many occasions growing up. He has a way of finding fault with everything. Mainly me,' he added wryly.

Was that one of the reasons why he stayed away in London?

'But his bark is worse than his bite; he does not mean it,' he said, stalking back towards her. 'He is old, hurting, he is just lashing out in his anger. There is a reason, a history for his antagonism towards you, and nothing to do with the war.'

What? she wondered. What possible excuse could he have for calling her *that*?

'Perhaps I shall tell you about it some time when you are feeling better. It will not excuse his behaviour, but it might go some way to explaining it.'

Seraphine sniffed, recovering herself. 'And you? Were you lashing out in anger, too, when you said those things about us?' She didn't know why she was bringing it up again, testing him.

He sighed, coming down on his haunches so he was looking into her eyes. His hands curled over the arm of her chair and she was acutely aware of the nearness of his fingers to her own. Her breath halted.

'I said those things before I knew you, Miss Mounier. In fact, I am ashamed of the things I said in that pamphlet. I did not mean them, just as I did not mean to duel with your brother. Not really. I hope you can finally accept my apology and we can now be friends. If you saw the things I witnessed over in France, you would understand why I might have thought it hard to believe that we could get along, but now I have come to know you, if only for the briefest amount of time, I realise how wrong I have been.'

She let his words sink in, nodding. 'It is hard for us to trust the English also,' Seraphine said, 'after the social ostracism we have suffered.'

'Then perhaps we can both try to put our past prejudices and grievances behind us and start again?' he offered.

She swallowed. She wasn't sure. She still didn't trust him.

'How is it you still have your accent, Miss Mounier, after all this time?'

She prickled. She would not apologise for it. 'I have probably retained it through spending most of my time with my aunt and uncle, and Henri, growing up—and because I never wished to lose it.'

He nodded.

'I thought you were in London anyway,' she said, changing the subject.

'I was,' he said, rising to his full height again, forcing her to tilt her head back to look up at him. 'How far did Mrs Dawson get with giving you the tour of the house?'

'We saw most of it. You must be very proud to own such a home.'

'I cannot take the credit for it. It is the Viscount's, not mine.'

Seraphine frowned. Did he not see it as his home, too? 'It was kind of you to let me borrow your mother's dresses. Although I think it may have made your father even more angry.'

'I'm sorry for her peculiar taste. You'll be pleased to hear I have collected some of your own clothes from Mayfair this morning.'

'*That's* what you were doing in London?' she asked, surprised.

'Yes. I told you, as I have told your brother, I mean to put things right. Starting with offering a roof over your head while I pay to repair your home. After all, the damage was probably caused because of the unwise, thoughtless things I said, sparking someone somewhere to do something foolish. I also intend to find out who. Your brother has agreed you will all stay here a while— at least until your uncle has recovered.'

'We cannot!' she gasped. 'You must know we cannot. Not now your father has made his feelings clear. We have stayed long enough.'

'I will deal with the Viscount.'

She pinched the bridge of her nose. 'What else?' instinct caused her to ask. 'What else do your amends involve?'

He slanted her a look.

'I have the feeling this is not the end of it. I am right, am I not? Tell me.'

A guilty look crossed his face. 'I promised your brother I would help to build up your reputation this Season. He tells me you are looking to find a husband.'

She inhaled, shocked and appalled. 'I do not need or want your help.'

'Nevertheless, he said I had hindered your chances by refusing to dance with you at Lady Bulphan's ball.

I fear he might be right. He said it was the least I could do to improve your standing in the *ton*.'

'Then I guess he failed to tell you I am opposed to the idea of being a wife?' she spat, launching herself out of her seat, suddenly furious—and mortified. How could Henri do this? It felt like such a betrayal.

'He might have mentioned you had shown some resistance. Yet he thinks you will come round to the idea.'

She tilted her chin up. 'He is wrong. I enjoy my independence. My freedom. I told him I would be happy being a governess, in fact. I do not need or want a husband and I find it rather liberating not living up to society's expectations.'

'Really? I would have thought it rather draining.'

'How would you know?'

A muscle flickered in his jaw. 'What if I could change their opinion of you—use my influence?'

She quirked an eyebrow. 'You do think very highly of yourself, Mr Hart.'

'On the contrary, it was your brother who suggested it, not I. I see no reason why we cannot get a handful of suitors calling at your door by the time you move back to Mayfair…'

'I am not interested in suitors!' she exploded, raising her hands, exasperated.

'What about having the ladies of the *ton* hanging off your every word? Lady Frances eating humble pie…'

'I do not care about her,' she said, shaking her head, yet his comment did raise a faint smile. She took a breath as she walked away from him, across the terrace, looking out over the manicured lawns and formal gardens to the more rugged parkland beyond, all bordered by dark forest. The stunning landscape, with the avenues of apple trees to wander and scrump, the lake shimmering in the sunlight and wildlife to entertain could almost trick her into thinking she liked this place—and the man who was set to inherit it.

She wondered if she was being selfish, turning down his help. Because she had others to think of besides herself. Other people like her. If he could build up her reputation, as he was suggesting, could she do some good with it, for the other émigrés in the *ton*? What if he had the power to help her change perceptions and reshape their lives? Wasn't it worth her swallowing her pride?

'This is a turnaround indeed, Mr Hart,' she said, turning to speak to him over her shoulder. 'That you want to help us.'

'I am not ashamed to say the events of last night were a wake-up call. They alerted me to an unsatisfactory situation—or should I say behaviour on my part. They have prompted me to remedy it.'

'But what of your reputation?' she said. 'Socialising with the likes of us.'

'I am sure it can withstand it,' he said wryly, the lines around his eyes and mouth crinkling as he smiled and came to stand beside her, looking out at the view. 'And I would be pleased if you said yes, if only to have an ally on the dance floor this Season.'

Allies.

Friendship with the man who had torn her down. Yet perhaps it was only fitting that he should be the one to build her back up.

'You sound as reluctant as me to be on the marriage mart.'

He shrugged. 'I care not for a love match. I merely need to find a bride the Viscount will approve of.'

'Thank goodness that rules me out!'

He grinned fully then and her stomach did a somersault.

She wondered why he wasn't interested in finding a bride he cared for. What reasons did he have to keep people at a distance? she wondered. Were they the same as her own? Fear of hurt and grief?

'Very well,' she said, sighing, making her choice. 'But I mean what I say. I am not looking for a husband. I am merely interested in expanding my prospects for reasons that I should like to keep to myself.'

His eyes narrowed on her.

'What? You think you are the only one with secrets, Mr Hart?' she said, glancing back at the house.

'And I shall let you keep them—for now,' he said, inclining his head. 'If we are to be friends, you do not need to use my title, Miss Mounier. I would much rather be called by my first name, not my family name, at least while we are here at Artington.' He retrieved something from his pocket. 'By the way, I found this for you.'

She looked down to see he was holding out her father's pocket watch. She glanced up at him, shocked. Where did he get it? Had he been in her room back at the house? Flustered, she wondered in what kind of state she'd left it. God knew she wasn't the tidiest person.

'Thank you. That is…most kind,' she said, deftly taking it from his hand, her gloved fingertips grazing his palm. She ran her hands over the smooth, worn metal. 'I am so glad, grateful to you, to have it back. It is very dear to me.'

'Yes, I know.'

She swallowed. 'Was there much damage?'

'To the first floor, yes. But I believe it is fixable. I have already spoken with the builders. I told them to make haste in putting it right. And your hand? How is it this morning?' His dark gaze lowered, as if he was trying to see through the material of her gloves.

'Also on the mend,' she said, smiling up at him for the first time.

'So let me get this straight.' Ezra was so stunned by Adam's story that he was yet to lay a card on their usual table at White's. 'You happened upon an incognito heiress while drunk at Lady Bulphan's ball, blurted out that you were on the lookout for one and on the back of that she has offered you a twenty-thousand-pound lifeline?'

'If he's prepared to parade her around Mayfair on his arm and knock her up,' said Hawk with his customary bluntness.

'Which shouldn't be a problem if she is as attractive as you say she is.' Ash fanned his cards impatiently to remind Ezra that they were supposed to be playing whist and it was his turn. 'Talk about the luck of the devil, Adam.'

Ezra shook his head in disbelief.

He laid his cards face down on the table, which was tucked away in the corner of the gaming room. A table where they had regularly poured out all their troubles to one another since returning from the war.

He couldn't believe Adam was getting married. He knew he had to find a bride this Season, yet it felt as if everything was changing—that he was losing his friend, being abandoned in favour of a wife, and he didn't like it.

He wanted to be pleased for Adam, but Ezra had an unsettling feeling of being left behind, that his friend was moving forward while he was stuck. Perhaps he was just jealous, especially as Adam really seemed to like this Miss Trym. And he wondered—was that what he wanted? To find someone he really liked, even loved?

Ezra dismissed the thought almost as soon as it entered his head. No. He'd let these four men into his life and they'd become his world. His happiness. But outside of his friendships he had always been reluctant to build relationships. He didn't need anyone else—he was stronger on his own. He knew the closer you got to someone meant a greater risk of being let down. If he kept people at a distance, they couldn't reject him, hurt him.

Deep down, he knew this stemmed from his childhood, but despite knowing it, he couldn't help or temper his feelings. Damn, his family had really taken a toll on him.

Would he still get to see Adam as much from now on? For surely his friend wouldn't have as much time for them when he was married? But he should give Adam a break. He knew his friend didn't have a choice, that his will wasn't his own. Even at the age of eight and twenty, they were being forced into a path—one that they didn't particularly want to take, but they had to, for the benefit of others.

His thoughts returned to this afternoon and his conversation with the Viscount. His guardian had been furious that Ezra had allowed a French family to stay in the cottage without his knowledge or consent. The man had reminded him that the estate, Ezra's inheritance, was all conditional. And the latest bargain was a bride, a respectable noble woman—which was ironic, given Ezra couldn't seem to stop thinking about the French émigrée his father had just turned out of the house. A woman the Viscount had made clear he didn't approve of.

He had raged that he would rather Ezra visit a brothel than bring a French woman back to Artington, calling it unacceptable, and Ezra had winced, wondering whether the Viscount had said as much to Miss Seraphine.

Was that why she hadn't been able to look him in the eye after crashing into his chest at full force, wakening every part of his body? But the truth was, he hadn't even wanted to visit one of those houses of assignation in the *ton* for some time, and he couldn't help but think it had a lot to do with his alluring guest.

The Viscount's cold, even cruel reception of her wouldn't have given her a great first impression of Artington. Ezra had almost forgotten himself and told her that he, too, knew what it was like to feel as though you didn't belong there, but he'd kept quiet because, he realised, he wanted her to like it at Artington while she was there.

He thought the place as a bit of a reflection of him. The hall had been revamped in the eight and ten years the Harts had been there, as if to create a better version of itself, yet it now had so many different elements, so many different faces, so many empty, lonely rooms, it wasn't quite sure what it was meant to be. Just like him.

Perhaps he shouldn't have brought Seraphine and her family there. Why had he thought it would be a good idea? Last night, he had tossed and turned, knowing she was sleeping just a garden away, unable to stop thinking about her standing before him in her nightgown, her heated eyes flashing in anger. He had even found himself staring out of his window to see if the candlelight in the cottage had still been on, wondering what she was up to.

Yet he knew he was being foolish. Nothing could happen between the two of them, no matter how much he was intrigued by her. For a man of his 'standing' to court an émigrée, he was certain it would all but ruin his hard-won reputation. And he wondered what his friends who were sitting around this table would have to say about it, after going to war with the French because of him.

'We were all idiots at twenty-one,' Adam was saying now as he gestured around the table to his friends. 'Joined up to fight Napolean expecting to be home within months and lived to rue the day.'

'You can say that again.' Ash toasted him with his glass. 'If I could turn back time, I'd try to talk us out of it.'

'If we could turn back time, you wouldn't need to,' Ezra said. 'If we knew then what we know now, none of us would have gone. And I am sorry that I goaded you all into it.'

There was a pause as they all took in his words, perhaps surprised by his apology.

'Hindsight is a wonderful thing—but sadly always comes too late to change things,' the steward said, setting down a bottle of whisky before offering them all a curt bow. 'Let me know if you need anything further, gentlemen.'

If Ezra were able to, he wondered what he would change. Would he change the past—that day the Viscount and his wife had come for him, if he could? Would he give up his wealth and inheritance to have his family back?

He would never have risked his friends' lives by getting them all to go to war.

And he certainly wouldn't have said those things in that damn pamphlet, stirring trouble, causing Miss Mounier and her brother distress. It played on his conscience because he liked her. A little too much.

He admired how loyal she was towards her family, especially her brother, coming to defend him at the duel. The way she'd bravely fought the fire, protecting her uncle, even though she'd got hurt. And he liked the way she wasn't afraid to stand up to the other women in the *ton*—and him. It was refreshing to socialise with someone like her, someone honest, someone different.

Perhaps that was all this was—what he was feeling. That it was a change from the norm. He was sure it would soon pass.

And the final thing he'd change? He'd tear up that letter. The one that had arrived at Artington this morning, the one that had been playing on his mind all day. It had been a moment of great elation and apprehension, after seeing the mail coach pull up, to hold the letter in his hand and see the familiar handwriting. His heart had hammered in his chest as he'd smoothed his fingers over the crisp parchment. And as he'd sliced open the envelope and had read the words, his world had imploded.

It was from his mother.

It was from his mother, informing him his brother had died fighting in the war, and that his father had also passed away in recent weeks—God rest their souls.

It was from his mother, telling him the responsibilities and burdens of his birth family had now become his own. That she needed his help.

He had read it over and over again, in shock. To have heard from her after all this time. To have been given the news about his father and brother—to find out they had died without him having seen them again, without being able to ask his father why he gave him up, without them having a chance to reconcile their differences—it felt wretched.

And to have heard from her, without as much as an apology.

When the Viscount had come to find him, to talk to him about the Mouniers, he had refolded the letter and hidden it away, to deal with later. But he didn't yet know what he was going to do about it. What he thought about it.

He felt the noose tighten around his neck, for if he was going to help them, he would need his allowance—and later his inheritance. He would have to do as his guardian had commanded and find a woman to marry, and soon.

He tried to shake away his melancholy thoughts as the talk around the table turned to Adam's own family—his brother had been diagnosed with a tumour and Ezra felt for him, for he knew they were close. He took another shot of whisky. Hearing about their relationship made him feel like a failure, for not having got in touch with his own brother in the past few years and now it was too late. For the relationship he had been denied with his sisters. And he thought perhaps if he had the slightest chance to get that back, he couldn't ruin that now.

If he had a chance to see his family safe, to rebuild

the bond with his siblings and maybe even his mother, if he could bring himself to forgive her, he would do whatever it took.

He would help establish Miss Mounier and her brother in the *ton*, but that's all. And he would turn his attention more seriously to finding a bride of his own, securing the line of succession, as the Viscount had dictated.

Chapter Six

'Tell me again why we must attend the ball at Vauxhall this evening?' Seraphine asked, as the three of them stepped out of Ezra Hart's coach in Lambeth.

'Because Hart is right—gossip will be rife about the fire in our home, Seraphine, and the sooner people see us back out in society, unaffected and with friends at our side, the sooner they will move on to talking about something else. And Vauxhall is the place to be seen,' Henri said.

'And tonight will be especially busy, as for once it is not raining,' Ezra said.

'Do we even have a ticket?' Seraphine asked.

'Yes. But do not worry, you are with me.'

They walked along the neat pathways, with tall, manicured hedgerows, passing ornamental plants and sculptures, and gently trickling water features. And as more and more people joined them, there was a palpable buzz of excitement in the air as they headed towards the bright lights and music.

They approached the manicured lawn, with a kaleidoscope of floral border displays, a large bandstand and platform, where dukes, earls and barons were already dancing with beautiful women dressed in a rainbow of silk under a starry night sky. As they drew closer, Seraphine felt the curious eyes of the other attendees turn to look at them, before the mutterings began.

'Everyone's staring. Are you sure you do not want to change your mind about this?' she whispered to Ezra. 'Most of the *ton* is here!'

But it was too late now, Miss Jennings and her father, the Baronet, were coming towards them and the men struck up a conversation about the weather.

'Miss Mounier, I am so pleased you made it this evening,' Miss Jennings said, sidling up to her, offering her a genuine smile. 'Would you like to take a turn—perhaps get some lemonade?'

'I would like that. Thank you.'

'You made quite the entrance this evening. I do not think anyone missed it—or the company you are keeping,' Miss Jennings said, smiling warmly as she took her arm and led her away from the gentlemen. 'Did you enjoy the opera the other night?'

'Very much so,' Seraphine replied. 'And you?'

'I did. Although I could not fail to notice your brother was alone for the most part. I was worried you were sick and your brother lonely.' Seraphine was a little worried where Miss Jennings was going with this, until she said, 'Is your brother not married, Miss Mounier?'

The lady blushed and Seraphine's face broke out into a grin. 'No, but I do believe he is on the lookout for a wife this Season.'

Seraphine had been worried she would miss having her aunt at the ball, but the older woman had barely left her uncle's side this week. He was recovering well, but it would be a while before he felt like getting dressed up and going out—in fact, she imagined he'd use it as an excuse for as long as possible!

It was nice to have a woman of a similar age to talk to and she realised her actions, and who she befriended, didn't just impact herself, but her brother's prospects, too. If he wanted to find a wife and settle down, she could at least try to behave for him, so he could secure his own match. She very much wanted him to be happy. And perhaps then he wouldn't be so focused on finding a husband for her.

Seraphine and Miss Jennings stood and watched the end of the dance together, admiring the many gowns and deciding on their favourites, before going to watch a female tightrope walker perform, looking up in amazement at how she maintained her balance on the wire. Just one misstep and she could fall. A little like her in society, Seraphine thought. Unlike the men, such as Ezra Hart—he had nothing to worry about. He could act as he pleased and still be held in high esteem because of his ancestry.

'Miss Jennings, Miss Mounier,' a man's voice interrupted them and they turned to see Lord Wentworth approaching. 'You are both looking lovely, this evening. I trust you are well.'

'Never better, Lord Wentworth,' Seraphine replied with a smile.

'I was hoping you would both do me the honour of a dance, if you have space on your cards this evening?'

They curtsied. 'Yes, certainly.'

Couples were getting ready to take up their positions

for the next quadrille and Lord Wentworth took Miss Jennings's hand and led her to the dance floor.

Seraphine smiled and headed to the drinks table to pour herself a glass of fresh lemonade, taking in a breath of the balmy evening air and the scent of the beautiful flowers in vases. It was rare to have a warm evening like this one. They had experienced daily frosts and near-constant rain so far this Season. People were calling it the year without a summer, so she knew she should appreciate it while it lasted. She was having quite a nice time, she admitted to herself.

'What are you doing here?'

Seraphine glanced up to see Lady Frances and her circle of friends on the other side of the drinks table. 'I did not know they were letting spinsters as well as the French in now.'

'It would seem so,' Seraphine said, taking a sip of the cool, bitter liquid, trying not to rise to the bait.

'We had all rather hoped you might have returned to France. Now that the war is over, do you not want to go home?' Lady Frances added, coming round the table towards her. 'Your head would look so lovely in a basket. Or are they not executing your kind any more? Shame.'

Hurt slammed through Seraphine's chest, winding her. She had heard some comments over the years, but none as cruel as that. She turned towards her foe, ready to retaliate, when Lady Frances purposely tipped a vase over on the table on to the skirts of Seraphine's dress, momentarily shocking her, as the cold liquid seeped through the material of her gown on to her skin.

'Oh, I am so sorry,' Lady Frances said, disingenuously, putting a gloved finger up to her lips. 'How clumsy of me—that French silk, it has a tendency to ruin as well. Just like everything from that country, it seems.'

Lady Frances's derisive laughter rippled around the group of ladies and Seraphine wondered how many more times she could find herself in situations like these, with people like this, who wanted to bring her down. How many times could she pretend to be all right about it for the sake of her brother and her family? She had tried, but sometimes it seemed futile.

She turned to go, needing to get away, fast, before she said something she'd regret, but came face to face with Ezra Hart, a strange expression on his face.

How long had he been standing there? Had he been listening?

His hands came up as if to steady her, being careful not to touch her, and she was horrified that she almost leaned into him, wanting his comfort. She stared up into his eyes.

'What you need, Miss Mounier, is to take a dance round the stage.' He was so close she could feel his warm breath on her face. 'After a few turns, I believe your gown will dry out in no time.' He held up his hand. 'Shall we?'

She looked up at him, surprised. Was he defending her, sticking up for her? It was such a turnaround from the other evening.

He inclined his head. 'Could I have the next dance?' he said, as if to make himself clear.

She nodded, mute, flustered. As she set down her glass and placed her fingers in his, they curled around her, and he began to lead her to the dance floor.

He released her and they took their positions opposite each other, waiting for the music to begin. Seraphine realised her legs were trembling—due to the anger, or the disbelief of what had just been said to her. But as she looked up at Ezra, she wondered if her jitters had more to do with the man staring back at her, his dark gaze focused only on her. Would she be able to remember the steps? She could barely think straight right now.

'Just follow my lead,' he said, as if he could sense her apprehension, that her thoughts were in disarray.

The music started and they began to move. She was aware that all eyes in the crowd were on them, no doubt shocked that the Viscount's son had asked an émigrée to dance.

'I know you can handle yourself, Miss Mounier, but are you all right?'

She nodded, still trying to find her voice. 'Yes. Thank you.'

'I am sorry for the despicable things Lady Frances said,' he whispered, before they were forced apart for the dance.

Was he angry—on her account? It was peculiar, as just days before he had been the one to cut her people down. Had his opinion of her changed in such a short amount of time? And was that so hard to believe, as hadn't hers mellowed towards him as well, despite her swearing they wouldn't?

'Lady Frances hates me,' she conceded. 'My presence here seems to offend her.'

'Hate you? No. She is just envious of you,' he said, as they came back together.

'Envious?'

Seraphine took a turn around him, before coming to stand in front of him again.

'Because you are the most beautiful woman here to-night. Something a little spilled water on a dress cannot change.'

Her breath halted. He thought she was beautiful? She swallowed.

'I believe every man in the grounds wants a slot on your dance card this evening, Miss Mounier.'

He walked around her, before coming back, and he took up her hand once more. She was suddenly excruciatingly aware of their fingertips touching gently through the silk of her gloves, the nearness of his broad chest and his now familiar, peppery scent drifting under her nose. If she needed a perfect distraction from the hateful things Lady Frances had said, this was it.

'I imagine I have you to thank for that. Who knew you were our key to acceptance and respect, Mr Hart? If I had known, I would have befriended you earlier,' she teased, suddenly feeling a little brighter.

He grinned. 'Do not speak such lies, Miss Mounier.'

She took her next turn around him, before coming back to her position.

'Lord Wentworth seems to have taken a keen interest in you.'

'And Miss Jennings.'

'Is he not a little old for you?'

Seraphine rolled her eyes. 'There is a lot to be said for an older gentleman. Wiser, more worldly.'

'Rich. A viscount… I thought you were not looking for a husband.'

'I am not.' She laughed. She was yet to meet a man who would marry her on her own terms and support her passions. She so very much wanted to continue with her charity work and help more people like her. 'What about you? I notice you are shirking your duties on the dance floor so far this evening, asking me to dance instead of other more suitable ladies and talking with the men. Who are they, the ones you have been speaking with?'

He glanced over his shoulder at where the others were standing, still talking. 'My friends. We met at Oxford and have kept in touch ever since.'

'You fought in the war together?'

'Yes.'

'You are close?'

'Like brothers.'

'Have you never had any siblings?' she asked, thinking that must have been lonely for him. But she realised she might have said the wrong thing when his dark brow furrowed. She couldn't fail to miss the way the corner of his mouth caught when he spoke of his family.

'Yes, when I was younger. But they are no longer around.'

'I am sorry,' she faltered, worried she had spoken out of turn.

'Not at all. My friends have more than made up for it.'

Too soon, the music came to an end and she smiled up at him.

'Feeling better, Miss Mounier?'

She had danced with many men over the years, but none whose conversation had changed her mood entirely, lifting her out of her dark thoughts. None whose touch had set her alight. It was disturbing.

'Yes. Thank you.'

'And look, your dress is almost as good as new,' he

said, his eyes roaming down over her body for just a moment, causing her cheeks to heat.

He led her back over to the drinks table where Miss Jennings was waiting and he lingered, holding her gaze and her hand a moment longer than necessary. 'Thank you for the dance.'

It was a while later when everyone was called to gather round the stage for a performance—a taster of a bigger show they were preparing to put on next year, if it should be a success tonight. The compère was warming up the crowd, getting them to boo and cheer, teasing them about what was to come, as the set and props were assembled.

Ezra and Henri found Miss Mounier and Miss Jennings in the crush, peering this way and that to get a better view of the stage, and Seraphine discreetly moved to the other side of her brother, allowing him to talk to Miss Jennings. Ezra sent her a knowing look.

'I did not take you for a matchmaker, Miss Mounier.'

'Just getting a little sibling revenge,' she said, smiling.

Ezra was envious of the relationship Seraphine had with Henri. He had missed the sibling banter when he'd left the rectory—the rapport he'd had between him and his older brother. He'd missed teasing his little sisters, or looking out for them, plaiting their hair. His close friendships with Hawk, Ash and Adam made up for it. But when Seraphine had asked him about his family, he had felt the familiar pang of regret. It reminded him of the letter, causing another searing pain in his chest, wondering what he was going to do about it.

'What do you make of the entertainment this evening, Miss Mounier?'

'There is so much to see and do.'

'Favourite part?' he asked her.

'Aside from the music, of course, I do not know—the artworks?'

'Do you paint yourself?'

'She draws,' Henri interjected. 'And very well.'

Ezra's eyebrows rose. 'Really?'

'Not well at all, my brother flatters me without good reason, but I do like admiring the work of others.'

The sound of a cannon firing made Ezra jump and the blasts of light and illuminations that suddenly lit up the outdoor pavilion prevented any further conversation. The crowd gasped and roared in excitement, but when Ezra saw men dressed in soldier attire race on to the stage, their weapons drawn, he felt his pulse quicken and his heart start to pound in panic, wondering what the hell was going on.

Then realisation dawned—they were re-enacting the battle he had fought in last summer, the use of pyrotechnics, horses, dancers and musicians bringing the spectacle to life.

And for a moment, he was horror-struck, as if he was back there, reliving it.

He'd had twelve months to get over what he'd seen during those long six years, but he'd come to realise he might never heal from it. It was like an open wound, constantly ready to bleed. It would be something that stayed with him for ever, taking up the dark places in his mind.

As the actors charged and the sound of clashing metal reverberated around the gardens, the familiar wave of panic began to take over—the palpitations, the breath-lessness. He recalled every one of the wounds he'd ex-acted or had inflicted upon him. He remembered every one of the fatal blows he'd made, the lives he'd taken—the last look in those men's eyes before their lids had closed upon the world. He began to feel sweaty, dizzy.

'Was it really like this?' Seraphine said, turning to look up at him. 'Was it so very bad?'

This performance glorified it. It was far worse. He felt nauseous.

'Are you all right?' she said, peering up at him. 'Can I get you something?'

'Forgive me, I need to—I need to go. Excuse me,' he said.

He pushed through the crowds, his heart racing, his mouth feeling dry, retreating into the gardens, away from the show. How dare these actors, these people, who had never been to the Continent, or even picked up a weapon, let alone take up arms against another man, try to explain to the crowd here what it had been like? He turned a corner, into a dark, secluded recess along the side of a tall hedge and crouched down, trying to get his breathing under control. His forehead felt clammy, his palms sweaty.

How would they know? How could they know what it had truly been like to take a life? And then do it again, and again, while fearing for your own and those of your men?

'It is just a play,' he kept telling himself. 'It's not real. It's over now. Your friends are safe. You're alive…'

'Mr Hart?'

He looked up to see Miss Mounier's frame shadowing the moonlight, as he heard more cannon fire go off in the distance. 'Are you quite well?'

Damn. He hadn't wanted her to follow him. He didn't want her to see him like this. He didn't want to seem weak. Not in front of her.

'Yes,' he said, drawing a hand over his face. 'Go back to the performance. I just needed a moment.'

But to his astonishment, she came down on her knees beside him, sitting on the grass.

'You will ruin your dress.'

She placed a hand on his cheek and turned his face to look at her. He tensed in surprise and she instantly lowered it again.

Ridiculously, he wished it back.

'Breathe.'

He swallowed and tipped his head back, shutting his eyes for a second.

'I imagine what you experienced over there—it was a whole lot worse than how they are portraying it. Glorifying it. The sights. The smells. The sounds.'

He nodded.

'Do you want to talk about it?' she asked.

He shook his head and so she just sat with him in silence for a while.

Eventually, he spoke. 'How can men who were not even there, who did not experience it, recreate something they will never know?' he said, as his world started to come back into focus. They hadn't experienced it—whereas he was still reliving it every night in his nightmares.

'I do not think they mean any harm. They are just trying to show what heroes you all are.'

'Or how lucky we all are—to have survived,' he said. 'The guilt I feel is immense—for being one of the ones to have made it home when so many did not.'

She considered him for a moment. 'I understand. You wish you could have done more. I feel the same about fleeing France. I am so glad we managed to get out when we did. But I often think about the people who got left behind. Who did not make it. Thankfully, I was far too young to remember much of it. Unlike you. What made you decide to sign up in the first place?'

'Young and naive, we all joined the cavalry to fight Napoleon just as soon as we had graduated from Oxford. It was my small, stupid way of rebelling against the Viscount. Of taking control of my own life.'

She tilted her head to one side, studying him. 'You do not get on?'

'What gave you that idea?' he said wryly.

And once again he wondered how the Viscount had thought they would ever stand a chance of forming a close bond, when he'd robbed Ezra of his family life and his home. He knew the Viscount thought he'd done him a huge favour, offering him a great fortune and land— but if he'd had any ounce of feeling in him, he might have realised it had also caused Ezra great suffering.

'I was not ready to return to Artington after university. I was not ready to leave my friends. I realise now it was foolish. I did not truly appreciate the dangers that lay ahead. I thought we would all return within months and I'd finally make the Viscount proud.'

'He must have been—surely?'

He shrugged. 'Perhaps, but by then it was six years later and I had paid a high price for it.' He raked a hand through his hair and turned to look at her. 'I took many lives out there in battle. I am not proud of it. I do not like myself much for it—or like to be reminded of it,' he said.

'I imagine you did not have a choice. Was it not a case of do or die?'

'You remind me of what I have done,' he blurted.

Her eyes went wide.

'Perhaps that is why I mistreated you so, said the things I did.'

'You have already made amends for that, Mr Hart.'

'Ezra.'

'Ezra,' she repeated. 'You saved me tonight from an enemy of my own.'

He was still angry about the way Lady Frances had treated her. He had stepped in and rescued her and he hoped their dance had helped to put it out of her mind. Now, it seemed, she was rescuing him back. Because it was helping him to talk, to listen to her voice, her sensible words. He realised she understood, because she had witnessed such barbarity, too. She, too, had lost along the way, but she had done what she'd needed to survive.

'Can you forgive me—for killing many of your kind?'

She placed a hand on his arm. 'They were not my kind. Not really. You forget those people, their cause, were responsible for murdering my family,' she said.

'Do your memories consume you, too, of that time? Do they ever come back to haunt you when you least expect them to—in the middle of the night, in the middle of a ball?' he asked, gesturing to the performance going on back there on the stage.

'I was only a child when things were at their worst in France,' she said. 'I remember some things—packing in a hurry, trying to flee before the Revolutionaries caught us. I knew something was very, very wrong. That bad things were happening, but not exactly what. I do not think I fully comprehended it until I was older. We were racing for the border, but my parents were seized before we got there.

'Somehow, Henri and I, and my aunt and uncle, managed to get away. We were told about my parents' execution later, by friends of my aunt and uncle. My aunt always says my father and mother sacrificed themselves for us. I take a strange comfort in that, knowing they loved me. That they died so Henri and I could live.' She placed a hand on his arm. 'Perhaps that is how you should think of those men out there—whatever country they fought for. They died so we could have a life.'

He nodded, looking down at her gloved fingers touching his arm.

'You must miss your mother.'

She removed her hand. 'I never really knew her. I wish I had. I wonder what she would have taught me about life, how she would have comforted me. Sometimes I used to make up stories in my head of what it would be like if she were here.'

He had done the same when he was a boy. He had missed his mother so much. The way she had held him on her lap, when he was sad—if he had cut his knee, or George had taken something that belonged to him. He remembered her smile and her laugh. He felt as if a piece of him was missing and it sounded as if Seraphine did, too.

His memories had faded over the years, but as he'd grown older, the resentment had simmered. Hurt and anger had taken over any feelings of love he had felt for her. He'd become bitter. And now he felt incapable of opening his heart to love—did Seraphine feel that way, as well?

His mother's letter hadn't covered any of what he'd needed to hear from her. That she was sorry. Why she did what she did and whether it was worth it. It didn't sound like it, if she was asking for his help now.

What he really wanted to know was, did she ever regret it?

'Are you feeling better?' Miss Mounier asked.

'Yes, thank you.'

'It is hard to talk about the bad things that have happened, but it does help.'

Finally, the fireworks and cannon fire stopped and the music returned to that of a cotillion.

'You had better get back. Lord Wentworth will be looking for you, expecting his dance,' Ezra said. 'You do not want to undo our good work by snubbing him now. But thank you. For coming after me.'

They both rose to their feet, and Seraphine dusted down her dress.

'I would appreciate it, Miss Mounier, if you did not mention this to anyone.'

'Of course not. And you can call me Seraphine, if I am to call you Ezra.'

He nodded. 'You had better go that way, Miss Seraphine,' he said. 'I will follow shortly. It will not do to be seen here together.'

Seraphine reached the lawn just as the dance was about to begin and, seeing her, Lord Wentworth greeted her, smiling broadly, glad she hadn't forgotten him.

'I wondered where you had got to, Miss Mounier.'

'There is so much to look at here, the art, the menageries, the illuminations, I admit I got quite distracted, Lord Wentworth. But I would not have missed our dance.'

'I am very glad to hear it.'

He took her hand and led her to the dance floor. He seemed like a kind man. She wondered how his wife had died and if he was still grieving. She made up her mind to ask Miss Jennings about it afterwards.

'What are your interests, Miss Mounier?'

He was keen to learn of her skills, she realised—perhaps trying to gauge her suitability for marriage. And she answered, in the way Henri and her aunt had taught her to, listing her accomplishments. But she wondered how her being able to sew or how many languages she spoke really mattered when it came to a partnership. Did a man not want a woman he could talk to, who had mutual interests? Or did he just want a wife who looked nice on his arm, who existed to benefit him?

It really was amazing how half the marriages in the *ton* lasted.

She wondered if marrying one of the gentlemen here would mean having to let go of her French connection— a huge part of her identity. And her charity work with people of her kind. Well, it was something she was not prepared to do.

Lord Wentworth was polite, asking questions, and she in turn listened as he talked, yet her mind was distracted. She was wondering if Mr Hart—Ezra—had returned to the gathering, and if he was back to feeling himself. She had known she shouldn't go after him, into the gardens—

that if anyone were to see them together, it would all but ruin her reputation, yet how could she not have? When the boom of the cannons had begun, she had seen the blood drain from his face, the colour of his skin fade to grey and his eyes had taken on a haunted look of fear. She knew that look because she had felt the same gut-wrenching fear when she had fled her home country.

She realised she was lucky—that she'd had Henri and her family to talk to growing up. That they had been able to express their shared pain—and she wondered if Ezra had had anyone he could talk to like that. Possibly his friends. She was glad he had opened up to her and was pleased she had been able to help to calm him. But she would feel better if she had seen him return to mingle among the crowds.

The dance seemed to go on and on and she became more distracted, glancing over Lord Wentworth's shoulder, feeling on edge. She even clumsily stepped on his toe at one point and had to apologise profusely. As soon as the music came to an end, she curtsied to Lord Wentworth and made her excuses, rapidly retreating to the company of Miss Jennings, asking if she'd seen her brother and Mr Hart.

When her new friend pointed them out, over on the far side of the gardens, her hand pressed to her heart and she felt her shoulders sag.

He was all right.

But her relief was short-lived as Miss Jennings was full of barely contained excitement, unable to wait to pull Seraphine to one side to reveal the gossip she had overheard.

When they had removed themselves from the throng

of people, out of earshot from the crowds, Miss Jennings whispered in hushed tones that she'd found out why Lady Frances despised Seraphine so much.

'Why?' Seraphine asked, perking up, leaning forward.

'Because, apparently, Mr Hart and Lady Frances have been courting!' Miss Jennings said, clapping her hands together, triumphant.

'What?' Seraphine gasped, her body stiffening and a fierce, unexpected pain in her chest winding her.

Surely it couldn't be true? She tried to keep her look of surprise in place even though she felt as if her face was falling. Surely he would have told her? And Henri would have known. He would have mentioned it.

'That is why she was so mean to you this evening,' Miss Jennings continued. 'She did not like the fact you arrived with him. And I would be careful—because she certainly would not have liked it when you danced with him.'

Seraphine thought she and Ezra were starting to become friends. Now, she wasn't so sure.

Would he really call on that woman? She couldn't believe it. Didn't want to believe it. Lady Frances had been so vile to her. Ezra had borne witness to it.

Her world spun on its axis once more. How had she missed the signs?

Yet he had told her he was seeking a match the Viscount would approve of. Lady Frances was an earl's daughter. She could even be considered pretty, if she wasn't so cruel.

'Courting? Are they really?' She was aware her voice sounded thick and hoarse. She hadn't seen them dance more than one set together.

'Yes, he called on her—the day of the opera. She said he arrived with the most magnificent bouquet of flowers.'

Seraphine swallowed, her lips pressing tight into a grimace. She took Miss Jennings's arm in hers, for support more than anything. 'Well, if your gossip is true, Miss Jennings, then Mr Hart has particularly poor taste. Come, I do not know about you, but all this talk has made me hungry. Shall we get some supper?' she said, trying to act as if she didn't care. And she really didn't. Did she?

'Yes, let's.'

Yet she didn't think she could stomach a thing. She suddenly felt nauseous.

Chapter Seven

For however long she was to be trapped here, on the Artington estate, Seraphine refused to give up her freedom, so she had decided to get away from the place—and Ezra Hart—for the day.

Last night, she had feigned tiredness in the carriage on the way home from Vauxhall, so she didn't have to make small talk with her brother and Ezra about what a success the night had been. And when Ezra had said goodnight at the cottage door, she had refused to accept his help down from the coach, or meet his gaze. She'd seen his brow had creased as a flicker of confusion crossed his face, but she didn't care—she ridiculously felt let down.

She had thought they'd made progress last night. She had been having a good time, despite Lady Frances's attempts to ruin her evening. Ezra had stuck up for her, and he'd asked her to dance. So finding out he had called on her enemy felt disloyal. She'd been fooling herself, it seemed. They weren't friends, not really.

She had been there for him when he'd been overcome by his memories, risking her reputation to go after him and follow him into the gardens. And she had opened up to him about her own past. As children, she and her brother had often shared their thoughts and fears, but now they were older, they rarely spoke about their childhood any more—she didn't want to burden Henri with her dark thoughts, her questions. But in trying to comfort Ezra, she had let down her guard, telling him about what had happened to her mother and father. Now she wished her confidences back, everything she'd revealed to him about herself, for he didn't deserve to know.

She suddenly felt a pang of loss for the woman who had given birth to her and all she could have learned from her if she'd still been around. What advice would her mother have given her about the Viscount's son?

She followed the footpath Ezra had described to her aunt at Lady Bulphan's ball—through Frampton and Fernside. She knew Henri would be cross with her for walking out without a chaperon, but she was determined to retain her independence and make her journey into the city alone. It was indeed a most pleasant walk, offering glimpses of Artington Hall all the way along, from different angles. History seemed to whisper to her from every stone, enticing her in, and she allowed her mind to drift, wondering what Viscountess Hart of Artington Hall would spend her days doing. The thought of Lady Frances presiding over this beautiful place was unbearable. Her touch would tarnish it.

Hearing the familiar birdsong in the trees, the scent of pine on the breeze, and the calming sounds of the River Fleet, she realised she was starting to like it here.

She liked Ezra.

She stopped suddenly on the path, her realisation shocking her.

She liked him. More than she should.

She had never meant for that to happen. It had crept up on her, taking her unawares. She had sworn to hate him. She had determined not to like any man—she didn't want to let anyone into her heart, for fear that she might lose them, as she had lost her family before.

These feelings for Ezra had come out of nowhere— and she wished them away. It was inconvenient. It was disturbing. She had thought herself incapable of having these emotions. It was frightening. And it was futile— because they could never be together, even if that was what she wanted, which was absurd. His father would never allow it. And anyway, Ezra liked Lady Frances— God knew why. He'd been secretly courting the one woman who seemed to hate her above all others. It was a wrench, yet she had no choice but to accept it.

What had he really thought of Lady Frances's joke about her head in a basket? She felt uncertain of him now. Had he danced with her out of pity?

She tried to shake her thoughts away. She wanted to maintain her independence and freedom, so she could keep control of her life, forge her own path and make her own decisions. Ezra Hart was certainly not a man who would entertain the way she liked to spend her days.

But she had never had these thoughts or feelings about anyone before—and suddenly she felt miserable. She walked on, harder, faster, pounding the path with her muddy boots, trying to stamp out her frustration. How could one man have had such an impact on her and in such a short amount of time? She didn't know how to deal with this apart from trying to banish her thoughts, block them out, as if they didn't exist.

As she came into the city and through the familiar neighbourhoods in Mayfair, she ducked into the church, picked up a basket, then carried on through the bustling streets, past the thriving market stalls, vendors shouting out about their wares. Some called her name and she waved. She did like it here, she realised. Yes, she moaned to Henri, often, about not fitting in, but she had created her own little community, where she felt at home. She had come to know these streets like the back of her hand.

Glancing about her now, she had the strangest feeling she was being watched, but she couldn't see anyone. She darted across the street, continuing along the pavement, until a carriage pulled up alongside her, startling her.

'Miss Seraphine.'

She reeled. Ezra. Had he been following her? She thrust her chin up in the air and barely glancing his way, she continued along the pavement.

'What on earth are you doing here?'

'Taking a walk,' she said haughtily, trying not to glance his way.

'Without a companion? In the city? Being seen unsupervised in the *ton* could ruin you, Miss Seraphine.'

His disapproval made her want to rebel even more. 'Well, it seems I now have you for that. Are you following me, Mr Hart?'

'These reckless actions of yours could cause a scandal.' She noted he'd ignored her question.

'Look around you. Who here will care? Besides, I know my way around these parts. It is quite safe.'

She continued at a pace and, to her annoyance, the carriage crept alongside her, keeping up.

'May I offer you a ride back to Artington?' he asked.

'No, thank you,' she said, turning her nose up in the air. 'I am going the other way.'

'Is there something wrong, Seraphine? It is just that I thought we had agreed to be friends.'

She liked the way he used her name for the first time, without her title, and the way it sounded on his tongue.

She turned to scowl at him. 'So did I.'

He stopped the carriage and got out. But she continued walking quickly, trying to get away from him. She crossed the road, to the other side, but irritatingly, his long strides allowed him to catch up to her easily.

'Have I done something to offend you?'

'Not at all.'

He overtook her and came to stand in front of her, blocking her path. 'Are you sure about that?'

She sighed. 'I do not understand why you are here, Mr Hart. Do you not have anything better to do? Should you not be calling on Lady Frances, in fact?'

His dark brow furrowed. 'No, why?' Then a kind of recognition dawned and she felt herself flush. She didn't for one second want him to think that she cared. But he was too astute. He leaned in to whisper. 'Do not tell me you are jealous of me calling on Miss Frances?'

'Not at all.' She shrugged. 'Just surprised to see you here at this time of day, that is all. Good day to you.'

And she ducked round him and continued on her way.

But within seconds he was back at her side, keeping up, like a buzzing bee she had to keep swatting away.

'You have obviously heard that I called on her,' he said. 'But it was just the once. And it should not surprise you. You know that I am looking for a wife this Season.'

'She is an interesting choice.'

'She is an earl's daughter. She is everything the Viscount would approve of.'

'Then I am pleased for you.'

'But after she was unkind to you that night at the opera, I broke it off. I have not visited her again.'

She finally stopped walking and looked up at him. 'You have no need to stop courting someone on my account.'

'I know that. But I will not have someone be rude to my friends. And that is what we are, is it not?' he said, raking a hand through his hair. And then he looked around them, at all the goings-on of the busy suburb. 'What in heaven's name are you doing here?' he asked, changing the subject.

She was still bothered that he had called on Lady Frances at all. Suddenly, she felt rebellion dart through her blood, wanting to test him. 'Do you really want to know?'

'Yes.'

'Then come and see. I am going this way,' she said, heading down a small passageway.

He looked around them once more. 'Why do I get the feeling I am going to regret this?'

She smiled. 'If we are truly to be friends, you should know this about me. Perhaps it will go some way to helping you understand why I agreed to yours and my brother's meddling. Why I agreed to smile and dance with the men Henri wanted me to last night. I guess we all have our reasons for why we do the things we do.'

Finally, they emerged from the passageway into a square. 'And perhaps you can tell me what it is that brings you into the city, too.'

'Seraphine, love. Over here!' a woman's voice called.

She tilted her head and led Ezra over to the tables where the volunteers were setting up.

'You're serving today, my dear.'

'Thanks, Christine. I have brought extra help, too,' Seraphine said, nodding towards Ezra.

The woman eyed him. 'He doesn't look as if he's from around these parts. He looks like he has some brains as well as brawn. You sure you want to get that suit dirty, love?' the woman asked Ezra and Seraphine tried to stifle a smirk. She imagined he'd never been called 'love' in his life.

Ezra raised his eyebrows and leaned in to whisper to her, 'I am not sure I do, no. What is this place, Seraphine? What are we doing here?'

His warm breath on her cheek sent a strange ripple of goose pimples across her skin. 'Aid—for French refugees,' she said, tilting her chin up, defiant.

His eyes widened and he looked around him again with fresh eyes at the people lining up in the square, some huddled around fires or shelters, others begging as people passed by, taking it all in.

'Some are sick, others have no money, or homes—and many have young children.' She rummaged around in her basket and drew out an apron, wrapping it tightly around her waist. 'I mix with your people, you mix with mine—seems a fair deal, do you not think? However, if you are worried being seen here might damage your reputation...'

His eyes narrowed on her. She imagined he was wondering how he could make a quick exit, planning his escape. 'These are not really your people. Not of your class, anyway.'

'They may have been once. Now people are just trying to survive. They need our help. The charm and safety of your estate, even the affluent suburbs of Mayfair, shields us from the reality that many impoverished French people live on the streets. Many left France with just the clothes on their backs—leaving behind homes and family. Now they are in dire need of food, clothes and friendship. They came here to escape the troubles and found new ones.' She placed her hands on her hips. 'Are status and reputation the only things of importance to you?' she challenged him.

'No.'

'Prove it,' she said, pulling out a second apron and thrusting it into his chest. 'Here, put this on.'

He picked up the lid of the cauldron and peeked inside, taking a sniff of the soup. 'Smells good. What is it?'

'Potato soup. It is not as grand as the white soup served in our houses, but it is comforting all the same. I cannot imagine you know what it is like to go a day without food, but these people do.'

His eyes darkened and the corner of his mouth caught. She had a feeling there was something he wasn't telling her.

'You presume too much. Are you forgetting we lived on rations during the war? We often had to add our daily rum tot to the food to make it palatable.'

'Of course,' she said, backing down a little.

She felt ashamed she had judged him.

'And you? Have you ever had to go without?'

She shook her head.

'Good.' He put the lid back on. 'You know, you make unconventional choices, Seraphine.'

And she knew he wasn't talking about the flavour of the soup.

'I am proud of them,' she said.

She hadn't really thought he'd stay. She'd expected him to throw the apron back in her face and walk away, so she was disturbed when he pulled it on over his head and tied it loosely around his waist, giving her a quizzical look. 'I will stay and help—if it means I will win back your good favour.'

And she found herself laughing, delighted.

'Do you come here, to do this often?' he asked.

'Once or twice a week—more if I can. I feel it is the least I can do.' She liked to feel she was doing something— and to be surrounded by people who never judged her. 'And I do not intend to stop, despite my brother's plans for me to marry.'

'I see. Does he know about this?' Ezra said.

'Yes. And he would never stop me doing something I am so passionate about. It makes me feel useful. I may be shunned in higher society, but these people have it far worse.'

She was surprised when Ezra rolled up his crisp shirt sleeves and came to stand by her side, serving up ladles of hot soup to the long line of people along with a handsome smile.

She couldn't believe he was there. Did he not have anything better to do? She almost wished he did—his presence was distracting her from being her usual chatty self with the regulars, his elbow brushing against hers every so often, sending ripples of heat up her arm.

She had thought him conceited and arrogant, but he obviously had a softer side—she could tell from how he talked to the children and was patient with the people in the line—and that, she realised, was all the more dangerous to her.

'What were you doing in the city, when you came across me today?' she asked him.

'I went to speak to the authorities about how they were getting on with their investigations about the fire the other night—whether they had made any progress.'

'Oh.' She had not been expecting him to say that. Did he still feel guilty for it? Was he still trying to make amends? 'And have they?'

He shook his head. 'Not yet. So I decided to make a few enquiries of my own.'

She looked up at him. 'And?'

He inclined his head, implying he had information, and her heart began to pound. 'I will share my findings with you later, when we are alone.'

Alone? She swallowed at the images that conjured up. They both knew very well they could not be alone. But she suddenly wondered what it would be like if they could be and she tried to stop her thoughts in their tracks.

When the masses had been fed, Seraphine sat with some of the families and spoke to them for a while, listening to their stories of what had happened to them in France, how long they'd been here—some for years, just like her—and how they had managed to get away. It was always devastating to hear which of their loved ones hadn't made it. It reminded her of her own loss. But it also made her realise how lucky she was that she and Henri had a home. Connections. Especially those in high places.

And she looked up at Ezra, who Christine had put to scrubbing the pans, and she cringed. Yet she didn't think he'd do it if he really didn't want to.

She took out her notebook and began to sketch a few of the families. Just a few days ago, he had been her enemy, now they were sharing jokes... The thought had her straightening and she reached over for her cup to take a sobering sip of water.

But she had enjoyed his company today—and she felt guilty for it, for taking pleasure in something while these people were suffering. She was desperately trying to cling on to her anger against him. It was easier than admitting she might actually be starting to care for him. Because the thought scared her, for she had never intended this to happen. She really didn't want to like him.

Why this man? she wondered. This man whom she had hated at first. Who was so dominant in the *ton*. Who was so beyond her reach. Who was out of bounds because of what she represented to his father and to society.

She needed to drum up some of her previous resistance to him. Letting him get any closer was dangerous, because it was inevitable she would lose him. He wouldn't stick around—he was going to marry another before the Season was out, meaning she would get hurt.

Ezra realised Seraphine smiled more easily among these people and he could understand that. There was no need to put on a front. They weren't judging, they were just grateful. And it made him feel good to do something for them—call it penance for the things he had said in that pamphlet. He hoped he had gone some way to redeeming himself.

These people, it seemed, made her able to be her true self, as he had used to feel among his siblings and his parents. As though he belonged. They had both been taken away from their homes, torn apart from those they cared about. Was that what made him feel he could share things with her, as he had done in the gardens at Vauxhall last night, thinking perhaps she might understand? She had seen him at his lowest, yet she hadn't judged him.

He was pleased she had come after him, just as she'd come after her brother that morning of the duel. Did it mean she was starting to care? She had sat by him, helping him through the moment until it passed, sharing her own fears—and the commonalities he shared with her had surprised him. There was something about her that made him let down his guard, open up. He had never allowed himself to be vulnerable with anyone else and he had worried she might use it against him, yet he didn't think she would. She was a good person. Kind. He didn't know many people who would give up their days to help others.

'Are you ready to go?' he asked her a while later, approaching her where she sat, sketching something in her notebook.

She snapped the book closed as he drew nearer. 'Yes.'

'My coach is probably still waiting where I left it.'

She gasped. 'The poor footman! I did not realise,' she said, getting to her feet.

And he grinned. 'You do know not everyone is your responsibility to worry about and take care of, Seraphine. He does get paid.' And then, feeling devilish, he grabbed the book out of her hand and spun around, turning his back to her, giving him a chance to flick through the pages before she could get to him, her hands trying to snatch it back.

'Mr Hart!' she warned.

'These are good,' he said, enjoying the feel of her arms brushing against his a bit too much.

'Give it back,' she said, her cheeks turning a delightful pink colour.

'Your brother was right. You do have a talent. You can really capture the expressions of people.'

'Mr Hart!' she warned again.

'Ezra,' he said.

She sighed. 'Ezra.'

And he grinned, finally handing it over. 'You should go to see that art exhibition at the Royal Academy. The new one that is about to open. Everyone has been talking about it. It will certainly be less taxing for you than today.'

She smiled. And he really liked it when she did. It made his heart beat just that little bit faster. 'I bet you have never had to work a day in your life before, have you?' she asked him.

'Does serving in the army not count?' he asked. 'Was that not the greatest service of all?'

She inclined her head, conceding. 'All right, I will let you have that one.'

'But I admit my fingers have never been so wrinkled from scrubbing pans before!'

They began to walk back through the square and down the streets they'd walked along earlier today. It almost seemed like a lifetime ago. He'd caught sight of her on the path leading away from Artington just as he'd been returning and he'd bade his footman turn around and follow her, wondering where she was going and on her own. She could be so reckless!

'I confess I thought you were boring. Haughty. Who knew you could take a step down off your pedestal and be normal?' she teased.

'I hide that side of me well.' As with other things, he thought. But the words she'd said earlier, about not seeing why a title made a difference, why it made a person better, or worse, had stuck with him. Did she really feel that way? It gave him hope.

'You were different today, too. More carefree.' He liked hearing her laugh—it made him do the same. 'Your brother says you shut everyone out—that you purposefully make yourself inaccessible at the events in the *ton*.'

Her eyebrows shot up. 'That is not true!' she said, wounded that Henri would say such a thing.

But when he gave her a look, she relented. 'If I do, it is a defence thing. Perhaps I do it before they have chance to alienate me.'

He shrugged. 'It was not a criticism, Seraphine, just an observation. I do the same.'

'You?' she asked, her gaze swinging to look at him. 'Why would you feel like you do not belong?'

'Perhaps we all feel like an imposter at times.'

He wondered if he should tell her, but instantly crushed the ridiculous thought. What good would it do either of them to reveal it now?

They reached the coach and the footman gave him a look.

'Sorry we were so long,' Ezra said.

'I was beginning to grow concerned, Master Hart.'

'Would you mind if we went past the house on the way home? I should like to see it, the damage, and find out how the builders are getting on,' Seraphine said.

'Of course.'

'And you must tell me what you discovered about the fire.'

He nodded before reaching over to the pocket in the side of the door, retrieving an empty glass bottle and handing it to her.

She took it from him, their fingers brushing.

'This is a bottle like the one thrown through your window the other night. What do you see?'

She gave an involuntary shiver as she held it. 'Nothing. It is just a normal bottle.'

He shook his head. 'No, it isn't. Look closer,' he said, leaning forward, turning the glass around in her hand.

'It is dark glass and of a unique design—only used for certain types of wine. See the maker's mark?' he said. 'It is expensive. Drunk only by noblemen who can afford it.'

She gasped.

'The perpetrators must have got the bottle from somewhere. There are not too many of them around. It gave me a clue as to who the authorities could go and speak to, starting with the makers of the bottle and who buys their wine.'

He sat back in his seat.

'Ezra, that is genius.'

'Like your friend said, I have brains as well as brawn.' He winked.

She laughed. 'Thank you. I really hope they catch them.'

'They will.' At least he hoped they would. He wouldn't

rest until the perpetrators had been reprimanded. It was the least he could do. Especially if they had acted after reading his words in the pamphlet. He needed to know they wouldn't strike again. That Seraphine was safe.

Sitting opposite her in the coach, she looked like a different person to the woman he'd journeyed home with after the ball last night. Right now, tendrils of her blonde hair were coming loose and her face was streaked with dirt. But she was no less attractive.

He liked the fact she didn't conform. He liked the way she wasn't afraid of her difference—that she was herself, no matter what people thought of her. That she wasn't willing to change herself for others and was determined to carry on with her charity work, no matter what. He wished he could be more like that. Somehow, she gave him faith that, one day, he could be.

Since he'd come to reside at Artington, he had lived in fear that he would be discovered, knowing he wasn't like the elite in society, that he was different. Despite what he'd told Seraphine when she'd questioned whether status and reputation were the only things of importance to him, it was what he'd been brought up to believe. He found it refreshing, even liberating, that she didn't.

When he was with her, he found he didn't worry quite so much about what people thought, especially the Viscount—or his threat. In fact, he wanted to ignore it, forget about his ultimatum. He was starting to like himself the more time he spent in Seraphine's company. Being with her reminded him of the freedom of his youth. She was good for him.

Seraphine had been right about Lady Frances. She was an interesting choice and one he was no longer inclined to pursue. When he'd called on her, when they'd sat in her drawing room and spoken—about the weather, about Lady Bulphan's ball, about her flower-arranging—he had felt nothing. Not a single spark. And the way she had gone on to treat Seraphine had put him off for good.

He glanced at the woman sitting opposite him, her hands gently clasped in her lap. If she had been jealous of him calling on Lady Frances, she must like him, he thought, settling back in his seat—the way he was beginning to like her?

He hadn't been looking for anything more than a respectable union of two noble families, yet he was starting to wonder whether that was enough. Whether he should hope for more.

He only wished he could learn to accept himself as she did. But he couldn't. He couldn't just shake off years of conditioning—the shackles of society the Viscount had placed around him since he'd become a Hart.

'You said you signed up as a soldier as you were running away from your problems. Your father...?'

He looked at her.

'Why do you still spend so much time away from home?'

He shrugged. 'We are just not that similar, he and I. And if I am not there, I cannot disappoint him.'

He didn't want to tell her the real reason he didn't get on with the Viscount—that they'd always had a strained relationship, because of how it had begun.

'Why would you disappoint him?'

He glanced out the window at the houses and people rushing past, going about their daily lives.

'Another thing you do not want to talk about? I thought we were friends?' she jested.

'It is because we are friends that I cannot,' he said, turning back to her. 'I admit I fear you will think less of me.' Because he didn't want the truth to change how she felt about him. He feared that it would. And he'd stayed and helped her today because he respected her, admired her, and he wanted her approval in return. He didn't want her knowing he'd pretended to be something he wasn't.

Looking back at Seraphine, there was a definite spark between them. He could feel it in the tension in the air. As if they were both constantly holding a breath—of hope, of excitement? It had been there since the moment they'd met. She was breathtakingly beautiful. Yet he knew these feelings he had towards her went against everything the Viscount deemed acceptable. Hell, even everything he himself thought was appropriate.

If anything were to happen, there would be those who wouldn't approve. There might be a lot of hostility towards them. He knew the men he'd fought with might see it as wrong. And those who had lost family out there on the Continent would wonder why he wasn't choosing one of their own.

If he was to make his feelings known, it would surely destroy his relationship with the Viscount, his chance of inheritance. He was expected to marry an English lady, the daughter of a duke, or earl. And he had to conform, do what was expected of him, as he always had done.

But he couldn't deny that he was starting to like Seraphine. A lot.

He was fighting it, wary about letting her into his heart, but he was starting to see her for who she really was—someone who was willing to help others before herself, someone strong yet kind. Someone who wasn't afraid to stick up for herself—or her loved ones.

He liked talking to her. He wanted to learn more about her and hear her opinions. And he wanted to share his own thoughts with her too. That was new to him— usually he didn't reveal anything of himself to anyone.

No one had ever cared to listen about how he felt about things as he'd grown up. The Viscount had always said he should be seen and not heard. He had kept himself to himself until he'd gone to Oxford and then his friendships, his debates in class, had begun to get him noticed. He'd realised perhaps he did have something interesting to say, that he could contribute and make a difference, and people wanted to listen.

When they'd gone to war, commanders had asked to hear his strategies, the soldiers had been enraptured by his rallying speeches and men had wanted to fight alongside him, for him. He'd been trusted, even by those above him. He had started to believe in his own worth, but it was easy to speak about things when they were about something other than yourself.

'Where are you from? I mean, I know you were not born in London. Was it Buxton?'

Her question surprised him. No one had asked that in a long while—not since they had first moved to London. Perhaps they had when they'd first moved here, but no more. It was assumed the Harts had always been at Artington.

'Yes, Derbyshire.' He didn't want to lie to her.

'Why did you move here?'

'For my schooling, I believe. They always wanted their son to go to Eton.'

She nodded.

Outside the window, he saw a child stumble and fall and a man pick her up and comfort her.

Not for the first time, he wondered if the Viscount had been a caring father to his son. He knew the man had loved his wife dearly. It was the only time he'd seen any tenderness in his personality, in the way he'd spoken to her. And he had been devasted when she had died. Was it just Ezra he couldn't show affection for?

Perhaps losing his son, and later his wife, had made him cold and bitter. Perhaps he regretted the fact they'd had to take in another man's son and make him their heir. It would explain the ill feeling that had always simmered between them.

If Ezra were to have a child, or even adopted one, he would never treat them as such. And he wondered, did he want to be a father? He had never thought about it before. Not even when the Viscount had started talking about him producing an heir.

Would he make a good one? He thought he could do a damn better job than the Viscount, or even his own father had done. He would certainly never abandon his own. He looked over at Seraphine and she smiled. She would make a wonderful mother—she cared about others more than herself. Yet was being a mother herself something she wanted after losing her own? His thoughts stopped him in his tracks. What was he thinking? He was daydreaming of the impossible—things that could never be. Things he didn't want to be, as they would lead to certain heartbreak.

And he knew he had to get serious. He had obligations, family he ought to take care of, responsibilities to take charge of. He knew he couldn't put off what the Viscount was demanding of him for ever, yet, even knowing this, he was drawn back to the woman sitting opposite him.

The rain was coming down hard, pounding on the roof of the carriage as they stepped out and raced towards the door of Seraphine's town house. Ezra held his cloak over her head as best he could as she fumbled with the key in the lock, laughing, before they ducked inside.

The ground floor was pretty much as it had always been. Cloaks hung on hooks in the hallway and shoes lay ready to be stepped into. On a chest, withered flowers still stood in tall vases. As they slowly climbed the stairs, men were working on the first floor, tending to the blackened walls, and Seraphine gasped at the damage.

'It'll be back to normal in no time, Miss,' one said.

'Mind your footing,' Ezra warned. 'Be careful how you go. It is not entirely safe yet.'

She couldn't believe the extent of the smoke and water damage to the walls and furnishings. And she wondered if the effects of the fire had changed the feel of the place for good. It felt different, or maybe she was just different—like a changed person to the one who had left here days before—and she wondered just how much that had to do with the man standing beside her, looking at her with concern.

Rainwater was streaking down his face and his tailcoat was soaked through.

'I just need to go and collect a few things from upstairs,' she said. 'I will not be long.'

'I'll wait for you here.'

Seraphine was relieved to see the bedrooms were still intact—only the windows were blackened by smoke. She retrieved a book she had been near to finishing, eager to read the end, and some extra gloves. Checking herself in the mirror, she realised she looked a mess. Whatever must Ezra think of her? Her hair was coming loose and she had streaks of dirt from the day's work on her skin. She poured some water into the basin, washed her face and refastened her bun. Taking a look in her wardrobe, she pulled out a classic pale-blue day dress and quickly changed out of her wet clothes.

Heading back downstairs, she saw her beloved piano in the salon and was overjoyed it was still in one piece. Distracted, she took a seat on the stool and, lifting the fallboard, ran her fingers over it, tinkling the ivory keys.

'Are you going to play, Seraphine?' Ezra said and she looked up to see him leaning in the doorway, listening, his damp hair ruffled, and her breath hitched. He had removed his tailcoat and was holding two steaming cups and saucers in his hands—and he looked extremely handsome. Her eyes slipped to his shirt, which had gone see-through down the middle, where it had been exposed to the rain, and it was clinging to his skin, hinting at the muscles beneath. Her pulse kicked up.

She looked away, closing the lid again and placing her hands on top, smoothing her hands over the sleek mahogany wood. 'I do not think the builders want to hear that! But I miss it. I am so glad it survived the fire. My brother bought it for me.'

'And I am certain he would not have if you could not play a tune,' he said, coming into the room. 'You are a woman of many talents.'

'Yes, my husband-to-be is very lucky, is he not?' she said, mocking herself.

He scowled. 'Here, to warm you up,' he said, passing her a cup of freshly brewed tea.

'Thank you,' she said, reaching for the saucer, their fingers brushing. She took a comforting sip of the hot liquid.

'That is a pretty dress. You know, we do have a piano at Artington you are welcome to play.'

'Yes, I saw. It is far grander than this. From France, I noticed?'

'That is correct.'

'I have been wondering, if your father so loathes our kind, why leave the French parts of the house—the windows, the French-style furniture, the piano—when he was rebuilding?'

'Perhaps, despite his ill feelings, he could not deny their beauty, their worth,' he said, holding her gaze.

She swallowed. 'Will you tell me about it?' she said.

'What?'

'Why your father so abhors us?'

He sighed and placed his cup down on a table.

'It is really the Viscount's father it has to do with. Do you really care to know?'

'Yes. Please.'

'Very well. His name was Benjamin Hart.' He came to sit next to her on the bench and she shifted up a little to give him more room—only their elbows still touched. Burned. 'When he was a young man, he went on a Grand Tour, spending much time in France. Once it was over, he returned to Artington, married an Englishwoman and they had a child—the Viscount. Only, it seems Benjamin could not forget the women he had met in France and, in secret, he organised for one of them to come over here. He paid to put her up in her own lodgings in the *ton*.'

Seraphine gasped.

Ezra lifted up the fallboard again, gently resting it against the wood, and he ran his long fingers along the keys, tunefully playing a scale.

'Do you play?' she said, turning to look at him in surprise.

'A little. Anyway, back to our story. When the truth about his affair came out, it destroyed his wife—she climbed the steps of the clocktower and, at the stroke of midnight, when she knew he was in the arms of another, threw herself off the top, falling to her death. It was always said she died of a broken heart, not the fall. In a way it was very clever, for every time her husband heard the chime of the hour, he would remember her. Remember what he had done. The pain he had caused her.

'Of course, the same was true for her son. Benjamin fled the country with his mistress, never to return, leaving the current Lord Hart in charge of the estate. He was just a boy, fifteen at the time, devastated about the death of his mother, and apparently he could never forgive his father for what he had done and has hated the French ever since, blaming them for turning his father against them.'

He played another scale, his beautiful fingers gently pressing the keys, and the movement of his hands fascinated her. Her skin erupted in goose pimples. He played skilfully.

'The young Viscount boarded up Artington and moved away, only returning when his wife convinced him they ought to, so I could go to Eton.'

'How tragic,' Seraphine said, shaking her head. 'I am so sorry. You must have known that letting us stay at Artington might bring up old wounds of the past.'

Ezra shrugged. 'I did not expect him to think all French women are the same.'

'What—that we all have such scandalous intentions?'

He grinned. 'I also did not think that you would meet him. He does not leave his rooms too often these days. He is rarely seen out in the *ton*. He is very fragile. Grief has changed him.'

'Ezra,' she said, warmth rushing through her at using his first name. It felt intimate somehow. 'Are you sure we should not leave the cottage?'

'No. I have spoken with the Viscount. You are staying now. I told him that it is only temporary anyway.'

And she nodded, taking that on board. It was the reminder she needed that she must not get too attached to the place—or to Ezra, for she would have to leave them both soon.

'Besides, I like having you there. You make the place less lonely.'

'And I appreciated your help today,' she said. She got up from the stool, putting some distance between them, unable to concentrate on anything but where the skin on her elbow was touching the heat of his skin through his shirt. And she wished he would stop running his perfect hands over the keys, playing the most exquisite scales. It was doing funny things to her insides.

He inclined his head, acknowledging her thanks. And

he finally closed down the piano. 'You said it would help me to understand why you agreed to your brother's meddling?' he said, rising to join her. 'Why you accepted my help to build up your reputation in the *ton*?'

She twisted her hands together. 'I accepted your help as, like you said, you are a man of influence. And I was hoping for your assistance. Not for myself, but for the people you met today, who are just like me.'

His brow furrowed, not quite understanding.

'They were forced from their homes amid the violence and they travelled a long way to get here in search of a better life. Like me. But some have not yet found it. There is so much prejudice and discrimination.' She stepped towards him. 'You have the means to help change that.'

His brows rose. 'Do I?' He shifted his weight, uncomfortable.

'You know you do. You could sway opinions. Make a real difference.'

'Seraphine, I am one man. You overestimate my influence. You already have a position of standing in the *ton*. Your aunt is an acquaintance of the Queen. I can help you...that was easy. You are beautiful, you have the means to socialise in high society. But them?' He shook his head. 'I am honestly not sure what I can do. There are too many of them.'

'But we cannot just sit by and do nothing. I will not,' she said, determined. 'If I can use my status, my voice, to get them any help they need—more money, a roof over their heads, or even food—I must.'

He drew a hand over his jaw. 'And what about a husband? Did you have any intention of going along with your brother's plan and finding one of those?'

She had meant what she'd said to Henri about not needing to find a husband. She had decided she would never marry. She had thought she would never feel the same way other men and women did towards each other. She had accepted she would never know that attraction— she had felt incapable of feeling it, or anything more.

Until now.

She looked up into Ezra's dark eyes. 'I told you I did not.'

He took a step towards her. 'I see.'

She launched herself away from him, wringing her hands. 'We were not talking about me. We were talking about them.'

He ran a hand around the back of his neck. 'What are you suggesting?'

'I do not know. Could you, is there any chance, you could speak to the Regent? Parliament? We could try to raise some money, set up a relief fund…'

'Seraphine, this is a lot to ask.'

'I know.' She bravely took a step back towards him. 'But would you just consider it? Please? For me?'

He came towards her, staring down at her for a long moment. 'I'll tell you what we could do. We could start small. But it might just work to get people interested.'

'What did you have in mind?'

'We will have a benefit ball at Artington—for the émigrés.'

'A ball?' she gasped.

'Yes, we will ask people to pay for their tickets.'

'But will people even come, given the cause?'

'They will come to see what a ball at Artington is like. I cannot remember there ever being one. Never in my lifetime. People rarely get to see inside the estate, let alone the house.'

'But what about your father?'

'I will tell the Viscount I am hosting a ball to find a bride—that will appease him. He does not need to know all the details…'

'Ezra, are you sure?'

'Yes.'

'Thank you.'

And then he laughed, shaking his head. 'Only you, Seraphine. Only you could have me hosting a ball. Mrs Dawson is going to be ecstatic.'

Chapter Eight

'I have been wanting to see it for a while, to see what all the fuss is about,' Seraphine said, excited. Ezra had agreed to escort her aunt and uncle—his first outing since the fire—and her and Henri to the Royal Academy Exhibition in Leicester Square. And it seemed half the *ton* had made an appearance on opening day. 'I have heard there are some exquisite pieces.'

'I must say it feels good to be up and about, out of bed,' Monsieur Auclair said, patting down his waistcoat, proving his burns were healing. 'Although I do believe I might feel worse again by this evening's ball.' He winked and Ezra smiled.

Ezra leaned in to whisper in Seraphine's ear. 'I think you might take after your uncle, Seraphine, in your lack of interest in these social events.'

She smiled. 'Perhaps. Although I think my tastes have changed quite dramatically this week. I confess, I may be starting to enjoy some of them.'

'Is that so? Well, then—what are we waiting for? Let us go and debate some art. Perhaps you will exhibit some of your own here one day.'

Entering the vast, but light and airy, gallery, Seraphine was pleased to see Miss Jennings and the rest of the women she had started to befriend. She noted Lady Frances was also in attendance, sulking on the sidelines. She couldn't believe just a week or so ago she had felt so alone and now she was surrounded by people she enjoyed talking to. Men and women alike.

'Miss Mounier, I took the liberty of purchasing you a programme,' Lord Wentworth said, approaching her. 'As a souvenir of today.'

She could almost sense Henri give a little cheer behind her, whereas Ezra could barely hold himself back from rolling his eyes, his lips pursed.

'Thank you, that is most kind.'

'Will you allow me to show you one of the works I find most intriguing?' Lord Wentworth said, leading her away.

The visitors strolled around the gallery at their leisure, perusing the artworks, stopping to listen every now and then to the guide who was telling them a little more information about each painting, and Seraphine found it all fascinating. There was a still life of flowers, landscapes—and scene after scene of Waterloo. Pictures depicting the battle, portraits of the generals who had died, and there was even a bust of the Duke of Wellington himself.

It all helped to build up a picture of what the war on the Continent had been like and the Royal Academy obviously thought artworks of the great battle would draw in the crowds. Looking around, she realised they had been right. The place was heaving.

But the more Seraphine studied the paintings, the more she realised she had made a mistake and her enthusiasm for the exhibition waned. She thought only of Ezra—and realised she shouldn't have asked him to bring them here. She felt terrible, wondering what impact viewing these scenes might be having on him and his memories.

She glanced over at him, concerned, but his back was turned, so she couldn't see the effect the art was having on him. She didn't want to cause a repeat of the other night. She excused herself from speaking with Lord Wentworth and slowly weaved her way across the room to Ezra, trying not to get brought into other conversations. As she drew nearer, she realised he was standing looking up at Henry Aston Barker's panorama of *The Battle of Waterloo*, transfixed, and she came to stand next to him.

'Are you all right?' she whispered.

'It is strange. To be surrounded by images of familiar places—where my friends once stood and fought and fell,' he whispered. And she could see it in his eyes, that each image struck a chord inside him, bringing back a moment, a feeling, as if he was back there, fighting. The scenes of devastation were incredibly moving, even for someone like her who hadn't been there, and it made her see the utter futility of war. She hoped there would never be another.

She glanced all around them, checking no one was in earshot.

'Did you know this is what it would be like?' she hissed. 'And if so, why on earth did you come?'

'*You* wanted to see them.'

'Yes. But that does not explain why *you* had to come. You do not need to be here. Not if it troubles you.'

A muscle flickered in his jaw.

'Do you want to leave?' she asked.

He shook his head.

From the point of view of someone who was beginning to know his behaviours from spending so much time in his company, the tension was visible in his neck and in the rigidity of his stance. Why was he being so stubborn?

Then she glanced away and her mouth gaped open.

Out of the corner of her eye, she saw Viscount Hart entering the gallery slowly with the aid of his cane. He was dressed more formally than she had seen him the other day, with a high collar and cravat, even a top hat. She looked up at Ezra, wide-eyed, then back towards the older man, shocked.

She knew the Viscount rarely made a public appearance and she wondered what had brought it on. Did he want to see the paintings, so he could imagine what Ezra had been through during the war? Was it an act of respect to his son?

Eza looked just as shocked to see him as she was, but instead of going over to welcome him, to say hello, suddenly, he was gesturing with his head that they leave. 'I have changed my mind, Seraphine. Come on! Let us go. This way.'

Giving her no time to think about it, he quickly moved into the next room and, for some reason that she couldn't fathom and knew she would question later, she instinctively followed him. The next gallery was far emptier than the last, but he walked straight through it, ushering her on into another, smaller space, which was empty. And once inside, he closed the door.

She looked all around her. The space was small, cramped, and she could hear his breaths coming in short, sharp bursts. She wondered if he was experiencing some kind of panic. Had those paintings affected him more than she'd thought, or was it the sight of his father, who had come here unannounced, that had him so worked up?

'Ezra, what are we doing?' she asked, alarm and a peculiar excitement racing through her.

He came towards her and placed his finger over her mouth. 'Shh.' And she went very still, her eyes wide.

They heard voices pass by the door.

'Have you seen Mr Hart?' someone was saying. 'If you do, can you tell him his father is looking for him?'

Ezra's peppery scent began to wrap around her in the confined space. But mainly she was aware of one of his large hands resting on the wall beside her head, his chest almost pressing against hers. And his finger, still brushing her lips.

She stared up at him, into his dark, troubled gaze in the dim light, trying to work out what he was thinking. What they were doing. If anyone saw them, found them here like this…

Up close, his features were even more striking. His dark eyes had tiny golden flecks in them and she could see a faint scar on his right cheek. She wondered how he'd got it. And she was acutely aware she'd never been so close to him before. Never been so close to a man who wasn't her brother or uncle before.

Her eyes dipped to his mouth, set in a hard line, his breathing ragged, and her heart picked up pace. Was he as aware of her as she was of him?

She struggled to think straight, his nearness scattering her thoughts. 'What are we doing in here, Ezra? We need to leave. Are you sure you are quite well?' she hissed.

'The Viscount is out there.'

'I know. I saw him,' she said, trying to remain calm.

'I did not know he was coming. I do not know why he is here…'

'And we are hiding—why? We are not children.'

'I was worried he would see us. You.'

'So?' She shook her head. 'I thought you had spoken to him. I thought he was all right about us staying in the cottage. Are you planning for us to stay in here until he leaves? This is ridiculous. I want to see the rest of the exhibition. I am not afraid of him.'

Was he?

She went to move, but Ezra's other hand came down on to the wall, trapping her between his arms. 'I told him I would not see you again, after the other day, when he saw you in the house,' he blurted out.

Her eyebrows rose, his words registering. 'What? He does not know we are still staying at Artington?' she gasped.

Ezra shook his head. 'No.'

'I see.' She tilted her chin up to look at him. 'So you lied—to him and to me.'

'I did not think you should have to leave. Especially as what happened was my fault. I did not *want* you to leave.'

'But you also do not *want* him to know that we are friends?'

'I told you about the Viscount's prejudices. I am trying to shield you from his judgement.'

'We were not doing anything wrong. Just looking at

the art.' Unlike what they were doing now. If they were to be caught here… Her mouth dried. 'And surely he would not have said anything. Not in public.' And then, looking up at him, seeing how ill at ease he was, realisation dawned. 'Are you embarrassed by me?' She pinned him in place with a challenging stare. Yes, that's what it was. He was ashamed to be seen with her, worried what his father might say.

'No!' He shook his head.

'I do not believe you,' she said, hurt tearing up inside her. She brought her hand up over his arm, gently lowering it, so she was no longer trapped. Then she pressed her fingertips against his chest. 'I am going back to the tour. You can stay in here if you would like to, hiding from your father, hiding from the world. But I refuse to do that.'

'Seraphine,' he said, gripping her arm, tugging her back.

'Let go of me!' she said, her skin burning where his fingers had touched her bare flesh.

He instantly released her.

'What? You think I am going to wait in here till you are ready to face them? Do you ever stop to think of anyone other than yourself? How your actions could have such a catastrophic impact? What if someone were to find us in here? What would they say?' She shook her head. 'From the moment I met you I knew you were careless, reckless. But this—'

She pushed past him, opened the door with force and shielded her eyes from the bright light that flooded the dim room. She turned back to look at him.

'Ezra, I think you are right. You should not have come today. I think from now on, you should learn when to stay away.'

Ezra was not in the mood for another ball. They were at the Jenningses' estate in Hampstead, and it was an impressive soirée. The Baronet's home, Bridford Hall, was the perfect setting for an event and the scale of it was incredible. Everyone who was someone was in attendance, but Ezra didn't really feel like speaking to anyone tonight. He didn't know why he'd come. Only, he couldn't bring himself not to.

Seraphine seemed to be growing in popularity by the day, his influence seeming to have done the trick, and she had a whole line-up of men asking for a slot on her dance card. He bristled with the annoyance of it. He'd done his job a little too well.

He knew he could join them and ask her to do him the honour of a dance, yet he didn't know whether she'd agree after what happened today at the Academy.

He was such a fool!

When he'd removed himself from that storeroom or cloakroom or whatever the hell it was he'd ushered her into and headed out on to the street, he'd tried to get himself in order. He didn't know what he'd been thinking.

He had never cared that much for art. And he had known the gallery would hold a showcase of pictures relating to the war. He had been aware the British Institution had promised a monied prize for a painting of a sketch of Waterloo for this very exhibition, so he had tried to ready himself for what it would be like. But Seraphine was right—he should have stayed away. He should have known what impact those paintings would have on him—his memories and his guilt. Yet, knowing Seraphine wanted to go, he had been prepared to put up with it, wanting to believe he could deal with it.

But the paintings had disturbed him more than they should. Yet as she had come to stand by his side, with the calming effect she had on him, he had realised they were just paintings. Many were theatrical, to be critiqued, not necessarily believed, or worth getting worked up over. But then, to see the Viscount arrive as well—it had shocked him to the core. It had made him forget all thoughts of the vivid artwork on display, the horrific memories of the war.

Ezra had struggled to comprehend what his guardian was doing there, what it meant. He should have gone over to him, welcomed and assisted him—that would have been the right thing to do, but instead, the same panic he'd always felt since he was that ten-year-old boy had exploded in his chest, knowing he might be rebuked, diminished in front of all the people of the *ton*. And thinking of the woman at his side—and the public judgement the old man might wreak upon them both if he was to step into the room and see them there together—he'd tried to steer her away.

But he hadn't thought it through.

She was right. It had been foolish. He had put her reputation at risk. His own reputation at risk. And for what? Because he'd been too scared to face the Viscount? Because he was still afraid of him? Shame on him.

What must Seraphine think of him now? A coward? A lunatic?

With a cool trickle of dread he recalled the moment

she had asked him if he was embarrassed by her. He wasn't—he just knew what the Viscount was like. But she hadn't believed him. And why should she? He'd lied to her about speaking with his father. About having permission for them to stay on the estate and, knowing her, it wouldn't sit right with her that they were staying somewhere they weren't welcome.

He'd ruined the whole bloody exhibition for her. He'd ruined his own day. Had he ruined their newfound friendship?

He looked over at her now, chatting to Miss Jennings and her brother and Lord Wentworth, and he bit down on the inside of his cheek. He wanted to be there, talking to them, talking to her, but it seemed she had replaced him with another.

'Did I not see you dancing with that French woman the other night at Vauxhall?' Ash said.

Ezra took a sip of his drink. 'You did.'

'And you were with her again at the Academy this afternoon. Before you just upped and left without saying goodbye.'

'I was.' And he couldn't stop thinking about how his chest had almost pressed up against hers, the perfect pallor of her complexion up close, her gorgeous blue eyes looking up at him, his finger pressed to her soft lips. He had wanted to run his thumb along the curve of her mouth. Now *that* would have been reckless.

'Is she not the one you snubbed the other evening at Lady Bulphan's ball?'

'She is. Look, do you have a point?' he snapped. 'Are you going to berate me for dancing with her?'

His friend reared back. 'No, I was merely going to

say I am surprised she has forgiven you. Especially after that piece in the pamphlet.'

Ezra leaned his head back against the wall. 'Me, too.' Although he thought he might have undone all his hard work with his actions today. 'Did I tell you she is currently living in the cottage at Artington?'

His friend gawked at him. 'No! You know damn well you did not. Ezra, you dark horse! Stay, as in…'

Ezra rolled his eyes. 'Just as a guest—with her family.'

'What the hell does the Viscount have to say about that?'

'He is not too pleased.'

'No, I can imagine.' Ash chuckled. 'How did this come about?'

'You heard of the damage caused by the fire to their home?'

'Yes.'

'I felt I might have been to blame—for the things I had said in that interview.'

'Quite likely!'

Ezra shrugged. 'So I said they could stay. Her and her family. To make up for it. Until the house is repaired.'

'You like this woman,' Ash said, crossing his arms and leaning back against the wall. 'I saw the way you danced with her.'

'Yes. No. I do not know,' he said, irritated. From the moment he'd seen her on her horse that morning, riding astride, rushing in to break up the duel, he'd felt a connection to her, a fascination for her, and he couldn't deny it any longer—the attraction was growing stronger all the time. He was struggling to keep his distance from her, as he'd proved today in that storeroom.

'You like her,' his friend reasserted. 'You could not keep your eyes off her the other night. You can't keep your eyes off her this evening.'

It was true. She drew his eye, like a moth to a flame. And she burned as bright in a stunning scarlet gown. But was she as dangerous to him as that blaze was to that creature?

'While all of this is true, it doesn't exactly help me on my mission to find a suitable bride, now, does it?'

'You could marry for love, you know,' Ash said.

Ezra scoffed. 'Love?'

But his eyes turned back to Seraphine, who was smiling up at Lord Wentworth, her eyes twinkling as bright as the necklace around her throat. 'The Viscount can barely contain his anger that I have allowed them to stay—imagine what he would say if I said I was marrying her.'

His friend grinned. 'I said you could marry for love. I didn't say that meant her. You put that connection together.'

Damn. Ezra put down his tumbler and drew a hand across his face. Did he care for her? 'Whatever this is that I am feeling, you know the Viscount's criteria for a bride. He would never agree to it.'

'Yes. But what is yours?'

Ezra scowled. He'd never really thought about what he wanted—only what the Viscount expected. What he demanded if Ezra wanted to inherit and see his family provided for.

'I do not know. I suppose if I had a choice, someone attractive. Someone who is not afraid to speak her mind and I can talk to, like I talk to you, and Adam and Hawk.'

'Lucky girl,' Ash teased.

Ezra ignored his jest. 'Someone who makes me feel… like I can be myself. That I don't have to hide. I am so sick of hiding,' he admitted. Doing so today in that room had made him feel as though he didn't like himself very much. He was starting to feel it would be better if he could be true to who he really was.

Ash looked towards Seraphine. 'And does Miss Mounier make you feel all of that?'

Yes.

But he felt a prickle of unease. 'You're making something out of nothing,' he said, swiping the air with his hand.

'Maybe. Or maybe not. I'm just saying don't let what happened in your past, with your family, affect your ability to trust people, to allow yourself to love, now.'

Was that what he was doing? His friend was right. He did struggle to trust people—who wouldn't, after what had happened to him? After the people who were meant to care for him the most gave him up, never to speak to him again. After the couple who took him in as their own couldn't love him and show him the affection he so desperately needed. Why would he want to open up his heart and love someone again?

'But she is French. I am sure Adam, Hawk, you… would all have a lot to say about that. They were the enemy.'

'That is all in the past. Stop making excuses, Ezra. Yes, she's French, but I'm sure if she could have joined the army and fought with us against Napoleon, she would have. I'm sure she suffered at the Revolutionaries' hands—that's why she's here. The émigrés were probably more anti-Napoleon than we ever were. Am I right?'

Ezra smiled, coming off the wall. 'You're always right, Ash.'

'And if you like her, we will like her. We are always with you, remember?'

Ezra felt a peculiar lump grow in his throat and he tried to swallow it down.

'You make it sound so simple,' he said.

'It is. You either like the woman or not. And if you don't make up your mind and stake your claim on her soon, I fear someone else will.' His friend inclined his head in the direction of Lord Wentworth, who was now leading Seraphine on to the dance floor, and a dart of burning jealousy took him by surprise.

'I have never seen you like this before. You've got it bad.' His friend stepped towards him and placed a hand on his shoulder. 'Ezra, we have spent too long during the war living in hell. Do you not think it is time to do something for yourself for once? This is your life. No one else's. And if the battles out there taught us anything, it's that life is fleeting and we should make it count. And you deserve to be happy.'

He glanced back at Seraphine. She was laughing at something the Lord had said and the man was taking her hand in his. Ezra's fingers bunched into fists at his sides, while a muscle flickered in his jaw. Seeing another man touch her—a viscount—was too much to bear.

'I hope you're going to take some of your own advice where love is concerned, Ash,' Ezra said, as the announcement came that a light supper of bread and cakes was soon to be served. 'For you deserve to be happy, too.'

They made their way over to the buffet table and he watched as his friend tucked in, but he was suddenly not hungry. As he glanced back at Lord Wentworth twirling Seraphine around the floor, his stomach swirled sickly in response and he didn't think he could stomach a thing.

Later, as the guests began to depart at the end of the evening, he saw Henri and Seraphine waiting for him outside. As she looked up when he approached, his heart lurched in his chest. It had been the worst evening—he hadn't spoken to her all night, just watched her dance and converse with others, and his mood was black. He was jealous and had missed her company and he rubbed his chest sympathetically.

Love. Could it be? Surely not. He rebelled against the thought even now. He had always fought against any such feelings. He didn't *want* to care for anyone in that way, as he knew love—feeling something for someone— could bring great pain and suffering. If he opened up his heart to love, there was a chance she could reject him, or leave him, and he could get hurt again. And he didn't think his heart could suffer much more pain.

He felt churned up inside, so unsure of himself. Of her. And of this burning thing between them. And what people would say.

Plus, he wasn't who she thought he was. If she thought his lie about the Viscount letting them stay at Artington had been bad, what would she say when she discovered the truth about him not having a title? About his humble background?

And yet they had both had their identities taken from them. If anyone could understand, he thought she might.

But he didn't know why he was thinking like this. Marrying someone he had no affection for would be so much less complicated, wouldn't it? And marrying an English woman so much simpler—which is why he hadn't argued against the Viscount's wishes. For if he did as he was told and took a wife he didn't love, she could never let him down. Given that Seraphine seemed to have had a wonderful night dancing in the arms of other men, after telling him she didn't want to marry, made him think she was lying, too, so he should not be thinking of getting any closer to her. He couldn't rely on her.

It was those sentiments that had him hesitating when she gave him a cool look and stepped inside his coach, followed by her brother.

He lingered by the door.

She stared at him, her understanding registering. 'You aren't coming,' she said, her voice flat. It was more of a statement than a question.

He tried to avoid her gaze, as she sat back in the carriage, hiding herself from him in the shadows, and he was unable to tell what she was thinking. He felt bad for his behaviour today at the Academy, for not speaking to her at the ball, for not asking her to dance—and yet he couldn't tell if she cared. She seemed closed off to him.

'I will be staying in London tonight.'

'Are you going on somewhere else?' Henri asked, surprised—and sounding slightly in awe. 'You devil, Hart!'

'I will see you both back at Artington tomorrow.'

Ezra closed the door and signalled for the footmen to set off, taking her away from him. He needed to think. He needed distance. Yet as he stood there, watching the carriage move through the gardens, reach the end of the driveway, then turn out of sight, he felt like such a fool, Ash's words ringing in his head.

'If you don't stake your claim on her soon, I fear someone else will.'

And he couldn't shake the feeling he was letting something precious slip through his fingers.

Chapter Nine

'Callers, for Miss Seraphine, *madame*.'

Madame Mounier clapped her hands together, absolutely thrilled that there was a whole herd of young bucks and older gentlemen out in the cottage garden, queuing up to see her.

'Shall we let them in?'

'Certainly, Aunt,' Seraphine said, dressed in the demure white dress she had been considering wearing to Lady Bulphan's ball. Smoothing it down, she sat on the chaise longue, her body rigid, ready to accept them.

'There's Lord Wentworth. Lord Barrington. Lord Smith. Mr Talbot. The list goes on,' her aunt said, peering through the window. 'Oh, Seraphine. You have done so well.'

Had she? Why, then, did she feel so miserable?

She welcomed Lord Wentworth with a curtsy as he entered the room and he offered her a bow and a warm smile in return. She liked the man. He was charming and she knew he had a fortune and a large estate in south London. Not that any of that really mattered to her, only to Henri.

She was still adamant she wouldn't marry, but she

knew if she were to wed, she could do a lot worse than this man. He was kind, he would treat her well—and they would have things to talk about together. Yet she did not see herself with him. She could not see him supporting her dreams and it was not this man that preoccupied her mind as her aunt offered him a biscuit.

She couldn't stop thinking about Ezra and what he was doing in London, and she hated herself for it. She didn't want to be in his home, without him, thinking of him, waiting for him to return. When had she started to care so much? She had tried so hard not to.

Even though she was weary from their day out at the Academy, and then the Jenningses' ball, she had tossed and turned in bed, staring up at the ceiling, unable to sleep. Her thoughts kept returning to the man she had spent the past few days with, his intense, deep-brown eyes focused on her in that small room at the gallery, his finger to her lips, and she wondered where he was and what he was up to.

When he hadn't got into the carriage with her and Henri last night, her heart had sunk. He hadn't been able to look her in the eye—and she immediately thought of his father's words about his women, her aunt calling him a rake, and she wondered if there was any truth to it.

She couldn't believe he'd been so reckless as to usher her away from the group and into that small room at the Academy—alone. Did he not care for the reputation he'd helped her build up this week? Yet she hadn't been afraid, not really—not as much as she should have been when thinking about them being caught there together. Instead, she'd only been frightened of her own feelings and how she'd wanted to lean in and get closer to him.

But then to learn that his father had forbidden him from seeing her, had wanted her and her family off his estate, and Ezra had lied about it. She had been shocked. And she wondered—if the Viscount didn't want them there, why hadn't Ezra turfed them out? She didn't understand it.

The final blow had come when she'd realised he was trying to hide her from the man, as if she was something to be ashamed of. It hurt, so much. And it made her think perhaps his thoughts and feelings hadn't changed—that he was still the narrow-minded man who had said those things about them in that pamphlet.

She had thought they were friends—had foolishly, somehow along the way, although she hated to admit it, begun to like him more than a friend. Now she felt wretched.

'Miss Mounier?'

'Sorry,' she said. 'Could you repeat that?'

'I wondered if you had enjoyed the Jenningses' ball last night? I very much enjoyed our dance.'

'As did I, Lord Wentworth.'

She had hoped Ezra would speak to her—try to explain, or at least make amends, but he'd avoided her all evening. He hadn't even asked her for a dance and she was disappointed he was breaking the camaraderie between them. The trust.

But the worst of it all was, as she had lain there in bed, she couldn't stop the strange feelings of frustration—the peculiar flickers of excitement—fluttering through her body every time she thought of him ushering her into that room, as if he needed her at his side in his panic. As if he wanted to be alone with her. Because although she knew it was wrong, it had also felt right—the way he'd leaned into her, his hands on the wall either side of her head, his face just a breath away.

His dark, handsome face was right there, at the forefront of her mind, his finger pressed against her lips. She'd felt her breasts tingle at his nearness, a maddening heat shift low in her belly and stoke between her legs. And she'd wanted things she had never wanted before. She had longed for him to put his hands on her. To press his lips against hers.

Placing her hands over her face, she had given a silent scream into the darkness. She didn't know what was happening to her and it scared her. Especially as he clearly didn't feel the same. For now he was doing God knew what at his bachelor lodgings in London.

She tried to shake off her thoughts and focus on Lord Wentworth. She didn't know when Ezra would be back, but she absolutely refused to sit around moping, waiting for his return. He had made it clear he didn't care about her and she needed to get on with her life. He wasn't here. These men were.

Perhaps Henri was right. Maybe it was time for a change, for her to grow up a little. If she chose wisely, was it possible she could marry and still keep a little of her independence? Only she couldn't imagine telling any of these callers about the charity work she so loved. She couldn't imagine any of them rolling up their shirt sleeves and helping her. Not like Ezra Hart.

But her aunt was right. She'd done well to attract such eligible men. Henri was proud of her, at last. And her brother was so important to her, she had to think of him and her family. Her prospects. Her future. Perhaps she did want more—a home of her own, a family. It would be nice to have children to care for. She was starting to think she would make a good mother. The children in the square in Mayfair seemed to like her. She couldn't let these silly feelings for Ezra Hart get in the way, especially when he did not care for her own.

So for the rest of the afternoon, with fresh determination, she decided to put on a good show, piling on the charm, never dropping her guard, asking the gentlemen callers questions, listening intently to their answers and smiling at everything they said.

That evening, she dressed in her imperial-blue gown—her favourite. They were going to Almack's Assembly Rooms on King Street and she was nervous. Almack's was different to being entertained at a high-society private soirée in someone's home. Here, only the crème de la crème of society was allowed a ticket and the likes of her family had never been on the guest list before.

She couldn't believe it when they walked inside, on trembling legs, no questions asked by the Patronesses. She guessed they had Ezra to thank for that, but she refused to let the thought of him dampen her excitement.

The huge ballroom was decorated in mirrors and medallions, the lanterns were lit with gas, not mere candlelight, and she had to pinch herself that she was here. She was glad to have her aunt back by her side and they scoured the room together, taking it all in, seeing who had come. And just like that first night at Lady Bulphan's ball, she spotted Ezra across the room. It was as if her eye was always drawn to him—could seek him out anywhere—and when he turned to look at her, his brown gaze colliding with hers, her heart almost stopped beating.

'You did it, Hart,' Henri said, clapping him on the back. 'The drawing room at the cottage is like a florist's. Seraphine had a queue of suitors at the place this morning. It is finally happening. I do believe my sister might just secure a marriage proposal this Season. Thank you,' the man said, shaking Ezra's hand. 'Thank you for all your help.'

A pit emptied in Ezra's stomach. 'I am glad,' he lied. Because it was the worst news—the worst thing that could have happened.

'Rumour has it, Wentworth is on the cusp of proposing. Can you believe it?'

He could. Wentworth was a smart man. And he would be a content man with Seraphine as his wife. Who wouldn't? Yet would she be happy to be his bride? He refused to believe it. She was too attractive for him. Too young. Too good for him. She was too good for them all.

Damn. He should not have stayed in London last night. He should have returned with Seraphine and Henri to Artington and then he would have been there today to fend off any suitors, or at least to preside over the proceedings.

Cold fury thrashed through him. He was livid with himself—and with her. Because he could not take his eyes off her, whereas she seemed indifferent to him. He had seen her enter Almack's this evening and their gazes had met across the room, causing his heart to pound that little bit faster.

His eyes had swept down, over her beautiful lips, her perfect body in that stunning blue gown—the one she'd worn that first night to Lady Bulphan's ball—and his whole body had gone up in flames, with desire and need, but she had turned away, abruptly, as if she was unaffected. Then she had continued to ignore him all evening. He clenched his jaw, his fists. And the more she spoke to other men at the ball, the more she danced, the testier he got.

He knew he should go over there and strike up a conversation, apologise, try to win her back round, yet he was uncharacteristically nervous. Because he wasn't sure how she'd react. He wasn't sure if she wanted him to. After all, she had told him in no uncertain terms to stay away. And he was worried he'd ruined everything, for good.

He'd spent the night at his lodgings alone, lying there awake, thinking of everything that had happened these past few weeks. He thought about what she'd said that day in Mayfair, when they'd been serving up soup together, about how she didn't think status was important. She was like a breath of fresh air. She wasn't the same as the other ladies in the *ton*. She didn't care for titles, or riches, and he wondered—could he tell her about his past? Could he confide in her? And he realised he wanted to.

What would she say? He wasn't sure. It was a risk, but one he thought he was ready to take.

The steward came round and topped up the gentlemen's glasses and Ezra took note of the bottle. The dark glass. The maker's mark. Interesting… Well, at least now he had a reason to talk to her. 'Could I borrow that empty bottle for a moment?' he said.

'Take it, it's yours,' the steward said.

When he saw her finish her dance with Lord Smith and exit the room, he saw his chance. Looking around to check no one was watching, he followed her.

'Seraphine,' he called, coming after her.

She glanced over her shoulder to look at him before turning round and moving with haste, continuing down the corridor.

'Seraphine. Wait! Where are you going?'

'It is stuffy in there.'

She stepped inside an empty room and he followed her, careful to close the door behind him.

She spun round to face him. 'What are you doing here, Ezra?' she said, her hands on her hips.

That gown really suited her. She looked so stunning, it hurt.

'You have been avoiding me all evening.'

'Like you were avoiding me last night?'

He looked around. They seemed to be in some kind of games room, set out with numerous tables where the men might later play cards.

She pinched the bridge of her nose. 'Look, what do you want?'

He took a step towards her. 'I wanted to show you this,' he said, holding out the bottle the steward had been carrying.

Her beautiful brow creased. 'Is that a different one?'

'Yes. They sell it here. I shall let the authorities know.'

She nodded, uncertain. 'Was that all?'

'I also wanted to tell you the invitations have all been

sent out for the benefit ball,' he said, putting the bottle down, floundering a little. He wanted to keep her talking. He didn't want her to go, not yet.

'Thank you. I was not sure if you still wanted to go ahead with it.'

'I do.' It wasn't the real reason he had followed her, but he knew the investigation, and him helping her with her charity work, were two subjects she couldn't be cross with him about. He hoped it would appease her, soften her towards him again.

'Did you miss me last night?'

Seraphine shook her head. 'You are unbelievable. I am not doing this again. We cannot be in here. I am leaving.'

She stalked past him, heading for the door.

'*I* missed you.'

There. He'd said it.

He turned round to face her and saw she had halted, her hand on the doorknob.

'I am sorry about the way I behaved yesterday, at the Academy,' he added quickly. 'You are right, I should never have gone. The paintings did affect me more than paintings should affect anyone.' She twisted her body to look at him and he shook his head. 'And then—to see him there. The Viscount. I admit I acted badly. It was wrong of me. I should never have separated you from the group or taken you into that room. But I am not ashamed of you, Seraphine, rather the opposite.' He took a step towards her. 'That is why I dragged you with me, into that room. I wanted you there. I am not ashamed of you, just ashamed of who I am around him.'

She shook her head a little. 'I do not understand.'

Ezra raked his hand through his hair. 'I want to explain it all to you. But first, I need to know. Have I lost your trust?'

She lifted one slender shoulder and let it drop.

'Where were you last night?' she said and then he saw her conflicted emotions cross her face, as if she hated herself for asking. But he was glad she had. It gave him hope. Hope that she cared.

He moved closer.

'It is not what you think. Seraphine, I slept alone.'

The statement hung in the air, like a great admission that there was more between them. That this one fact was what was important, causing the tension between them, and was what they had both been thinking about.

She stared up at him, her big blue eyes uncertain.

He ran his hand around the back of his neck. 'I am sorry about the way I behaved yesterday—and last night. The truth be told, I did not like seeing you talking with those other men and later, dancing with them at the Jenningses' ball. I was jealous,' he said simply. 'And I hate the fact they called on you today.'

'I thought that is what you wanted—for me to meet people,' she said, exasperated.

'Things have changed.' He frowned. 'I do not like it. Not any more.'

She swallowed. 'You danced with other women. You did not dance with me,' she said accusingly.

He closed the distance between them.

'I wanted to dance with you, I just didn't think it was a good idea,' he whispered. He felt his heart pound harder, knowing he was getting closer to saying what he wanted to say.

'Why not?' she asked, breathless, staring up into his eyes.

'Because I knew that one dance would not have been enough and I would be in danger of wanting to dance every dance with you for the rest of the evening.'

He saw her swallow, her throat work.

'Seraphine… When I look at you, all I see is danger. Danger to my very sanity and being.'

'Ezra,' she breathed.

Then he reached for her. He took her cheek in his hand, his thumb gently stroking the corner of her lips, giving her chance to say no. And when she didn't, when her chest rose and fell in a hectic rhythm, he knew she wanted this as much as he and he lowered his head, pressing his lips softly, reverently, against hers, and her eyelids fluttered shut.

For a moment, her breath caught and he thought she might protest, pull back, but then her mouth, her body, relaxed beneath him, sank into him, and he brought his other hand up to hold her face as he deepened the kiss. Her lips parted, allowing him to slide his tongue inside her mouth, wanting to taste her, to claim her, and her hand came up to curve over his shoulders, clinging on.

It was the most sensual moment of his life, as her tongue tentatively pressed against his in response, her fingers stealing into the hair at the base of his neck, and suddenly, everything was forgotten—the smouldering rage he'd felt when those other men had pursued her, the anger at everything the Viscount, or Lady Frances, even himself, had said about her, the frustration of not being able to touch her. It was all converted, transmuted into desire as she kissed him back so passionately it left him breathless.

She tasted like sweet lemonade, smelt of lilies, and it was the most truthful, passionate kiss he'd ever shared and he wanted more. He wanted to get closer still. He lowered his hand to her waist, carefully drawing her body into him, and she gave a sharp inhale at the sensations of their bodies meeting, her soft chest crushed against his solid muscle, but rather than his actions scaring her off, her other hand came up to curve over his shoulders, holding on, holding him close.

His fingers drove into her hair and her head tipped back in surrender, allowing his mouth to steal from her lips to ravage her jaw, her neck and lower, placing kisses over the exposed skin above the neckline of her dress, before coming back, finding her lips once more, and she moaned, softly.

The sound of a door opening startled them, causing them both to freeze, forcing him to pull away and end the kiss, and he stared down at her, his breathing, his mind, in chaos.

He knew he shouldn't have done it. It was wrong. Yet he didn't think anything could have prevented him from doing so and it had been momentous. Significant.

Seraphine stepped back, unsteady on her feet, dropping her hands from his shoulders and looking up at him in flustered dismay.

'No one can find us here like this,' she whispered, aghast. Her blue eyes were two huge pools of distress— and she was trembling, from the kiss, or from fear of being caught, he couldn't be sure.

But she wasn't saying it shouldn't have happened.

He reluctantly released her from his hold, but not before lingering, holding her fingers in his, squeezing them gently. 'You go. I will follow after.'

She nodded and opened the door a little, tentatively looking up and down the corridor, before opening it and slipping through.

'Seraphine,' he whispered and she glanced back.

'We will talk about this later.'

Chapter Ten

'We have been invited to dine with Hart at Artington tonight,' Henri said, leaning in the doorway of Seraphine's bedroom in the cottage. 'I am inclined to say no—that we should go to the ball in Soho and keep up the interest with Wentworth and Barrington and the rest. One of them must be so close to proposing. Any day now. What do you think?'

Seraphine tried to keep her look nonchalant as she stared at her brother's reflection in the dressing-table mirror. She continued to brush her hair, feeling as if her heart might leap out of her chest. She couldn't believe Ezra had invited them to dine with him—at his father's house—after what had happened between them last night.

'I do not think it would do any harm to have a night off,' she said carefully. 'We do not want the Lords getting complacent now, do we?'

Henri nodded. 'It is just, well, Miss Jennings will be there, too. At the ball.'

Seraphine grinned. 'You like her!' she said, spinning round on the stool to face him.

'I do,' he said, blushing just a little. 'Only I am not

sure her father would think I am good enough for her. I am sure he'd much rather she wed someone like Wentworth, or Barrington—or even Hart! In fact, why Hart has not shown an interest in her is beyond me.'

Seraphine's stomach did a flip. Whatever was the matter with her? At the mere mention of his name, she seemed to lose control of herself.

'She is very beautiful, is she not?'

'She is. And kind. And I am pretty sure the feeling is reciprocated. She asks about you all the time, so I would not worry. You are a good man, Henri. Miss Jennings knows her own mind—and she seems to have her father wrapped around her little finger. Have you told her how you feel?'

'Not yet, but I think I have made it pretty obvious. I am concerned I have been too eager, in fact—not mysterious enough.'

'Then perhaps we should not be in attendance at the ball tonight, keep them guessing. Maybe it will make her miss you and she will realise how she feels.'

He nodded. 'Very well. I shall accept Hart's invitation.'

Seraphine's stomach rolled once more and she felt slightly guilty that she'd manipulated Henri into agreeing to the dinner invitation. But she did know Miss Jennings liked him back. She knew he didn't have to be concerned.

'It will be nice not to travel into London for once. I am sure Aunt and Uncle will appreciate that, too,' Henri said. 'I do not know about you, but after all these social events, I am pretty tired. I am looking forward to the Season being over and having a quieter winter.'

'Do you know if Ezra has mentioned this dinner to his father—whether the Viscount will be around?'

Henri shrugged. 'I do not know. Why do you ask?'

'I just wondered.'

Seraphine looked back at herself in the mirror. She felt different. Did she look different? She wondered if her brother could sense that about her. She brought her fingers up to touch her lips. They felt bruised, swollen.

When she had stepped out of the ballroom last night and heard Ezra softly call her name, her pulse had pounded. She had turned round, schooling her face, not wanting him to know she was pleased to see him there, that it was what she had been hoping for—for him to come after her. She had been so desperate to talk to him again.

'I slept alone,' he had said.

Those three small words that had hung in the air between them meant so much, calming her biggest fears and revealing his feelings. It had changed everything between them, illuminating how they both felt, and her face flushed at the thought.

She had never been kissed before and when Ezra had bent his head, lowering his lips to hers, for a moment she had been shocked at the exquisite sensations rippling through her. She had thought about protesting, knowing it was wrong, that they shouldn't be doing it—that it would bring shame and scandal upon them both if they were to be found together in a romantic embrace—but she hadn't wanted to stop him or push him away. Instead, she had melted in his arms. She couldn't do anything but.

It had felt glorious as his tongue had moved inside her mouth, his fingers stealing into her hair, sending goose pimples erupting all over her body, and when his heated lips had moved down her neck, pressing against the upper swells of her breasts, her body was set alight.

She had wanted like never before.

And now, to be invited for dinner?

She was still burning in all the places where he had held her in his arms, she could still smell the warm, clean peppery scent of him and taste the spicy flavour of him on her tongue. And she was desperate for it to happen again. At seven and twenty, she was starting to feel as if she'd wasted too much time already. She'd been missing out.

When he'd returned to the ballroom last night, he had gone back to talk to his friends, as if it had never happened, but his eyes had sought out hers and he'd inclined his head, his heated gaze burning into hers. She had tried to get her pulse back under control and gone to the drinks table to pour herself some lemonade and await her next dance. They hadn't spoken again until the carriage ride home, when Henri had chatted them both half to death about Miss Jennings and how much he liked Almack's, and she and Ezra had listened, nodding. But she had been so aware of him, his nearness, his scent, as he sat next to her, their eyes occasionally meeting, their arms brushing. And she had felt a longing, deep in her bones, to get closer to him.

She hadn't been able to sleep, thinking of him lying in bed in the grand house just across the parkland.

She hadn't seen him all day, so by the time she dressed for dinner, she was going out of her mind. She wondered how she would be able to look him in the eye after she'd behaved so wantonly, pressing herself against him, kissing him without restraint. Yet she needed to see him to know if he still felt the same. To know if he wanted to kiss her again and what it meant, or if he regretted what had happened.

She was afraid. Afraid to look at him—because in one look she'd know. But in one look, her brother, and her aunt and uncle, might also see the heart of her and she was terrified she might give herself away.

If Henri were to find out, if he were to discover that something had happened between them, he would be horrified—especially as he was so certain she was about to receive a proposal from Lord Wentworth or Lord Barrington. He would demand satisfaction—he would insist Ezra married her to protect her honour, or they would no doubt face each other off again in a duel in Hyde Park. She shivered at the thought.

Ezra must know this and she wondered what he intended to do. He must know they shouldn't have been alone. That they shouldn't have touched or kissed. Yet he'd offered her no promises of security.

Dinner. How would she be able to eat anything in his presence? She'd barely touched a morsel all day, her stomach in knots. And it churned even fiercer when Ezra's carriage pulled up outside to take them across the parkland.

Artington Hall glowed gold in the early evening sun, bats flitted across the sky and Seraphine wondered when it was exactly that this place, and its master, had taken up residence in her heart.

As they pulled up parallel to the door, she saw him. Ezra was right there, standing on the steps ready to greet them, looking more handsome than she'd ever seen him, dressed in a white shirt and navy waistcoat, with a matching fitted tailcoat. She savoured the sight of him, thinking he looked more male, more virile than ever before. He welcomed her aunt, and uncle, Henri, and then he turned to her, staring right at her, saying her name and welcoming her, too.

'Hello, Seraphine.'

An emotion that felt suspiciously like love bloomed in her chest and she wanted to throw her arms around him and tell him how she felt, but she could barely move, her legs were trembling too much. It was a struggle to walk when he ushered them inside for drinks.

As he held out his arms, gesturing for her to go through the door before him, she found herself searching his face, looking for clues, but it was hard to tell how he was feeling—he was the perfect host, a pinnacle of propriety and good manners.

'I hope you are feeling more yourself this evening, Hart,' Henri said.

She swung to look at him.

'Quite well, thank you.'

'Have you been ill?' she asked. The very thought of it, and her not knowing, was troubling to her.

'Hart had a turn at the ball last night. Had to disappear for a while to get some air. It was a crush in the place.'

She met his gaze, then turned away, flushed. 'Oh.'

His eyes glittered down at her. 'I recovered quite quickly, I assure you.'

The incredible dining room had been dressed in flowers and the soft glow of candlelight, and the starters of soup were soon served.

'What is it, Mr Hart? It is delicious,' her aunt said, tasting the dish.

'White soup. A recent favourite of mine.'

It drew a secret smile, but while Seraphine appreciated the sentiment, she could barely bring herself to swallow it down. She took a few mouthfuls, then lowered her spoon. If he would just give her a sign, some clue as to how he was feeling...

Ezra was sitting opposite her and all she could think of was the distance of the table between them. She watched his tanned fingers toy with his glass. Once, twice, his long, outstretched legs brushed hers under the table and she reluctantly moved her feet away. Was it hot in here?

Being this close to him, surrounded by others, not being able to talk to him properly, was torture.

'Where is your father this evening?' she asked. 'I hope he did not mind you having guests.'

'On the contrary, he is out this evening. A rarity, so I seized upon the opportunity to have you over.'

'We are yet to meet your father,' her aunt said. 'We would very much like to thank him for his hospitality.'

'I shall pass on your thanks, *madame*.'

'I suppose we need to decide which one she will marry,' Henri said, slapping his hand down on the table, making Seraphine jump.

The main course had been a grand affair—an array of sumptuous dishes featuring game, vegetables, pickles and jellies, and now they were all full, patting their stomachs and sitting back in their seats.

'I think Wentworth,' he said decisively. 'What do you think, Hart? He has the title Seraphine deserves, the fortune—and reputation. He is a capital fellow and Seraphine likes him well enough.'

Ezra glanced across at her and she took a large sip of her wine.

'You speak as if we are making a business arrangement, Henri,' her aunt chastised him.

'Most marriages are those of convenience, are they not? Affection comes later.'

'Is that the case for you and Miss Jennings?' Seraphine shot back at him. 'I do hope her father does not think the same as you, Henri, and thinks she should marry for status rather than how she feels for the man.'

Her brother scowled.

'We married for love,' her aunt said, reaching for her husband's hand.

'Well, you might have. I merely tolerate you,' her uncle jested and her aunt tapped him lovingly on the arm.

'I think Seraphine needs to narrow down the qualities she is looking for in a husband,' her aunt continued. 'To help her decide.'

Seraphine met Ezra's eyes again over the candlelit table and heat soared through her body.

'Perhaps. And then we can pick the one she likes the most. I hope she picks the one with the grandest title.' Henri winked.

Suddenly, something shattered. And they all looked over at Ezra to find he had smashed his glass between his fingers. His hand was bleeding.

Seraphine gasped at his injury and instantly got up and reached for her napkin. Without thinking, she came round the table and took his left hand in hers, wrapping the material around it to stem the flow of blood.

It reminded her of that first night he had brought them here, when he had done the same to her. Had she liked him even then?

'Forgive me,' he said, staring into her eyes. 'I do not know how I managed that.'

'Clumsy of you, Hart!' Henri said. 'Are you all right?'

'Yes,' he said, as Seraphine tucked in the end of the material before reluctantly pulling away. She stood, staring down at him before moving away, her breathing ragged, then returned to her seat, her fingers trembling, tingling from his touch. It was just a scratch, but the sight of his blood had disturbed her.

The servants began to clear away the dishes and poured more wine, fetching Ezra a fresh glass.

'Shall we change the subject?' Seraphine said. 'All this talk of me is making me quite weary. Let us talk about the Artington ball tomorrow, instead. How is Mrs Dawson faring? Is there anything I can do?'

'I believe she has it all under control, but could no doubt do with your help on the morrow.'

Seraphine managed to relax a little, once they stopped talking about her marriage prospects, and after tending to Ezra's hand, her fingers brushing his skin again, seeing the heat in his eyes as he'd looked up at her, she had begun to enjoy herself, too.

They ate ice cream for dessert, flavoured with lavender, and it was divine. It reminded her of Lady Bulphan's beautiful borders, the night she and Ezra had met in the gardens.

When darkness descended and the clock tower struck eleven, Henri made a move to go. Resigned, Seraphine reluctantly stood. There was nothing she could do about it, it wasn't as if she could linger there without the rest of them, so she followed as they exited the dining room to wait for the carriage to arrive.

'Before we go, would I be able to borrow a book from your library?' Seraphine asked Ezra, as they walked towards the hall. 'I finished mine. And it is good to have something to read when I lie awake at night.'

'Struggling to sleep?' he said, his eyes shimmering at her.

'A little.'

'What kind of book would you like?'

'She likes those romance ones. You know, the ones that are published anonymously. I doubt you have any of those, Hart.'

'I am surprised. I thought you read only political literature,' he teased. 'But by all means, go and take a look in the library next door. Help yourself to whatever you would like.'

'I will not be long,' she said to the others, as she headed down the now familiar corridor, making her way into the library. She ran her fingers along the spines of the books, wondering which one to choose. There were so many of them. Did Ezra get a chance to read much?

She glanced over to Ezra's study and remembered the book she'd seen lying on his desk. Curiosity got the better of her and, wondering what he was reading, she stalked over there.

She picked it up and studied the title. She was keen to know what interested him. She touched the embossed lettering—*A New View of Society* by Robert Owen—

but as she opened the cover, a letter fell out, drifting on to the floor.

She bent down to pick it up and the parchment opened between her fingers, allowing her to read the first hand-written line.

> *Dear Ezra,*
> *I know this letter will come as quite a shock to you, as we have not been in contact for so long, but I'm afraid I have some news to impart, my son. The saddest of news.*
> *Your brother George fought in the war with the French and was in the infantry at Waterloo. Did you join in the fight and did you see him there? We were informed he died from his wounds in Brussels three days later. We miss him dearly and your father never quite recovered after he died.*

Seraphine gasped. She knew she should close it, quickly put it back and pretend she had never seen it, but she could not stop herself from reading on.

> *Your father then passed not three months ago. It was his heart, the doctor said. And now, we look to you for help, my dearest boy.*
> *We hope you now understand the reasons why we did what we did and that you can forgive us. We hope you can find it in your heart to help me and your sisters in our time of need.*
> *Your mother,*
> *Mrs Whittaker*

Seraphine lowered the page, her heart pounding. She didn't understand.

Why was a woman called Mrs Whittaker calling Ezra her son? Why was she telling him his father and his brother had died, if he was Mr Hart—the Viscount's son?

It made no sense.

Unless…

Unless he wasn't the Viscount's son.

Her mind whirred.

He had never referred to him as his father. Or the Viscountess as his mother, for that matter. She had always thought it a little odd, but had put it down to their strained relationship.

But they looked nothing alike. There were no similarities between them at all. Maybe in the way they were both proud and imposing—they could both be formidable— but not their features.

She raced from the study back into the library and looked up at the paintings on the wall. The one of Viscount Hart. The one of the Viscountess. And the one of Ezra. There was no resemblance, nothing at all, and her forehead crumpled in confusion and doubt.

If he wasn't their son, who was he?

She lifted the letter in her hand again. Whittaker, it said.

Was he born a Whittaker? If so, he would never be Viscount. Was he even set to inherit the Artington estate, or his father's fortune? And why hadn't he told her?

'Seraphine?' His voice came from the doorway.

As she spun round to face him, he stared at her and she knew she looked shocked, guilty. His gaze dropped to her hand to see the letter she was holding.

He flinched, his eyes lifting back to hers. She thought she saw a flash of fear, before he frowned.

She had no words of explanation. She shouldn't have looked. She had no right. And yet…all she could think of was that he'd lied to her. Kept something from her.

'I went to choose a book, but saw there was one on your desk. I wanted to see what you were reading. When I picked it up, this letter fell out,' she said in rushed explanation.

He crossed the distance between them so fast, she felt giddy. Suddenly he was right there, his body almost pressing against her. 'You were prying?' he said, snatching the letter from her hand. 'I thought I could trust you.'

She reeled, winded, hurt by his harsh tone. 'And I you, Ezra *Whittaker*,' she spat.

A muscle worked in his cheek. He ran a hand through his hair. He stared at her for a long moment.

'Does it matter to you?'

'What?'

He clicked his tongue. 'That I don't have a title.' His voice sounded strange. Hoarse. Strained. 'I need to know. Does it matter to you?' His face was harsh, his lips a thin line.

She shook her head slightly. 'The title doesn't. The lie does. You lied to me, pretended to be something you are not.'

'Seraphine, are you coming?' her aunt called from along the corridor and they both turned in the direction of her voice.

'I will tell you everything,' he said, momentarily leaning in, his voice a low whisper. 'But you must never speak of this to anyone. Promise me.'

His words sent a shiver of unease through her. 'Ezra, you are scaring me.' Who was this man standing before her?

'Seraphine?' her aunt called again.

'Meet me by the lake. After everyone is in bed, when the clock strikes midnight. I will explain it all. Now go.'

Seraphine wrapped Ezra's coat—the one he'd lent her the night of the fire—tighter around her body. She had waited until her aunt and uncle had gone to bed and Henri had stopped bashing around, until the cottage was still, before she deemed it safe to leave.

She reached the lake just as the clock struck midnight and she shivered, knowing now what that meant. What Ezra's grandmother had gone through at this time and how distraught she must have been to feel she had to take her own life.

Only, she wasn't his grandmother, was she?

And the poor boy that woman had left behind wasn't Ezra's father.

And if that was the case, who the hell was he? This man she had grown close to. She needed to know. She wanted answers. He owed her that.

Finally, she saw him, a lone figure striding down the hill towards her. And as he drew closer, she could see he had removed his neckcloth and waistcoat. His shirt was loose, his coat thrown over the top, and he took her breath away, walking towards her in the moonlight. Only, she didn't even know who he was—this stranger who had her feeling this mixed-up tangle of emotions.

'Thank you for coming,' he said as he approached. He looked serious, intense.

'How could I not?'

'Shall we sit?' he said, motioning to the bench a little further round the lake. And they began to walk over to it in silence.

She cut right to the chase. 'Ezra, why do you have a letter from a woman called Mrs Whittaker calling you her son?'

He sat on the bench and she came down beside him. He ran his hands over his thighs and she realised, he was nervous.

'That letter is from my mother.'

Her brow furrowed. 'But the Viscount…'

'Is not my birth father.'

There was a long silence as she took that in. 'I do not understand,' she said, shaking her head.

'You asked for my help to build up your reputation in the *ton*, but the truth is I was born beneath you, Seraphine. I am not of upper-class breeding from birth, like you. I have had to earn my place in the aristocracy.'

She couldn't believe what she was hearing. 'Please, tell me everything.'

He gave a short, sharp nod. 'It is not easy for me to share this, but I will.'

'Because I found that letter?'

'No,' he said, raising his hand to take her chin between his fingers, turning her face to look at him. 'Because I want you to know. I was just waiting for the right moment, the right words, for the courage to come.'

He took a deep breath and began. 'The truth is, aged ten, I was gifted by my parents to my father's patron, Viscount Hart. The Viscount and his wife had a son of their own, but he died just after his tenth birthday and they were grieving his death. We lived on their estate in Derbyshire, in the rectory, and I was made their legal heir, taken away from my home and my family and brought here, to London, in return for my father receiving a living for the rest of his life.'

He said it so matter of factly, as if it was the norm, it took a moment for Seraphine to realise what impact, what damage, that might have done to a ten-year-old boy.

Her heart went out to him. 'How did you feel, being taken away from home at such a young age? Did you even know the Harts?'

Ezra shook his head. 'No...' he laughed bitterly '...they were strangers. I left my family to be with people who thought they wanted me. Only it did not work as they had hoped—they had wanted an heir, but they realised I would never replace their son. I was really just a reminder of what they had lost, leading to a rather cold upbringing. And I felt as if my parents abandoned me. I never saw or heard from them again and I have never been able to forgive them for it. I have been angry with them for so long. They separated me from my older brother and my two sisters and left me in the company of strangers and, I realise now, it damaged me.

'I lost the ability to trust people. And I never again wanted to get close to anyone, to care. I kept to myself, did what I was told, went to boarding school. But I felt lost, never myself. It made me feel like there was something wrong with me, because they gave me away. And I never felt as though I could fit in here. I did not feel I deserved this place, or the fortune that lay in store for me.'

No wonder he felt as though he didn't belong. No

wonder he'd said he felt like an imposter. The things he was saying, it sounded as if she was speaking herself.

'Going to war was the only way I felt I could take control of my own life. It was a risk I was prepared to take so I did not have to come back here after Oxford. For so long I have kept people at a distance, believing if my own parents can let me down, anyone can.'

Now she understood why he was so fiercely self-reliant. Because choosing to be alone was better than chancing rejection. And she could understand that—because she had been doing exactly the same, pushing others away before they could hurt her, too.

'I was just as shocked as you were to read that letter,' Ezra said. 'I had thought I would never hear from them again. And reading that my father and my brother have passed and knowing I did not get a chance to reconcile with them, it is hard.' He shook his head. 'I never got the chance to ask my father why he did it. He died thinking I was angry with him.'

'I am sorry about your father and brother, Ezra,' she said, placing a hand on his arm. 'It is a tragedy you did not get to see them again. But I am sure they knew you loved them and forgave them, in your own way. I am sure your father was proud of you.'

He grimaced. 'Despite my anger that my mother has only got in touch because she wants something from me, for some ridiculous reason, I still want to see her, speak with her, needing something from her—needing answers. There really must be something wrong with me.'

'I do not think you are ridiculous, Ezra. It is only natural you should want to speak to them to find out why they did what they did. And you cannot blame yourself for the choices they made, or how the Harts behaved. They were the adults; you were the child. They are responsible for this situation, not you,' she said.

He shrugged. 'I could not help but wonder, why me? Did they not care for me as much as my other siblings? Why send me away?'

She frowned. 'I understand. And yet,' she said slowly, carefully, 'have you ever wondered whether the opposite could be true?'

He looked at her. 'What do you mean?'

'That maybe, just maybe, they loved you so much, they were willing to sacrifice their own happiness to give you, and their other children, a better life? That even though it hurt you, they thought they were doing the right thing?'

He swallowed.

'We will never know why our parents behaved the way they did. But I sometimes wonder why my parents had to die,' she said. 'Why they were seized, when we were so close to the border, so close to getting away. And I think in my heart of hearts, I know. I believe they gave themselves up, to give me and my brother a chance to get away.'

He looked at her, taking in her words.

'There is always two ways of looking at things. And I have to think my parents were killed that day so I could survive—and that is what they would have wanted. The same goes for you. Rather than focusing on the bad, the feelings of rejection, perhaps you should focus on the fact you were also chosen. That your mother and father knew you were strong enough to do this—and that now you might be able to help your family in return. And even though the Harts struggled to be parents to you and the Viscount perhaps feels regret for that, they are still willing to entrust everything to you. Maybe you should start believing you are worthy of everything they want to give you, Ezra.'

He tipped his head back, closing his eyes, as if letting everything she'd said wash over him. And they sat there in silence for a while.

She watched the ripples of water caused by the fish in the lake, considering the effect their parents had had on their lives and the effect they had had on each other.

'Why have you never told anyone that you will not be Viscount?' she asked.

He turned to look at her. 'When I came here, I took the Viscount's last name of Hart and people assumed I was their son. They just went along with it, never correcting people, so I did, too. The longer the lie has gone on, it has felt like too big a secret to reveal. The estate is not entailed, so the Viscount can leave his properties and fortune to me on his passing, but his title will fall into abeyance—as far as we know, there is no other living heir. People will then find out about my humble beginnings and I dread that. I feel ashamed about it.'

'Why did you not tell me sooner, Ezra?'

'I thought it would change how you saw me. It has been drummed into me from an early age how to behave, to convince people to believe the lie, to appear more than I am—but deep down, I felt I did not measure up. The Viscount was always watching. I was never to let him down. I was always having to meet his expectations. Society's expectations.'

'Are you scared of him?' she asked.

His lips twisted. 'I was. Not so much any more. But for now, he still holds all the cards, he always has. There is always a condition—some expectation. And the latest is that I find a bride and marry this Season... He has even threatened to deny me my inheritance and strip me of his lands if I don't comply, reveal my true heritage.'

She swallowed, taking that in. 'Surely he would not, after all this time?'

He shrugged. 'I do not know. But you were right the other day. I have been brought up to believe that status means so much to a person's worth. I am unsure how I would feel now if it was all taken away. And...and I have never wanted to disappoint him.'

That explained a lot, Seraphine thought—about the way he had behaved all week, why Ezra acted the way he did at the Academy.

She watched the little wading birds, experts in disguise, blending in among the pebbles. She realised Ezra had tried to do the same. As had she. She had tried and failed to fit in for so long. They had a lot more in common than she'd first thought, she realised now. They had both loved and lost their parents. They had both been uprooted and struggled to find a place for themselves since.

She thought back to when she and Ezra had first met and she'd accused him of being privileged. But he hadn't always been.

'I am sorry I lied to you, Seraphine,' he said, running his hands over his thighs again. 'But I never wanted to let anyone know the truth. Especially not you. The one person whose opinion I actually care about.'

She released a breath she'd been holding all day. So he did care. 'Do you really think you need a title to be somebody special? Do you not think you are enough as you are?'

'I have only started to believe that might be true since I met you.' He cleared his throat. 'About yesterday,' he said.

And she stopped breathing.

'I should not have done that. I should not have kissed you.'

Confusion swept through her.

'I wanted to, but I should not have. Not there. Not like that.'

She turned to look at him. 'No? Then how?'

Ezra's heart thumped wildly in his chest. He so desperately wanted to touch her, to wrap his hand around her neck and pull her towards him. He wanted to kiss her again, to know she still liked him, that seeing that letter hadn't changed things between them, but he needed her consent first.

'I should not have asked you to meet me here tonight. I am doing everything all wrong. But I did not want you to go to sleep tonight without me explaining. I did not want you to go to bed thinking ill of me, thinking you didn't know me, after I had kissed you. But it is dark— late. You had better go now.'

She nodded slowly and stood, her back to him, staring out over the lake, and his heart felt like it was being wrenched out of his chest. She was leaving him.

And then she turned. 'Ezra, do you not want to kiss me again?'

His pulse pounded and he felt a rushing in his ears.

'More than anything. It is all I have thought about all day. All this evening. But—'

'Then why don't you?'

He curled himself up off the bench towards her, towering over her, staring down into her eyes. He took her left hand in his, his fingers caressing hers. Had she really just asked him to kiss her again? After everything he'd just revealed about himself?

'Is your hand all right?' she said, lifting it up to inspect the cut from earlier.

'Yes, it was foolish of me. But Henri would not stop talking about you and those other gentlemen...'

She shook her head. 'And yet I can only think of you.' She pressed her body closer. 'Ezra, please kiss me.'

He brought his hands up to hold her jaw and, as he drew her face closer towards him, her eyelids fluttered shut and his mouth came down on to hers.

His fingers lightly grazed the corners of her mouth as he kissed her, softly, slowly, and her lips parted, allowing him to deepen the connection, pressing his tongue inside her mouth, stealing her breath away. And she responded, her silky tongue carefully caressing his as she moved her hands beneath his cloak, wrapping her arms tightly around his waist.

He drew his arm around her and hauled her closer, his other hand trailing down from her face, over her jaw, his palm flattening against the base of her throat, where he could feel her pulse fluttering wildly.

She broke away from him slightly, to stare up at him, before placing her hand over his, moving it down, over her breast, and his breath stalled.

'Seraphine...' he said.

'I want to feel your hands on me, Ezra.'

His lips moved over hers, but this time it was a deep, open-mouthed kiss that went on and on as his fingers caressed the bare skin at her neckline, his hand cupping the weight of her breast beneath, and she moaned, her legs buckling beneath her. Then he was dragging her backwards, lowering himself on to the bench, bringing her down beside him.

He kissed her again, need lancing him as he ravaged her mouth, her neck, her exposed skin at her cleavage, and she was pushing him back, so he was lying on the bench. He pulled her down on top of him, protecting her from the hard metal slats beneath him. And as she tugged at his shirt, pulling it out of his breeches, her fingers delving beneath to curl over the warm, taut skin of his chest, his muscles tensed at her touch.

'Seraphine, what are you—?' He shook his head. 'Do you even know what you are doing?'

She shook her head.

'Driving me mad, that is what,' he said, his head tipping backwards, closing his eyes. He placed his hand over his shirt, over her hand, to still her roaming fingers. And he forced himself to say the words he didn't want to say. 'We should stop.'

She rested her head down on his chest and when he opened his eyes, her head tucked under his chin, he looked up at the stars. It was beautiful. Hundreds of them, glittering in the black, velvety night sky, shimmering down on them.

He put his hands on her hips, grazing them with his fingertips, then increased the pressure. 'Turn around,' he said, moving her round in his arms, so she was lying on top of him, so her back was against his chest, her bottom settling into his groin. 'Look.'

She tipped her head back and he brought his hands up to unpin her hair, the silky blonde strands falling down, and he buried his face in her neck, drawing in the sweet lily scent of her.

'It is beautiful.'

'So are you.'

'Do you believe in signs? In fate, in destiny?' she asked.

It was like the heavens were telling him this was how it was meant to be—that the stars had aligned. 'I do now.'

She turned her head, bringing her hand up to hold his cheek. Just as she had that night at Vauxhall, saving him. And his mouth found hers again and they kissed, slowly, reverently, his arms wrapping around her waist. This time, he gave in trying to fight it. Or stop it.

He took a moment to stray from her mouth, his lips roaming down her neck, kissing her skin, moving to the base of her ear, then he came back to her lips again, claiming her mouth once more. And she recklessly writhed on top of him, a low moan escaping her throat, snapping his resolve for good, and he felt himself harden beneath her. Could she feel it? He wanted her to.

One hand came up to trail over her ribcage, to cover her breast, caressing, peeling down the material to expose as much of her as the silk would allow, so he could touch her swollen flesh, her nipple springing free, and she gasped as his thumb brushed over the taut rosy tip. His other hand roamed lower, down, flattening over her stomach, smoothing over the silk covering her thighs, all while his tongue was still stoking her mouth, sweeping inside in wave after tumultuous wave.

'Ezra,' she breathed.

He smoothed up her dress, slowly, drawing the material over her knees, then her thighs, gathering it at her hips, until his fingers, finally, felt skin, the smooth, soft skin of her exposed thigh. As he brought up his knee beneath her, holding her one leg aside, his hand, now trembling, dipped, curving over her soft, intimate hair. Their mingled breath was suspended as his fingertips, ever so gently, slid between her parted thighs, touching her most intimate, secret places, and she whimpered.

'Is this all right?' he whispered. He needed her permission to take possession of her innocent body, even if it was only with his hands.

Seraphine nodded. She couldn't speak as his fingertips pressed against the place where her excitement, her frustration, had been building all week—and with a precision she hadn't been expecting. She gasped. How did he know where she wanted him to touch her?

She tried to squeeze her legs together, as unbearable, overwhelming pleasure crashed through her, but he wouldn't let her, resolutely holding her leg apart with his knee. And there was nothing she could do but tip her head back in surrender against his shoulder, as his fingertips swirled around her, as he kissed her neck, crushing her breast in his other hand, teasing her nipple, making her wetter, making her squirm on top of him. And then he dipped lower, moving his finger to her entrance, making her breath hitch as he pressed gently inside her body.

She gasped out her pleasure as his finger slid inside her, at the sensations he was causing as he breached her innocence—and needing him to know how she was feeling, wanting to make him as wild as he was making her, she moved her hand between their bodies, where the hard ridge of him was pressing into her lower back. She had no clue what she was doing, but she curved her palm over the length of him and squeezed and he groaned.

And as his finger plunged inside her again, his tongue in her mouth became more insistent, demanding more of a reaction, before he came back to stroking her intimately, bringing with him a fresh rush of moisture, as he touched her just as softly, just as tenderly, as before. And it tipped her over the edge. His fingers rolled over her and her breathing quickened. Intense pleasure surged through her and her whole body tensed as she panted, crying out her first ever climax.

When she opened her eyes moments later, she felt herself falling softly down to earth. She could feel his heartbeat thudding against her back. And his hand was still right there. He released her breast, pulling her gown back into place, and lowered his knee, letting go of her leg, before he smoothed down the material of her skirts. She bit her lip, unsure what she was meant to say or do, still in awe about what had just happened.

'Are you all right?' he whispered.

Her body flushed with warmth and love, and she twisted her head to look at him. Dark, uncertain beautiful eyes stared back at her. She turned her whole body to face him, resting her cheek on his shoulder, her hip on the bench. 'Yes,' she said shyly.

And when his arms came up to wrap around her

waist, she enjoyed the feeling of being held in his embrace, feeling the hard muscles of his body against hers. All of them. And she wondered, what should she be doing? She wasn't sure. Should she, did he want her to touch him back?

She smoothed her hand tentatively over his chest. He felt as if he had been sculpted by one of those artists at the Academy, his body was honed to perfection. Then she roamed lower, her fingers trailing to his waist.

But he caught her hand with his.

'Ezra?' she asked. 'What do I do?'

He brought her hand up to his lips, and gently kissed it.

'As much as I want to show you, Seraphine, I do not think this is the right place for it. It is late and I do not want this to be a quick tryst on a cold bench, do you? You mean more to me than that.'

'But—'

'Let us just…wait,' he said, gathering her to him, pulling her into his chest and stroking her hair.

Chapter Eleven

It took all day to prepare Artington Hall for the ball, hours to arrange the endless bouquets of flowers and light all the chandeliers. The dance floor had been chalked, champagne glasses filled, fruit and pastries laid out and the dance cards placed perfectly on a table in the hall. Peering out of the window, seeing the first of the carriages come down the drive, Seraphine held her stomach and nodded to the band to start playing, before checking the footmen were in position, ready to welcome the guests.

She couldn't believe Ezra had left her to sort everything—as if she was the lady of the house herself. But everything was ready and Artington Hall looked magnificent. And despite her nerves, Seraphine was so pleased Ezra had stuck to his word and that it was really happening—that they were having a benefit ball here to raise money for the émigrés. There was just one thing missing—him. Where was he? The guests were about to arrive and at the moment they had no host!

She hadn't seen him all day, not since last night. And she was beginning to think he had abandoned her, that even if he couldn't get out of hosting the ball, he hadn't been able to bring himself to come.

'He will be here,' Mrs Dawson said, placing a reassuring hand on her arm. 'He is not the kind of man to let anyone down.'

And Seraphine didn't think he would. Not really. Not after he'd gone to all the effort of sending out the invitations—even to the palace. And not after getting the Viscount to agree to hosting the event in the first place. She couldn't believe the old man had gone along with it, but he had—on the condition Ezra find a bride tonight.

It was the talk of the *ton*. The most talked-about ball of the Season so far, one that everyone wanted a ticket to. And not only because Ezra Hart was hosting a benefit ball for the émigrés—a most unusual situation—or because it was at Artington Hall, which was so rarely seen by the public, but because rumour had it that tonight was the night the Viscount was going to choose a wife!

She hoped the rumours were wrong. She couldn't bear it if he danced more than one set with anyone, not in front of her. Not after the things they'd done together last night—not after she'd practically begged him to put his hands on her and let him touch her so intimately. Her cheeks flushed at the memory, at the exquisite sensations he'd created. And she would have done more. It was he who had been restrained. He who had said they must wait. But wait for what? She had wanted. She still wanted.

Seraphine could see Lord Wentworth getting out of his carriage, Sir Allan Jennings and his daughter, too, and there was Lord Barrington. Her heart was in her mouth. But none of them was whom she was looking for.

Where was he?

She had woken this morning in her own bed in the cottage and sat bolt upright. She had still been wearing her dress, the one she'd worn to dinner, and she wondered how she had got there. The last thing she remembered was being tucked up next to Ezra's body on the bench, enclosed in his arms, listening to the sound of his breathing, enjoying the feeling of his chest rising and falling beneath her, and she had let her eyelids drift shut.

She had arrived at the hall early this morning, as she'd arranged with Mrs Dawson, to get everything ready, but the woman had informed her Ezra had gone to London and wouldn't be back until early evening. Had he been avoiding her? But he was taking it too far—now she was starting to worry. Did he regret what had happened between them last night—was that why he'd stayed away all day?

Then, glancing around, she saw him coming towards her down the hallway.

He was here!

And he looked incredible, dashing in a new dark suit, which hinted at his muscular body beneath. Muscles she knew what it felt like to be pressed tightly against. Her mouth dried. None of the decorations or chandeliers— the splendour of Artington Hall tonight—none of it drew her eyes as much as he did.

As he approached, his eyes, burning almost amber in the flickering candlelight, met hers and her heart stuttered. His eyes swept over her in approval, his gaze darkening, and she felt a responsive heat flare low in her belly.

She couldn't believe the story he had told her last

night, of the young boy who'd had his heart broken when he'd been taken from his parents, separated from his siblings, raised by strangers. And she realised he must have been lonely, growing up here, never having someone to love and cherish him as he deserved. Mrs Dawson had probably done as good a job as any.

Seraphine wondered under that strict, formidable exterior whether the Viscount had loved him, in his own way. But unwittingly, he had caused him great damage. She could see now why Ezra struggled to trust, why he had gone to war, why he cared for his friends, his comrades so much, and why he stayed away from this place. She understood him so much better and realised he had been brought up to see that status and reputation were everything. She hoped she had started to persuade him to think differently. If only so he could stop being so ill at ease with himself. Perhaps if he knew how much she cared for him, she could make him see his own worth.

She could still feel the taste of his lips on hers. Last night had been wonderful—the way he'd touched her, she had never thought it could feel so good. The way his fingers had stroked her skin, pressing inside her body, had been exquisite and she wanted him to do it again. Her face flushed at the thought, just as he approached.

'I like what you have done with the place!' he said, grinning.

And just at that moment, the guests began to pile through the doors, pulling them apart, as they did their duty and welcomed them. The hall was bustling—it was as if it had burst into life for the first time in years, just like she felt about herself.

Suddenly, trumpets resounded around the hall and

excitement filled the air as people turned to each other, whispering, knowing what that sound meant, but not daring to believe it. And then the master of ceremonies confirmed it—he announced the arrival of the Prince Regent and everyone flocked out on to the steps to see the royal carriage pull up outside.

The crowd fell silent as His Royal Highness stepped out of the carriage.

'Did you know he was coming?' Seraphine whispered, coming up alongside Ezra.

'I sent the invitation, I never expected he would make an appearance.'

Ezra stepped forward to receive the Prince and took a bow.

'Your Royal Highness, you are most welcome.'

'Mr Hart, thank you for having us.' He looked up at the hall and around at all the guests. 'I came to tell you, I respect what you are doing here, for the émigrés.'

'Thank you, sir. May I introduce Miss Seraphine Mounier?' he said. 'A good friend of mine, and your hostess for this evening.'

Seraphine curtsied.

'Miss Mounier, delighted to meet you. I would be honoured if you would assist me in opening the ball by giving me the first dance.'

Ezra stood on the sidelines, watching the dance. Watching her. He had intended to dance the first dance with Seraphine this evening, but he knew she could not have denied the Regent.

Seraphine was dressed in a white-silk gown decorated with embroidered landscapes and figures, almost like a batiste. He'd never seen anything like it before and she looked stunning. He couldn't take his eyes off her. Her eyes were shining, and her face was radiating joy. She looked lovely. She captivated him completely.

He couldn't believe she had accomplished this so successfully. And despite the jealousy twisting in his stomach now she was dancing with the Prince, smiling at whatever the Regent said, he was proud of her.

He glanced around him, anxious for the dance to come to an end. Henri seemed to be just as in awe of Seraphine as he was. As he peered over at Lady Frances, she looked as if she had swallowed a lemon. He had to stifle a laugh.

He had resented being in London all day, but the authorities had requested his help with their investigations. While he wanted to be useful and he knew they were getting closer to catching their man, he had wanted to get back to Seraphine.

It was strange. Usually, it was all too easy to stay away from Artington, but that wasn't the case with Seraphine here. He liked the place so much more with her in it. And he realised he would like to have her at Artington, always.

He couldn't stop thinking about last night.

After all these years of hiding his true self, feeling ashamed and worrying the truth would come out, it had felt liberating to tell Seraphine who he really was. That he didn't have to feel as though he was lying to her any more. It somehow made him feel like a free man, as if the chains had finally been cast off. He had half-expected to be shunned by her, but he should have realised she was far too kind to do that. More than that, she had helped him accept himself and even want to like himself for who he was.

He'd come to realise the only approval he needed was that of the people he cared about. No one else mattered.

As for the rest of the *ton*, Seraphine had coped with discrimination about who she was for years. If she was strong enough to put up with it, it made him realise he could be, too. With her at his side, he would face whatever came his way.

He should never have touched her. But once he had, he knew he couldn't stop. He'd wanted to give her pleasure. He'd wanted to show her how he felt about her with his mouth and his hands. He'd never felt that way with a woman before. Usually, it was about his own satisfaction, nothing more.

He'd wanted to take her back to his room, lay her down on his bed, peel off her clothes and show her what else he could do to her. How else he could tease and please and satisfy her. And he'd wanted to settle his body between her legs and thrust inside her, to take her innocence and claim her as his own. But he'd known that he couldn't. Not yet. Because it wouldn't be right.

His gaze raked over her again. She was a natural beauty, with her slender curves, breasts he'd held in his palms last night strapped into that low-cut dress, yet he knew she was strong. He'd seen her handle a fire, ride a horse, put on a ball and serve the masses in the city square—and still put him and her brother in their place. He admired her so much. But most of all, he admired her mind and her kindness. The way she always cared about others more than herself. The way she cared about him, even after what he'd shared with her last night. That she had accepted it, that she hadn't judged him—that she had even offered him a different way of looking at it.

That's what she had done since he'd met her. She'd offered him an alternative perspective of the world. She'd given him a reason to live again. To love again?

Seeing it her way, he had been able to let go a little of his anger, a little of his pain. And he wondered if he might finally be ready to reply to his mother's letter.

The music finished and the Prince led Seraphine over to the drinks table, where the servants swiftly poured them both a glass of champagne. When he saw them clink glasses, he crossed the room so fast, it was a wonder he didn't crash into anyone, knocking them over.

'Ah, Miss Mounier, I think perhaps I may have taken up a little too much of your time, given the way Mr Hart is looking at me,' the Regent said, looking vaguely amused. 'Thank you for the dance and the most exceptional ball.' He nodded to them both and went to move on. 'Oh, and I have not seen the Viscount in Parliament recently, Mr Hart,' the Prince said, turning back to him. 'We could do with an opinion from Artington on many matters, I feel.'

'Thank you, sir.'

Then he was gone to mingle with the many others who were all seeking an audience with him. While Ezra knew most men in this situation would have been reeling, proud to have royalty at their ball, to have been given such a compliment by the Prince, he only felt respite— relief that he had Seraphine back to himself. At last.

'You are looking very French this evening,' Ezra said. 'And I mean that as a compliment.'

She laughed. 'What you see is what you get, I guess.'

He hoped so…he wanted her, badly.

Yet her statement struck a chord. For he had been pretending to be something he wasn't his whole life. He'd tried to be the child the Harts wanted. He had found his place among his friends, where he could be himself, but apart from that, he had lied for years to himself and others. But after telling Seraphine the truth last night, he felt so much better about everything and realised he didn't want to lie any more. He just wanted to be himself—with her.

'How was Mrs Dawson today?'

'She was pretty wonderful, actually. Organising everybody, keeping your father occupied. I do not know how she does it.'

He was relieved the Viscount had decided to stay in his rooms tonight and not make an appearance at the ball. If he'd seen the number of French guests Ezra had invited, he might have had one of his fits of rage.

'Did she look after you, like I asked her to?'

'Yes. But Ezra, where were you? You…left me. I woke up back in the cottage,' she said, lowering her voice.

'Yes, I know. I carried you there, put you to bed.'

'You—what?'

He grinned.

'What if someone had seen?'

'I was careful. They did not.'

She glanced around and he wondered if she was trying to distract herself from her heated memories of last night, as was he.

'Where were you all day?'

'The authorities asked me to meet with them. They have made some progress with their enquiries.'

'Really? What did they say?'

'Let us talk about it later. Not here.'

She nodded. 'I cannot believe you invited so many French people,' Seraphine said, changing the subject and looking around the room. 'I dread to think what Lady Frances is thinking.'

'This *is* a benefit ball for émigrés, is it not? The intention was to raise awareness of the émigrés' plight. I did not think it would hurt to be a little more inclusive and diversify the aristocracy.'

'Thank you, Ezra,' she said, turning back to him, tears in her eyes. 'For doing this. I think you may have finally redeemed yourself for your words in that pamphlet.'

'I am glad. But I confess my thoughts were not of redemption. I believe I only held this ball so I could dance with you, so you had better have a slot saved on your dance card for me, or I shall be very put out.' He grinned.

The band was getting ready for the next set and he held out his hand. 'It was my intention to ask you for the first dance this evening, but you had a better offer. So could I have the second dance of the evening?'

Her face broke out into a smile and she placed her fingers in his. 'Certainly.' He led her to the dance floor, knowing all eyes were on them.

'I thought we would try a waltz this evening, what do you say?' and he inclined his head towards the band.

'All right.'

He slid a hand around her waist, pulling her into his shoulder, and she gasped.

'People can see.'

'What can I do? It is the scandalous nature of the

dance,' he said, as he tugged her tighter, their hands entwining, forming an arch.

Right now, he didn't care if anyone saw. Or what they thought. He wanted this. *Her.* He wanted her with him, or as close to him as etiquette would allow.

'I thought you cared about your reputation.'

'Maybe I am learning to take a leaf out of your book.'

If she was worried what the *ton* would think about this, he couldn't wait to hear the collective gasp around the room when he asked her to dance the next set, and the next, making his intentions—and affections—known.

As Ezra continued to turn her about the room, his hands on her body, his dark eyes looking down at her, never breaking eye contact, she stared up at him, smiling. She was having the best time. She couldn't believe Ezra had introduced her to the Prince. Introducing her meant he was vouching for her social standing and she appreciated it—him—so much. She had been flattered when the Prince had asked her to dance, entering into the spirit of the evening, affirming her status in the *ton*, yet she had only wished to dance with Ezra. Now, all her dreams were coming true. She was so pleased to be back in his arms, basking in the warm glow of his admiration.

But then something in the doorway caught her eye. She saw a figure approach the ballroom door and she faltered.

Ezra saw the consternation on her face and glanced in the direction of where she was looking. There, standing in the doorway to the ballroom, dressed in his finery, holding his cane, was the Viscount.

Their movements came to a halt as the man glowered

at them and Ezra stared back. Had he seen something between them?

Seraphine wondered how Ezra would react. She knew how the man impacted him. She knew the Viscount didn't approve of her. Would the Viscount cause a scene? She held her breath.

Yet just as quietly as he had come, his expression unreadable, the old man turned around and walked back down the corridor, without even coming into the ball.

Ezra looked down at Seraphine, his brow furrowed. 'Perhaps I should go after him. Maybe I should check he is all right.'

She nodded.

But before he had the chance, a huge explosion of glass shattering pierced the air and the guests screamed, cowering together as the music screeched to a halt. There was a breath as hundreds and hundreds of glistening shards and splinters rained down on the ballroom before coming to settle on the floor, tinkling like piano keys.

Ezra threw himself around Seraphine, protecting her from the fragments, as they hunched down in the corner.

Seraphine looked up to see the ballroom window had been smashed—that a brick had been thrown through it. And then, through the jagged gaping hole, she saw a group of men running, coming towards them across the lawn. Men with makeshift weapons in their hands. Her breath caught in her throat.

Ezra was up like a shot and Seraphine saw the instant change in him, from man to soldier, as he pushed her back against the wall, the concern in his eyes matching her own. 'Stay back. Stay down, out of sight. I don't want you getting hurt,' he said. And she nodded, watching aghast as he moved with speed and power over to the Regent, checking the Prince was unharmed, calling on the other men to assist him in moving the man into the library.

Then he was back in the ballroom and she watched in horror as he removed his jacket, rolled up his sleeves and reached for a sword off the wall, ready to fight.

There were a dozen of them heading this way, clambering through the broken window, and although Ezra had told her to leave, she couldn't move. She couldn't bring herself to look away. She had to watch; she had to know he was all right. As the intruders came further into the room, Ezra and his friends, even Henri, approached them without fear and a brutal fight ensued. She saw the warrior in Ezra instantly, his instinctive, skilful precision with his sword, as he led the others in combat. And she knew then what an asset he must have been on the battlefield.

As he took one brute down, then the other, a third began to think better of it. He dropped his weapon and began to flee. But Ezra charged after him, through the glass, over the immaculate manicured lawns, catching up with him, tussling him to the ground. They began fighting with their fists, the man's hand smacking into Ezra's jaw and Seraphine winced and gasped at every strike and blow. Henri was getting up off the floor, having knocked out his opponent, and the other men were finishing theirs off, too, tying up their wrists and hustling them together, waiting for Ezra to end it.

Finally, he struck the last blow and the man went still, collapsing back on to the ground. She could have wept with relief. He was safe.

It was over. These men had been stopped from whatever it is they were hoping to achieve.

Ezra and his men helped the Prince's guards to bundle them into a carriage to take the offenders to London, where she hoped they'd be reprimanded. She shivered to think what could have happened.

She watched as Ezra and his friends came back into the room, congratulating each other and slapping each other on their backs. 'What a rush!'

'We've still got it.'

'Saved the day!'

But as Ezra looked across at her, meeting her gaze, she knew the ball was ruined.

All around them, shards of glass lay strewn on the floor like rubble. The musicians had disbanded and the guests were still huddled together in shock in the library. She doubted they would be in the mood for any more dancing, or supper tonight. And she wasn't sure they would want to return to Artington Hall any time soon.

Ezra was relieved to see Seraphine standing there, leaning against the wall, looking at him, safe and unharmed. It was a similar relief to what he'd felt when he and his men had reached the city of Brussels—the general hospital—after Waterloo and he'd realised Ash, Adam and Hawk were still alive. When they'd found each other and embraced, laughing, knowing they'd somehow all survived, it had been a moment of great elation. That the war was over and they'd all made it through.

He met her gaze, wanting to cross the distance towards her and gather her into his arms, yet he saw the Regent coming out of the library, surrounded by his guards, and he knew duty meant he had to speak to the Prince first.

He realised how much he'd changed in the days since his duel with Henri in Hyde Park, when he'd been seeking his next burst of exhilaration, needing that sense of danger to feel alive, feeling that was all he knew. Now, he didn't care for violence—he only cared that Seraphine was safe.

He approached the Prince and braced himself for the reproof he knew he was due.

'Mr Hart.'

'Sir.' Ezra bowed. 'I am sorry for the disruption to this evening's proceedings.'

'Who the devil were those men, Hart?'

'I do not know, sir, but we intend to find out. They have been chained up in a carriage, set to return ahead of you to London.'

'You have reprimanded them all?'

'Yes, sir.'

'No one got hurt?'

'No.'

'Well done.'

He didn't want his Prince's praise. Yes, he'd got the Regent to safety, but truth be told, when he had seen those men approach, he had thought only of protecting Seraphine. And right now, he just wanted everyone out of here so he could check she was all right.

He might have known something like this would happen. And the thought that those men had come here to cause trouble because of her, maybe even to harm her, sent shivers down his spine. He was so glad he and his friends had apprehended them. He wondered if they were the same men who had set fire to Seraphine's house. If they were, the truth would out and he would make sure they would pay for their crimes. This vandalisation and violence against the people he cared about had to stop.

He thought about all her efforts today in preparing for tonight and, looking around him at the devastation, he was sure she must be upset and in shock from what had happened.

'Well, Mr Hart, I dare say this is the most excitement I have seen in a while,' the Regent said. 'But I hope you do not mind if I take my leave now? In fact,' he said, projecting his voice out to the room, 'I think we should all call it a night. Mr Hart has a lot of mess to clean up.' The man held out his hand for Ezra to shake. 'And thank you, for your hospitality and your protection. It will not be forgotten.'

'Thank you for coming, sir. And I sincerely apologise, once again.'

And with that, everyone began to take their leave.

Ezra saw his guests out to their carriages, reassuring some of the women who were most shaken by the evening's events that the criminals had been apprehended, while listening to the opinions of others who were aghast at the violence, the destruction caused and the damage to the ballroom—all the while speculating on why it had happened.

'Too many French attendees, no doubt,' he heard Lady Frances say. And he felt sorry for her, that she never had anything nice to say, and that it must stem from being so deeply unhappy in herself. He realised what a lucky escape he'd had in not pursuing her.

He'd made so many apologies, trying to explain to

people what had happened, attempting to appease them. He had no doubt it would be the scandal on everyone's lips for some time, for the *ton* would always talk. He was getting a taste of what Seraphine had had to put up with all this time.

When he saw the last carriage weave down Artington drive, he turned to head back inside, weary.

His diligent staff were still there, sweeping, mopping, not really knowing where to start—and Seraphine. Seraphine was still there. And his heart pounded with alarm when he saw who she was talking to—the Viscount.

Ezra stiffened, taking in the scene before him. He hoped the man wasn't being unkind—he would be sorry. Ezra would rise to her defence, there would be an argument, and that was the last thing she needed right now.

'Lord Hart,' he said as he approached, coming to stand by Seraphine's side.

'Ezra. Miss Mounier and Mrs Dawson have filled me in on what happened this evening.'

'I shall get the window fixed,' Ezra said, thinking that's what he must be concerned with, and the man nodded.

'The Prince Regent was unharmed?'

'He was fine. In fact, he left in good spirits. I think he rather enjoyed the excitement of the evening,' Ezra said, his lips twisting.

The man nodded. 'You lied to me, Ezra. About the purpose of this event.'

'I told you it was a benefit ball.'

'You also told me you intended to find a bride.'

He swallowed.

'We shall discuss it tomorrow. But right now, I am

going back to bed. I am glad this was not any worse than it could have been, for your sake.'

Ezra nodded, then blew out a long breath, turning around to the staff. He pinched the bridge of his nose. 'Please, everyone, let us leave this for tonight. Go to bed. Get some sleep. It has been quite a day and none of this is urgent, we will sort it in the morning.'

One by one they all began to put down their brooms, buckets and mops and retire.

Everyone but Seraphine.

He held her in his gaze, coming towards her.

'Are you all right?'

'Yes. You?' she said, her brow crinkling. 'You're bleeding.'

He put his hand to his forehead and when he brought his fingers back down, he realised she was right.

'Come and sit down. I will clean it up,' she said, leading him into the library. And he liked the fact she cared.

'The Viscount—what did he say? Did he treat you kindly?'

'Yes, he was very civil. I think, in fact, he was worried about you.'

Ezra scoffed. 'About the window more like.'

She shook her head. 'I am not so sure.'

He sagged down on to the chesterfield as she fetched a bowl of water and a cloth, soon returning. She slipped off her shoes and came to sit beside him and gently pressed the cloth to his temple. He blanched.

'Sorry, this might sting for a moment,' she said.

'Henri went with the coach, taking those men to London,' he said.

'I know, I saw.'

'And your aunt and uncle, I sent them in a carriage back to the cottage. They were pretty shaken up.'

'Thank you.'

'I hate not being able to ensure the safety of the people I care about. I think it stems from the war and being unable to save my men.'

'But you did ensure everyone's safety. I saw you. You were amazing out here,' she said. 'The Regent even thanked you.'

'It should never have happened in the first place. Perhaps I should have put more security on the gates.'

'The Regent's guards were here. They would not have allowed him to attend if they had not secured the perimeter and deemed it to be safe.' She put down the cloth. 'Ezra, who were those men? What did they want?'

He shrugged. 'I do not know.'

'Please, do not lie to protect me, Ezra.'

He sighed. 'Anti-émigrés, I think. They probably did not like the fact I was holding a benefit ball.'

'I am so sorry,' she said, shaking her head and getting up, picking up the bowl and setting it down on the table. 'I should never have got you involved. I should never have asked you to do this for me.'

'If I remember rightly, this was my idea.' He watched as she dried her hands on her skirts, before wringing them together. 'So we are both blaming ourselves. A lot of good that will do us. Come here,' he said. He took her hand, tugging her gently back towards where he was sitting. 'It is all right.'

'But it isn't all right. I cannot believe they caused such damage. I feel awful.'

He tutted. 'It is not your fault, Seraphine.'

'I could not bear it if anything had happened to you...' she said, tears welling in her eyes.

'Hush, now, nothing did.' He pulled her closer, his hand curving around her thigh, just under the curve of her bottom, drawing her body closer to him, so she was standing between his knees, his dark, heated gaze looking up at her.

Ezra's movements were slow, as if he was giving her time to say no, to change her mind, and her legs trembled hard. But she knew she wanted this to happen. She wanted to feel his hands on her again. She had been desperate for a moment alone with him, all evening, so she could kiss him again. She knew it was wrong, yet it didn't feel like it, it felt so right.

He rose to take her in his arms, holding her for a long while, giving her the comfort she needed, until she took a step back and looked up at him, placing her hands on his cheeks. Almost reverently, he lowered her face towards her, kissing her. As their mouths clung, as his tongue swept inside her, she gasped at the thrilling and tender feelings rushing through her body.

'I missed you today,' he said, pulling away slightly, smiling against her mouth.

'I missed you, too.'

And he kissed her again, but this time, it was different. It was raw, it was open-mouthed and passionate, and he drew her up against his hard, muscular body, every part of him, and she felt the instant flicker of excitement down below.

'Seraphine,' he breathed, tearing his mouth from hers. 'We need to talk about this.'

'And we will. Later.' She kissed him again and he succumbed for a moment, before breaking away again.

'Seraphine.'

'I want to do this, Ezra.'

He pulled away from her slightly. 'Do you even know what *this* is?'

'Yes.'

'How do you know?'

'I do read.'

His eyebrows rose up. 'What do you read?'

'Books.' She gave him a secret smile.

'Not the kind I have in my library, clearly. And what did these books teach you?'

'Things…but I'm sure you could teach me better.' And she took his hands in hers and placed them on her breasts.

'Show me.'

He groaned and placed his forehead against hers. He raised his hand into her hair, and pulled the pins out, one by one, letting the silky, blonde strands tumble down around her shoulders, his hands loosening the tendrils and sending tingles through her body.

'I want you to be sure. There is no going back.'

'I am sure, Ezra,' she whispered.

He took a step away from her and, for a moment, she thought he was saying no. But then he brought his hands up to his neckcloth, and began to loosen it, slowly undoing it before pulling it off. He shrugged his arms out of his tailcoat and threw it over the side of the chesterfield, before moving to the buttons of his waistcoat.

She stood watching him, the slow removal of his clothes doing something profound to her insides, melting her stomach, and she felt liquid heat pool between her legs. She couldn't move her gaze from him as he stalked back towards her. She didn't want to miss a moment.

He took one of her hands in his and gently slid her glove down her arm, smoothing the silk off her wrists and her fingers, his dark eyes unmoving from hers. He did the same with the other one and her heart was pounding so hard she thought it might leap out of her chest.

'Turn around,' he whispered. Placing his hands on her shoulders, he twirled her. He swept her hair aside, giving him access to the fastenings at the back of her dress. He kissed the exposed skin at her shoulder as he loosened the silk bow around her waist, pulling the end, and she gasped, before his fingers began to pop open each of the tiny buttons. 'This is tricky, especially with trembling fingers.'

And she was glad he was admitting he was just as nervous as she was.

When the last one came undone, she held her breath and he smoothed the shoulders down over her arms, letting the material fall away from her body and down into a pool on the floor. Dressed in only her shift, he pulled her back against his chest, letting her feel what she was doing to him, what reaction she was causing in the lower half of his body. She turned her head to face him and smiled, and his mouth found her lips again, as his hands found her breasts, and she whimpered as he kneaded her soft, swollen flesh.

'I need to see you,' he said. 'I am going out of my mind.'

His words gave her the courage to turn and face him. And he gripped her arms, holding them up above her head, before he released her and gathered the material of her shift at her hips and lifted it up and off her, leaving her standing there, in just her stockings, naked before him.

He drew in a ragged breath, as he raked his eyes over her.

'You are perfection,' he whispered.

And she shivered under his gaze, in the cool air and glittering candlelight of the library.

His hands came up to cup her breasts again and he kissed her on the lips before dipping his mouth to her breast, taking one rosy peak inside, and she held his head to keep her from falling, or to hold him in place, she wasn't sure. She tipped her own head back as she delighted in all the delicious sensations he was causing.

'Ezra,' she breathed.

'Take off my shirt,' he said, raising his head, and they broke apart just long enough for her to help him bring the material up over his chest and head and discard it.

Her eyes widened at the sight of his magnificent body in front of her. He was all beautiful, sculpted muscle, and she tentatively ran her palms over his chest. He had lots of scars and her fingers trailed over them, wondering how he got each one.

'Are they all from the war?'

'Yes.'

But he didn't want to talk, as suddenly he was lifting her, his hands curving over her bottom. She gasped as her hands came round his neck, her knees round his hips, as he carried her, naked, over to the piano, setting her down on the polished lid, her stockinged legs hanging over the side.

He removed her hands from his shoulders and, holding her hands in his, he pinned them behind her back as his mouth worked its way down her neck to her heaving chest again, laving her breasts, her taut nipples with his tongue, and she arched into him, wanting more, groaning with pleasure.

He came closer, his body moving between her legs, and he released her hands to push her knees further apart.

'Do you want me to stop?'

She shook her head. 'No.'

His thumbs pressed against her slick heat, rolling over her tiny nub, as they had done last night. Only this time he could see her, splayed out before him. He could see everything he was doing, everywhere he was touching, and her face heated, her chest rising and falling rapidly.

'You are so damn beautiful,' he moaned. 'Lie back.'

Eyeing him warily, she lowered herself on to her elbows.

'All the way.'

And she did as she was told. 'What are you going to do?'

'Trust me?' he asked, his mouth curling up on one side.

And she nodded.

He ran his hands over her bare stomach, making her muscles tense, and over her breasts, her nipples prickling under his touch, before his palms roamed up to her throat, then back down, over her ribs, her hips, her thighs, leaving no part of her untouched. And just as she thought she couldn't take it any more, he bent his head and she bucked, raising her bottom off the slick wood, shocked as his mouth touched her where his thumbs had just been, the tip of his tongue curling round her, explicitly, as his hands pushed her knees wider apart.

He licked her slowly, gently, and it was so sweet, so torturous, it felt wildly intimate. When he kissed her, fully, his hot mouth covering more of her, she grabbed his head and he seemed to lose all restraint, ravaging her until she came apart, her thighs quivering, her bare buttocks squirming around on the piano. And as she cried out her climax, his hand came up to wrap around her mouth to silence her, until the last tremors of her orgasm faded away.

She felt dizzy with elation and satisfaction as she lay there, sprawled out on the piano, her breathing nowhere near normal, until he took her hand and pulled her up to sitting.

'Did your books teach you that?' he grinned wickedly.

She shook her head, eyeing him shyly. 'You know very well they did not. I did not know about that.'

He grinned, resting his forehead against hers. And he moved her hand to place it over the hard ridge of him. 'I want you so badly, Seraphine.'

And she nodded, biting her lip, understanding, but not sure what to do.

'Where I touched you with my fingers last night and just now with my mouth, I want to be inside you, with my body. Is that what you want, too?'

She nodded. 'Yes.'

He moved her fingers to the fastening of his breeches, showing her how to set him free. And once they were loose, he released her for a second, to tug off his boots, losing his balance, and she helped to steady him, both of them laughing, before they sobered with desire and he pushed down his breeches, stepping out of them.

He stood before her naked and he took her breath away. He was the most magnificent man. Then he was carrying her again, through the air, her legs wrapped around his waist, and he lowered them both down on to the rug in the middle of the grand room.

He came down on top of her, his bare chest against hers, his naked thighs on hers, and as his knees parted her legs, allowing him to come down between them, he stroked her hair away from her shoulders, smoothing it away from her breasts.

'Nervous?'

'After what you just did?' She smiled and shook her head.

'This is different. It might hurt at first,' he said, his voice hoarse.

'Thank you for the warning. I am sure I will be just fine. I am in safe hands.'

He rested his forehead against hers, then, as he took himself in his hands, running the tip of himself along her silky thighs up to her wet, silky entrance, she felt heat, and need, lance her.

'Seraphine?' And as he said her name, she knew he was asking her a question, asking permission once more. 'You can still change your mind.'

She shook her head. 'I don't want to change my mind.'

To prove it, she brought her hand down between them to cover his, wrapping her fingers around him, guiding him, doing this together, and then he was right there, at the centre of her world.

He kissed her slowly on the mouth, deeply, as he thrust

inside her, and the shocking breach had her tensing around him, making her cry out, making him groan, and his head came down to rest against hers, to stare into her eyes, as her hands came up to wrap around his shoulders.

'All right?'

She nodded.

'I'm inside you,' he whispered, as if he wasn't able to believe it. 'You feel like heaven.'

As she began to relax around him, getting used to the sheer size of him buried inside her, he started to move, gently surging further in, and she couldn't believe it when her body accommodated him. Then he slowly slid out before thrusting inside her again, all the way back in, breaking down any last barrier between them. This time all she felt was pleasure, great pleasure racking through her body at his invasion. At the intimacy. At the fact they were joined together, at last. And she never wanted to be parted from him.

Their chests, their stomachs, even their brows were slick with sweat as they writhed together on the floor. And he kissed her forehead, her mouth, her neck, moving her arms up above her head, entwining their hands. She looked up at the mirrored ceiling and saw herself spread out beneath him, their bodies a tangle of limbs, his body moving on top of her, as she thrashed beneath him, and she felt overwhelmed with the beauty and onslaught of it.

Then he began to move faster, harder, demanding more, wanting to be deeper than she thought possible, accepting nothing less than as if he wanted to be a part of her. She knew he wouldn't stop until he'd wrought every last drop of pleasure from her body. As he surged once more, slamming into her, she screamed out her release, calling his name, the sheer force of her love for him bringing tears to her eyes as he exploded powerfully inside her.

Seraphine clung on to him until the shudders racking her body finally subsided, and Ezra's own hectic heartbeat began to settle. It had been incredible. It had never felt so good. He had never felt as if he'd fit so perfectly with a woman before and it had never meant so much. He hoped it had been as good for her.

He raised his head and stared down at her. 'How are you?'

She nodded. 'Good. You?'

'I'm all right.' He grinned.

Gently, he eased out of her and came to lie at her side, his hand curving over her stomach, his fingers lightly grazing her hip.

'Tell me,' he whispered. 'Was it like *that* in your books?'

And she sighed, happily. 'No, I only read about the facts. Not the feelings.'

'It is never usually like that in real life either.'

He kissed her and tugged her into his body. He realised he loved this woman who had saved him, making him want to live again, making him happy. She was helping him cast off all his doubts and making him feel he could be himself—someone he wanted to be, someone he could be proud of, without a title.

He wanted to stay like this, with her, for ever. And although he knew that probably wasn't practical, he knew the only thing that would come close to it was if he married her. Then he could be with her, always. He could make love to her, always.

Just the thought caused a stirring in his groin again and he was shocked that he wanted her again so soon, after his thorough taking of her already. He knew he probably couldn't do it again, she might be sore, but it didn't diminish his desire for her.

Slowly, he lifted himself up, resting his head on his elbow, staring down at her, and he felt a little guilty that her first time had been on the floor. He got up and held out his hand to pull her up and walked her over to the chesterfield.

He lowered himself down, bringing her down on top of him, on to his lap, her knees straddling his thighs as she wrapped herself around him, her arms draped over his shoulders, her head nestled into the curve of his shoulder. He covered them with a blanket, so she wouldn't get cold.

They lay like that for a while, and he thought this was what contentment felt like, to have the woman of your dreams, naked, wrapped around you. To be able to kiss her and touch her, and do whatever you liked to her, until you both soothed the restless tide inside you, feeling satisfied, complete, until you had the strength to do it all again.

His hands came round her to hold her buttocks, stroking her soft skin, and she nestled into him further. His heart rate kicked up.

'I thought you were asleep.'

She shook her head.

'Not tired?'

And she lifted herself away from him a little.

His eyes dipped to her breasts, the apex of her thighs near his hardening groin.

'Maybe you haven't worn me out enough yet.'

And his pulse went into overdrive.

'Really?'

And she grinned, seductively.

'Well, I'll have to see what I can do about that.'

And he lightly ran the tip of his fingers between the crevice of her buttocks, and she gasped, perhaps wondering what he was going to do to her, what he might teach her next.

'You're good,' she said, narrowing her eyes at him.

'You just have no one to compare me to.'

She shook her head. 'You're too good and you know it. It would imply a past—a past I do not think I want to know about.'

And as if to punish him for it, she raised herself up, taking him between her hands, and lowered herself down on him, and he groaned, tipping his head back, closing his eyes in surrender.

'Dear God, woman, what do you do to me?'

She kissed his eyelids gently.

Then he opened them. He looked into her eyes. 'I knew nothing. Felt nothing, until I met you. It is as though I have been numb. For years. You have brought me back to life.'

She whimpered as she lowered herself further, as she took him fully inside her, grinding her thighs down on to his.

'Can you feel this?'

And he moaned, resting his forehead on hers. 'It feels

too good. Is it the same for you? Do I fill you up, Seraphine? Make you whole? That is how it feels for me.'

And she kissed him, hard on the mouth, giving him his answer, as her tongue slid in and out, and she tortured him by rotating her hips, moving on top of him, slowly, too slowly, making it last. If it had been up to him, he would have thrust inside her, taking his release, demanding hers.

But she moved her hands up to her hair, lifting it up as she rode him, and she was so beautiful, so perfect, he wondered what he had done to deserve her. This.

He dug his hands into the flesh on her hips, hard, fastening her to him, and he took her breast in his mouth, suckling her. But it wasn't enough. He wanted more. Everything she could give him. And suddenly, he felt frantic, desperate with need, and his control snapped. He grabbed her by the buttocks and lowered her back on to the floor, coming down after her, slamming so hard inside her, he shocked them both with the most earth-shattering climax as they came together, crying out each other's names in unison.

Chapter Twelve

The early-morning sun streaming through the library window woke her and Seraphine sat up, holding the blanket over her naked body. She looked down at the man still sleeping next to her on the chesterfield, his handsome features gently softened by slumber.

She raked her hand through her dishevelled hair and down over her face. She wondered what time it was—would the servants be up yet? She didn't want anyone to come in here and find them like this.

She took a moment to gather her thoughts, looking around for her clothes. She couldn't believe everything that had happened in the past day. The ball. The attack. The Viscount speaking with her, the Prince Regent dancing with her and Ezra, making love to her—with his mouth, with his body, twice.

It had been glorious, everything she'd hoped it would be and more. She had read bits and pieces, her aunt and Henri had hinted at things, and she knew the details of what a man and woman did together, but she had never known how it might feel. That it could feel so wondrous.

She stole another look at Ezra and emotion soared through her at how far they'd come. Their relationship was like the fire that had burned through her home in Mayfair. Their first meeting had been angry, and brutal, setting her ablaze. She had hated him yet admired him, was attracted to him all at once, the feelings sweeping through her so fierce, so unexpected, so untameable.

Last night, it had been explosive, intense, beautiful. He had built her up from the ashes, where he had first found her, and she had risen like a phoenix, and yet...

She knew a fire must always be put out. It could be dangerous. Destructive. Just look at what had happened at the ball last night. Those men had come to the house, in the middle of the ball, causing trouble, picking a fight—because of her.

Ezra could have been hurt.

She loved him, she realised. So much. He had seen her at her lowest and he had been there at her brightest moment. She loved him. And she thought he loved her back. Only, he had offered her no words of love. He had behaved as if he loved her, kissed her and touched her as if he did, but there had been no promise of a union or a future together. He had not spoken any words of marriage. Suddenly she felt vulnerable. A little like a fool. She had opened herself up to him, allowed herself to fall in love with him, given him everything—her virtue, her honour—but asked for nothing in return.

And all at once, she felt unsure. Of him. Of the things they'd done. It shocked and disturbed her how much she wanted a proposal from this man. She had never wished to be a wife before and now, in the space of a few short days, she was daydreaming of becoming his bride, the woman at his side.

She didn't want to regret the things they had done together. She wanted to remember it, relive it, always, but she had to wonder—what were his intentions?

A chill rippled down her spine.

She looked up at all the intimidating portraits of the Hart family, who had borne witness to their lovemaking, and his words from the other night flittered through her mind.

'There is always a condition—some expectation. And the latest is that I find a bride and marry this Season… He has even threatened to deny me my inheritance and strip me of his lands if I don't comply, to reveal my true heritage.'

Suddenly she realised with blinding clarity why he hadn't asked for her hand in marriage.

He couldn't.

Because the Viscount would never allow them to be together. Yes, he had spoken to her last night, been civil, but he wanted Ezra to marry a woman he deemed respectable and she wasn't that. And certainly not now, after having given up her virginity.

If Ezra chose her, he would have to give up everything else.

She stared down at him.

Would he? For her?

But she couldn't ask that of him. It was too much. Too much to ask him to put aside the needs of the Viscount and his inheritance. It was too much to request he didn't help his family and to deny him the reunion he so desperately craved. She studied his face—the faint lines around his eyes, the scars here and there—and she wondered what he had been through, what he had suffered, out there on the Continent. She knew she didn't know the half of it. Yet the wound of his family abandoning him seemed to run the deepest. She didn't want to be the reason he didn't get to see his mother and sisters again.

She shook her head, reality dawning on her.

She couldn't ask him to leave this place—everything he had spent the past years working towards. Everything he had suffered at the hands of the Viscount's cold treatment had to mean something. He deserved to be the master of Artington. It was his destiny.

And he deserved to find happiness. To have some peace—and being with her would just cause more pain, more animosity, more problems. Look what had happened last night. She stroked a finger down his face—over the bruise he'd sustained from protecting her and everyone else. He could have been hurt—because of her. And she couldn't live with herself if anything happened to him. Because yes, the perpetrators had been reprimanded, but there were many more anti-émigrés out there who might cause them harm.

If them being apart meant he would be safe, then surely it would be worth the pain of giving him up.

And that's how she made her decision. Her decision to leave him.

When Ezra woke, a smile of satisfaction on his face, he turned, patting the chesterfield, trying to find Seraphine lying beside him, but he quickly realised, she wasn't there. He sat up and got the fright of his life when he saw Mrs Dawson staring down at him.

'Have too much whisky to make it up to bed, did we?' she asked, her eyes raking over his bare torso. And he pulled the blanket up to cover him.

He looked around, anxiously, wondering where Seraphine had gone. Had she heard the housekeeper approach and hidden somewhere? He looked over his shoulder at the piano—there was no sign of her clothes. No sign of her anywhere.

'Is anyone else up yet?' he asked.

'It has been a slow start this morning, but we have made some progress on the ballroom. It was quite the mess.'

'And Miss Mounier. Has she made an appearance this morning? She mentioned something about coming to help,' he said, lying.

'I believe she left, Master Ezra. Early this morning.'

His brow furrowed. Had someone seen her leave him? Had she gone back to the cottage?

'Her brother returned from London and they left soon after this morning.'

'Left? Left to go where?' he asked, panic exploding through his veins, as he tried to reach his breeches.

'Back to Mayfair, I think. She left me this to give you,' Mrs Dawson said, handing him a letter and he immediately snatched it up.

She wouldn't have left him, would she? Especially not after last night. His world began to spin on its axis.

He opened the parchment, the paper he recognised from his own desk.

Dear Ezra,
Thank you so much for your kind hospitality.
*   Now our uncle has recovered, and the house in Mayfair has been repaired well enough, we felt it was time to leave. Henri and I discussed it and we feel we cannot bring any more trouble to your door.*

Thank you so much for hosting the benefit last night. I shall never forget it.

I wish you every luck in making a match to secure your fortune and help your family.

Yours,

Seraphine

He scrunched the letter up in his fist.

Blinding hurt and rage crashed through him. He'd wanted to make her his since the moment he'd first seen her and now that he had, now that he had everything he wanted within his grasp, she had left him. Abandoned him, and the betrayal, took his breath away.

She had left him, without as much as an explanation. Just like his parents. And he felt as if he couldn't breathe. He'd never felt pain like it—not on the battlefield, nor at the hands of his father and mother. She hadn't even said goodbye. Not properly.

Last night had been the best night of his life. He'd taken her innocence, making love to her, over and again, showing her how much he cared.

Had it not meant anything to her? It had meant everything to him.

Anger lashed through him. How could she do this?

He threw off the blanket and stalked over to his clothes, pulling on his breeches. Maybe it was a good thing. He had had her, his desire would soon be ebbing away. That is what usually happened. He could move on, marry someone the Viscount deemed appropriate.

He tugged on his shirt, drawing the buttons together. But who was he fooling? He knew now that his desire for Seraphine would never fade. He would never have enough of her. Because he loved her, with every fibre of his being. And he wanted her with him, always.

The very thought of doing *that*, being intimate with anyone else, ever again, was sickening to him. He could never. She had ruined him for anyone else.

He opened the letter again, smoothing the parchment to read the words again, trying to calm himself down.

If she was worried about his safety, and that of his home, because of what had happened last night, she had no need. He was sure the culprits of the Mayfair fire and the attack last night were one and the same and they had now been apprehended. He would make sure of it himself by going to speak to them and the authorities today.

As for his family...he needed to speak to the Viscount. They needed to sit down and talk. He needed to tell him how he felt—that he wouldn't marry anyone, unless it was her. Surely the man wouldn't strip him of his land and fortune because of it? But if he did, so be it. He had made it on his own before, when he was in the army, and he could do so again. From now on, he wouldn't live by anyone's terms but his own. Seraphine had taught him that.

He would find a way to look after his family with or without the Viscount's money—because there was no way he was going to wed another and sacrifice the one woman he actually loved. He had found love and, this time, he was damn well going to keep hold of it. He would not make the same mistakes he had made before. He would not harbour his hatred and resentment. He would talk to her, ask her why. And sooner rather than later.

He realised this was exactly who she was. Seraphine

was always putting others before herself. She was one of a kind. Putting his needs first. Is this what his parents had done?

But did Seraphine not know she was his greatest need? Like his parents had been?

Without her, he had nothing.

Chapter Thirteen

Ezra knocked on the door of the Mouniers' Mayfair mansion the following Friday afternoon. He had half-expected to find a flurry of other gentlemen callers, thinking that he'd have to wait in line, but he was surprised to see there were none.

There was even a look of surprise on the housekeeper's face as she let him in, seemingly baffled that the mistress should have a caller, and he wondered what was going on.

As he climbed the stairs of the house, he realised it looked nice. A fresh lick of paint had given it a new lease of life. He hoped Artington would soon be back to looking its best, too. They were working on the window in the ballroom, trying to get it looking as good as new. Better, in fact, now some of the other cracks had been healed within its walls.

Entering the drawing room, he couldn't remember a time when he'd been more nervous. What would Seraphine and her family make of him just turning up here? How would he feel when he saw her again? The last time he'd seen her, he'd been storming her body, taking her with him to the stars.

'Hart!' Henri said, coming into the room. 'I could not

believe it when they said it was you. You do not have to pretend to call on my sister to come and see us, you know. You can come any time. What brings you to town? Here, take a seat. We have not seen you at any of the social occasions this week. We have missed you, good fellow.'

The housekeeper passed him a cup of tea and Ezra perched on the sofa, holding the saucer in his hand and bringing the cup to his lips, taking a sip.

'We were sorry we left in such a hurry last week, but Seraphine was in quite a state—insistent we had caused you too much grief already. I had not realised the Viscount did not want us there,' he said. 'You should have told us so, rather than us outstaying our welcome.'

Ezra heard Seraphine before he saw her, her laugh drifting into the room first. Then she was there. Seraphine was coming into the drawing room alongside her aunt and when she saw him, she stopped dead, staring over at him, and he got up out of his seat so fast he spilt his tea in its saucer.

His blood rushed in his ears. She looked like perfection in a pretty white gown. He wanted to haul her to him and chastise her—to tell her never to leave him ever again. Instead, he just stood there, gripping the handle of his teacup.

'Madame Auclair, Miss Mounier.'

'Hello.'

And he wondered how he was going to get through this. But he had to draw strength from everything that happened this past week. Mainly from the words of the Viscount.

He had gone to find the man in his rooms the morning

Seraphine had left, and he had prepared a great speech in his mind.

He'd burst into the old man's chamber and placed his hands down on the table where he was eating his breakfast.

'I have come to tell you that if I must choose between my inheritance and my feelings for Miss Mounier, then I will choose her. I will leave Artington with just the clothes on my back, forget about the inheritance and earn the money for myself—and my mother and sisters who have written to me—another way. I may never be the Master of Artington Hall, but I will be the master of my own fate.'

The Viscount had continued eating his toast and gooseberry jam.

'For the first half of my life I have mainly done what others have told me to do, what they have expected of me, but for the second half I should like to be happy. Miss Mounier makes me happy. She understands me like no other person. I can be myself with her. And I will not give her up.'

The Viscount had finished his mouthful and swallowed it down with a sip of his tea. 'All right then,' he'd said, placing his cup down.

Ezra had stilled, coming off the table. 'All right then?'

'If you want to marry her, then I think you should. I accept it.'

Ezra had looked at the man, perplexed. This was not how he'd thought the conversation would go. 'All right I should marry her and you want me off the property right now?' he asked, uncertain of what was happening.

The old man sighed. 'No. I mean, marry her and be

happy, Ezra. I think she will make a good home for you both here at Artington.'

Ezra had reeled. 'This is a turnaround. I do not understand.'

The man had sighed. 'I am glad that you are finally sticking up for something you want, Ezra. You have always done as I have asked, wanting to please. I know you have always been angry with me, for taking you away from your home and your family, and I probably deserved your hatred. I was so lost when our boy died, we were trying to fill a void. But it was not fair of us to put that burden on you—to ask you to make us happy again. To ask you to love us, when instead you were upset and wanted to push us away. We realised that quite soon after we had brought you here, but by that time it was too late to go back. We had made a commitment to you and your family. And I really thought I could mould you into the man I thought you could be. Last night, I finally saw that man. I have seen glimpses of him since you came back from the war, but I saw him in his entirety for the first time last night, when you hosted that benefit ball. When you danced with the French woman in front of everyone. In front of the Regent.'

Ezra had swallowed.

'This woman, Seraphine, she has done what the Viscountess and I never could. She has helped you to accept who you are. She has helped you be happy here. I am glad to see that at long last. Now come, join me. Sit down.'

And Ezra had slumped into the chair beside him, stunned.

'We were so desperate for our child back, the Viscountess and I, I am afraid we were selfish. We did not think about the implications for you, Ezra—we just thought we would be giving you a better life. That you would want it—this grand hall, the wealth. I had not appreciated you would miss your brother and sisters—your parents—quite so much, perhaps because I had been an only child. Perhaps because I was not close with my own mother and father.'

Ezra had tried to swallow down an enormous lump in his throat.

'But we did love you, Ezra. We wanted you. And we never regretted our decision to take you on, not for one moment. I am sorry if I was overly harsh with you at times, we just wanted the best for you. I admit we got things wrong. I was so determined to take the correct path, to be a proper parent, unlike my own, that I was much too stern with you.

'But from the moment I saw you, I knew you could run Artington. Seeing you do well at Oxford, what you achieved on the battlefield, the fact you have a commendation from the Regent in the war, it is all very impressive—and I am sorry I have not told you before. I came to see that exhibition at the Academy the other day as I wanted to understand what you had been through a little more. I was sorry I missed you there.

'And then there is your compassion for the émigrés—seeing the way you looked at Miss Mounier last night, it reminded me of the way I felt about your mother. I loved her so very much. And I will not deny you that. I realised the depth of your love for her when I saw you together. That she was not just another of your women. And you are a good man, Ezra, you deserve to be happy.'

'Even though she is French?' he asked.

'*C'est la vie!* I know she is a good person. I like her.'
The man smiled, leaning in, his eyes crinkling. 'I heard
the things the Prince said to you last night, about what a
good thing you have done, and I have to agree. It made
me realise what I have known all along—you are the
only man I would ever leave my estate to, Ezra. I am
proud of you.'

It had been a great moment of understanding and for-
giveness between the two of them and they had gone on
to spend the rest of the morning talking and getting to
know one another better. Later, they had drafted a response to Ezra's mother, saying they would help. And
it had felt good, doing it together, putting down the pen
and sending it off with the mail coach. It felt as if he was
taking a step towards a new, bright future.

He thought of those words of pride the Viscount had
said to him now as he looked at Seraphine and it gave
him the hope, and courage, to proceed with what he had
come here to do.

What was he doing here? Seraphine wondered as she
stiffly sat down on the chesterfield in the drawing room,
her hands tightly clasped in her lap, the air thick with
tension. She couldn't bring herself to speak.

Taking in his dark, dashing looks, his long fingers—
fingers that had explored her body just days ago—she
felt the china of her teacup tremble in her hand. She
thought he looked more handsome than ever.

'The events of the other evening were terrible, weren't
they, Mr Hart?' her aunt said. 'I do hope you've managed
to get Artington Hall back to looking its best.'

'Absolutely, *madame*. Almost everything is back to normal.'

Was it? Was he?

She hadn't been herself since she'd left him. Even now she wanted to stand up and announce that she had made a mistake, that she had never meant to leave him, but instead she just sat there. She couldn't move. She could barely breathe.

All she could think of was the way his body had fitted inside hers, moving so perfectly, the scene of them lying under the mirror in the library, and she felt her cheeks redden. How could she have behaved so brazenly? And why had she run from his arms? Because pushing him away before he had the chance to do the inevitable to her was far better than chancing rejection, wasn't it? She wouldn't have been able to bear his dismissal of her— not after the things they'd done. She'd had to make it her decision. She'd had to make the choice for him.

'Did you hear they connected the men who descended on Artington the night of the ball, with the men who set fire to your house?' Ezra said. 'They were from the same group and have all been apprehended. They were men I knew from Almack's, who used to drink the expensive wine there, hence the use of the dark-green bottle. I must apologise to you all once more in case I had any influence on their actions. I hope I have made amends by helping to catch them. They are all serving time in jail now, for their sins.'

She knew Ezra had played a part in their conviction and she was so grateful to him. That now they could feel safe once more in their home. Only, why did it feel like the walls were closing in on her, the space smaller? She missed being at Artington, she realised.

She missed him.

'We had heard and we never blamed you for any of it, Hart. So no apology is necessary,' Henri said.

'Might I ask where Lord Wentworth and Lord Barrington and the other callers are today?' Ezra asked.

'Well, that is a story and a half!' Henri said, displeased, throwing Seraphine a dark look. 'My sister refused to receive any more gentlemen. She said she refused to compromise her ambitions and insisted I stop this farce of finding her a husband. She is determined to be a governess instead. What is a man to do? You know how stubborn she can be, Hart.'

Ezra stole a glance at her and she caught his gaze, before looking away.

'Yes, I know,' he smiled wryly.

'What about you, Hart?' Henri said. 'Rumour has it you were to announce your bride-to-be at your ball the other night. The proceedings probably scuppered your plans.'

'On the contrary, they did not.'

'Seraphine, why don't you show Mr Hart the piano—perhaps play something for him?' Seraphine's aunt said, interrupting.

Memories crowded her of the night they'd spent together, the things he'd done to her on top of the Viscount's pianoforte, and she turned to look at him, wide-eyed, and he stood, abruptly, and everyone stood with him.

'Actually, your question, Henri, and your lovely offer, *madame*, bring me to the reason I am here. I was wondering, might I have a moment alone with Miss Mounier?'

Silence reigned over the room.

'Yes, yes, of course,' her aunt said, sending Seraphine a look and trying to usher a very reluctant Henri out.

'Whatever is going on?' the man said, looking between them both.

The older woman managed to bundle him out of the door and it closed, leaving Seraphine and Ezra alone. He turned to look at her.

She wrung her hands.

'You left me,' he said, the hurt audible in his voice.

And when she stared up into his eyes, she realised what she'd done and she wondered why she hadn't thought of it before. She'd abandoned him, just as his parents had. And she felt awful. Only probably just like them, she hadn't wanted to. He must know she hadn't wanted to. She was just doing what she thought was right—for him, for her.

She took a step towards him. 'I thought that was for the best.'

'How?' he said, lifting his palms to the ceiling. 'How could that possibly be for the best?'

'Ezra—your family. The Viscount. The violence. You must see the odds are all stacked against us.'

'Did you really think I would put my hands on you, sleep with you, do the things I did to you that night, Seraphine, and not marry you?'

'What?' Henri exploded, behind the door and they heard a commotion, as Seraphine's aunt was clearly trying to hold him back from knocking down the wood.

Seraphine gasped, her hand coming up over her mouth, looking between the closed door and Ezra. 'I never asked for a proposal.'

'I know you didn't, but you're damn well going to get one anyway,' Ezra said, closing the distance between them. 'And I hope you will say yes, because I cannot go another day without knowing you will be by my side every day for the rest of our lives. There is no one else I want to be seen with, to spend my life with. It is you or no one.'

The breath left her.

The door handle rattled as a skirmish carried on outside.

'I slept with you because I love you, Seraphine. I should have told you that at the time. I did not because I was too interested in showing you rather than telling you how I feel. And perhaps I had not quite worked out in my head how I was going to deal with the Viscount about it all.

'But listen,' he said, raking a hand through his hair. 'Before your brother manages to break down the door and tries to kill me, I spoke to the Viscount about you, about the situation. I refused to marry another and he has agreed we can wed. You know I cannot offer you the title you thought I would bring. His title. But I can offer you a home, a fortune. *Love.* Because I do love you. So much, Seraphine. I love everything about you. The way you always think of others. Your accent. I love that you are French.' He grinned. 'Your stubbornness—and your passion for helping people. And I want to be there by your side as you continue to do so.'

She swallowed. Did he really mean it?

'I had thought us both incapable of love because of our past hurts, but you have helped to heal my heart, to show me I have a future, that I have so much love to give, and I do not want to waste another second not being able to show you how much I care. I know you are afraid of letting me into your heart, for fear that you could lose me, as that is how I feel about you. But I would rather love you and lose you one day, hopefully in the much-distant future, when we're old and have lived our lives to the full, than waste the years and be miserable without you. Now please, put me out of my misery and say you will be mine, as I cannot breathe without you.'

And she smiled. She couldn't believe he'd uttered the words she had been longing to hear.

'I never wanted a title,' she said, coming towards him, shaking her head. 'I didn't even want a husband, not until I met you.' She came closer. 'You are all I need, Ezra.'

'Is that a yes?' he said, breathlessly. 'Are you saying yes?'

Her face broke out into a grin. 'Yes, I will marry you, Ezra,' she said, throwing her arms around his neck, and he picked her up and spun her round, burying his head in her neck.

When he put her feet back on the ground, she raised her hand to cover his cheek. 'You're right, after losing my parents, I have been afraid of caring for anyone again. Of opening up to anyone, especially here. I never thought I would find the kind of love my parents shared, or meet anyone who would understand me. Who would finally make me feel as if I belonged. As if I had found my place, my home. But you, Ezra, you have shown me all that is possible and more.

'I told my brother to send away any other callers as no one could ever compare to you. It was you or no one. I left you the other morning because I thought that was what was best for you, what you wanted. But I felt more distraught every step I took away from you. I will always put your feelings before mine because I love you. So much. But I have missed you this past week. I have felt like a part of me was missing.'

'We are whole again now.' And he took her face between his hands, bent down and pressed his lips against hers.

The door suddenly crashed open, Henri practically falling through it. 'What the devil?' Henri said. 'I feel as if I have missed something. Something huge.'

Ezra and Seraphine grinned.

'You have,' they said in unison, unable to take their eyes off each other.

'Lord Mounier, I wanted to ask you if you would give me your sister's hand in marriage,' Ezra said, taking Seraphine's hand.

'Seems like it is a little late to be asking my permission to do anything! I thought you two loathed each other,' Henri said, looking between them both.

'No,' Ezra said, shaking his head, staring down at Seraphine. 'You are wrong. I believe I loved your sister from the first moment I laid eyes on her.'

Seraphine's heart was thudding in her chest.

'I mean, I would say yes, willingly,' Henri bumbled. 'But you know my sister—she knows her own mind. And...'

Seraphine slid her arms round Ezra again and he kissed her, a deep proprietary kiss.

'And, well, it looks as if she has already made her decision.'

Epilogue

The wedding had been an incredible day and they'd hosted the reception in the grounds of Artington. All of the *ton* had been in attendance, including Ezra's most faithful friends, Adam, Ash and Hawk, and even some of the families from Mayfair who Ezra and Seraphine had got to know better over the past few weeks, when they'd helped out in the square as often as they could.

It had been the icing on the cake that Ezra's mother, and sisters, had arrived a few days before, and while Ezra and his mother had taken long walks getting to know each other again, and he'd spent afternoons playing Pall Mall with his sisters, Seraphine had been delighted to settle the three women into their new home in the cottage on the estate.

It had been an emotional reunion when the carriage had pulled up and Ezra's mother had stepped out. She had broken down, saying there hadn't been a day when she had not thought of Ezra. She had suffered greatly for what she had done, but their reasoning had been as Seraphine had thought—they'd seen an opportunity to give Ezra a better life. One they could never have provided for him. And they had thought the Harts would take good care of him. They had refrained from writing, or visiting, hoping it would allow Ezra to move on with his new family. They had never imagined the pain he had endured.

The Viscount himself was in fine spirits in the church and at the wedding breakfast, even standing up to make a toast to his beloved heir, Ezra.

And Seraphine had been overjoyed when Henri found her and revealed he had finally plucked up the courage and asked Miss Jennings to marry him—and she had said yes. Everything was turning out perfectly.

They served their favourite white soup for their wedding meal and their first dance had been a waltz. But all the guests were stunned when the sound of the royal trumpets had resounded around the ballroom and the Prince Regent had arrived, wanting to pass on his best regards in person.

'I have a wedding gift for you, Mrs Hart,' the Prince Regent said. 'I wanted to tell you in person that I have decided to set up a relief fund for those émigrés still struggling to fit into life here in London. We will call it the Hart Foundation. You inspired me, Miss Mounier. You are an ambassador for a brighter future. I hope you shall have an annual Hart Foundation ball here at Artington and that my small contribution will make a great difference.'

'Thank you so much, Your Royal Highness.'

'And I have something for you, too, Hart,' the Prince said, handing Ezra a letter. 'It is not urgent, so open it tomorrow.'

Ezra put the sealed envelope into the pocket of his coat. 'Thank you, sir.'

'Now, go and dance with your wife.'

And he did. Ezra twirled her round the ballroom under everyone's envious, watchful gaze and he smiled down at her, the love shining out of his eyes. 'I am so proud of you,' he said. 'You are indeed a representative for a brighter future. My brighter future. And I cannot wait to start working on that bright future tonight, when we are alone.'

And she laughed. 'I can't either. I am counting down the moments.'

Much later, when the last of their guests had departed and they had said their goodbyes, Ezra took her hands in his and stared down at her. 'Alone at last,' he said with a smile.

'Whatever will we do?' she asked.

He grinned, as he began to lead her up the stairs, the ripples of excitement stoking between her legs as they drew closer to their new bedroom that looked out across the estate. Taking her by surprise, Ezra scooped her up, lifting her off the ground and making her squeal. Kicking open the door, he carried her over the threshold.

The moment he set her down, her hands were on him. Seraphine had had to be restrained all day, but now she could finally be herself, with him, free of restrictions. Ezra drew her into his arms as his mouth came down on hers, his fingers eager to remove her gown.

'You looked stunning today, but you are even more beautiful with nothing on,' he said, practically dragging the material off her skin, over her head, and she laughed at his eagerness as he cast the gown aside. 'I want to make you mine,' he said, turning her round and drawing her back against his chest.

'I am yours.'

'I want to make our vows complete.'

He lifted her shift and tugged it off, too, discarding it, and drew his fingers down the sides of her naked body, making her shiver.

He stepped back and began to unpin her hair, letting the tendrils fall down her back, almost to the top of her bare buttocks.

When he was done, she turned and began to remove his clothes. She had become more experienced at doing so these past few nights, when she had sneaked along the corridor to his room, when all was quiet. Hand over her mouth, he had teased and pleased her, driving her to distraction as she'd thrashed against the covers, until the early hours, when she'd reluctantly had to creep back to her own bed.

Tonight would be the first night she didn't have to leave him and she was excited about all they could do together through the dark hours, but also about waking up and seeing his handsome face lying next to hers on the pillow.

Shrugging his shirt off his shoulders, she ran her palms over his chest, pressing her lips to his warm, solid skin. She was beginning to learn all his scars and how he'd got each and every one. She was determined to know every inch of his skin.

Moving her fingers to the waistband of his breeches, she smiled up at him as he sprang free from the confines of the material and she heard him suck in a breath as she pushed the material down his legs and he stepped out of them. She took him in her hand and he groaned, resting his forehead against hers.

In one swift move, he grabbed her wrists and toppled her on to bed, coming over her, and he pushed her thighs apart with his knees, opening her up to him. His fingers roamed down to stroke between her legs, to check she was ready for him—but he was beginning to realise she was always ready for him and he loved that.

He kissed her, a deep, slow, open-mouthed kiss, before he pulled away and stared down at her. He was ready to take his wife, to claim her as his once more, but a thought had struck him.

'You know, we have never discussed if we want to be parents,' he said.

She stared up at him, surprised. 'Well, do you? Want to be a father?'

'Yes,' he said. 'Do you want to be a mother? I know we have both suffered great loss, but we now know love can help us to overcome anything. And I think we both have great capacity to take care of a child, or two, or maybe even three. If we can.'

She laughed. 'I am actually relieved you said that because I'm wondering if it is a bit late to be having this conversation,' she said.

His brow furrowed. 'What do you mean?'

'I mean… It has been weeks since the Artington ball and I have not had my courses this month.'

He blinked and she bit her lip.

He lifted his head slightly. 'Do you think you might already be with child?'

She nodded. 'Yes.'

He lifted himself off her completely and sat up.

'Seraphine!' He looked shocked. 'That's—that's amazing news,' he said, tears filling his eyes, his emotions threatening to overwhelm him.

She raised herself up to sit beside him. 'Are you pleased?'

'Pleased? Yes. This is the best news. I love you so much.' He laughed, letting his tears fall and roughly swiping his cheeks. 'You will make a wonderful mother.'

She placed a hand on his cheek. 'And you will make a wonderful father.'

'We can do this, together,' he said, kissing her again, curling her back against his body, so they were lying like spoons. 'We're going to give this boy, or girl, the childhood we never had. We're going to make them so happy.'

'Like you make me,' she said, her eyes glowing up at him with affection. 'I love you, Ezra.'

'And I love you. I will try to be the best husband to you and father to our child, Seraphine.'

'I know. And can you start by showing me the best husband part now?' She grinned, wriggling against him.

'You still want to do this?' he asked, flattening his hand down over the curve of her stomach, then lower, threading his fingers through her intimate curls.

'Definitely,' she said, bringing her hand up over her shoulder to hold his head. 'I have waited all day to do this. You cannot get out of it now.'

'It will not hurt you or the…the baby?' he asked, his fingers parting and stroking between her folds.

She shook her head, laughing. 'No.'

He drew her leg up over his thigh, opening her up to him, and needing no further encouragement, he thrust gently, entering her from behind while his fingers continued to tease her. And she moaned softly, 'Oh, Ezra.'

'I want to show you how much I love you,' he whispered. And with every long, steady torturous penetration of her body, she felt it. His adoration for her, his commitment, his promise.

As she took him inside her, meeting his every thrust until she came apart under his exquisite touch, and she felt his own release deep inside her, she hoped he could tell how much she trusted him, how much she valued him, and that he was the only man she would ever allow inside her body, letting him take ownership of her and her heart.

Ezra awoke early, wrapped around his naked, pregnant wife, and for the first time in for ever, he felt content. He had everything he wanted, right here in his arms.

He drew in the scent of her hair. Lilies. And he drifted back off to sleep for a while. But when he next awoke, he remembered the letter the Regent had given him yesterday. Seeing the envelope poking out of his discarded jacket's pocket, he gently removed himself from the bed to pick it up and rip open the sealed parchment. He read the words and sat down, shocked.

'What is it?' Seraphine asked and he turned to look at her. Her gorgeous sleepy blue eyes were watching him from the bed, obviously seeing the conflicted expressions crossing his features.

He shook his head.

She threw off the blankets and stalked around to him, naked, coming up behind him, wrapping her arms around his neck to scan the letter over his shoulder and read the words out loud.

> *By the Grace of God, King of the United Kingdom of Great Britain and Ireland*
> *To Our Trusty and Well-Beloved Ezra Hart*
> *It has pleased us to recognise your distinguished service, unwavering loyalty, and exceptional contributions to the realm during the war. We, by the authority vested in us, do hereby grant, create and advance you to the rank of Baron and do grant unto you all the rights, privileges, and honours appertaining thereto.*

She gasped. 'The Regent has made you a baron for your service in the war?'

'Yes, but read on. There is more.'

> *It has also pleased us to recognise your distinguished service and unwavering loyalty to the Crown, saving the Prince Regent's life at a recent gathering. We, by the authority vested in us, do hereby grant, create and further advance you to the rank of Viscount, and do grant unto you all the rights, privileges and honours appertaining thereto.*
> *We command you to take your seat in the House of Lords, to bear the title with honour, and to faithfully discharge the duties incumbent upon you.*
> *God Save the King!*

'I have been given a further promotion to Viscount Hart—a title awarded for loyalty to the Crown, for protecting the Prince Regent at our ball. Finally, I feel as if I have earned my place in the world.'

She smiled. 'Ezra, this is wonderful news. I told you a title makes no difference to me, but I do know how much this means to you. Congratulations. You so deserve this.'

'Thank you. I cannot quite believe it.'

She came round towards him, and lowered herself into his lap.

'I thought you would be happier. Was this not always your dream?'

'I thought it was. Until I met you. Now nothing else is as important as us,' he said, dropping the letter on to the floor. He ran his hand down her chest to her stomach, resting his hand there. 'And our family.'

And as she took his face in his hands and kissed him, he knew the upbringing they'd both had, him being given up by his parents and being raised by the Harts, and Seraphine losing her parents in the Terrors—all that had happened had led him to her. The Revolution and the war he'd fought in all had a purpose. It hadn't been for nothing. And he would not change any of it. For it had brought him Seraphine. To a family of their own. It had all led to the greatest love anyone had ever known.

* * * * *

If you enjoyed this story,
keep an eye out for the next book in the
A Season to Wed miniseries,
coming soon!

Their Second Chance Season
by Ella Matthews

The Lord's Maddening Miss
by Lucy Morris

While you wait, check out
Sarah Rodi's previous
Viking romances

'Chosen as the Warrior's Wife'
in Convenient Vows with a Viking
The Viking and the Runaway Empress
Her Secret Vows with the Viking